★ AMERICAN ★ TRIBUTE ★

ELAINE CAMP
Right Behind the Rain

D0204499

Silhouette Special Edition

Published by Silhouette Books New York

America's Publisher of Contemporary Romance

For the *Collegian* Bunch.
Friendships forged by a burning passion
for the written word. The flame still burns.

SILHOUETTE BOOKS
300 East 42nd St., New York, N.Y. 10017

ISBN: 0-373-09301-2

First Silhouette Books printing April 1986

America's Publisher of Contemporary Romance

Printed in the U.S.A.

AMERICAN TRIBUTE

Where a man's dreams count for more than his parentage . . .

Love's Haunting Refrain, Ada Steward #289—February 1986
This Long Winter Past, Jeanne Stephens #295—March 1986
Right Behind the Rain, Elaine Camp #301—April 1986
Cherokee Fire, Gena Dalton #307—May 1986
Nobody's Fool, Renee Roszel #313—June 1986
Misty Mornings, Magic Nights, Ada Steward #319—July 1986

ELAINE CAMP

dreamed of becoming a writer for many years. Once she'd tried it, she quickly became successful, perhaps because of her reporter's eye, which gives her a special advantage in observing human relationships.

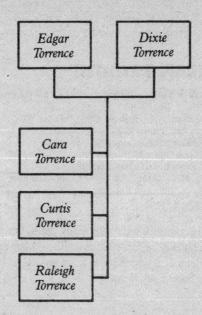

Chapter One

March—it comes in like a lion and goes out like a lamb.

How true, Raleigh Torrence thought as she marked off the first few days of March on her desk calendar. This March had roared into being, clawing and ripping up her life. Oh, how she hoped it ended as a meek, gentle lamb. Flipping back the pages, she glanced through February, which had passed in a gray blur. She stared at one particular page in February that had only one notation: Curtis's funeral.

Raleigh closed her eyes for a moment, remembering the cold, blustery day when she'd said her final goodbye to her brother. It had been the saddest day in her life, and only an undercurrent of rage had propelled her through the funeral and the days following it. Opening her eyes, Raleigh stared at the calendar page as biting anger tore through her again. She picked up her pen and wrote

"Why?" on the page, underlining the word three times in mute frustration.

"Lunch call!"

The merry voice, out of sync with her dark memories, roused Raleigh, and she blinked her hazel eyes and looked up into Cathy Carlsbad's smiling face. The young redhead leaned forward, waving a hand before Raleigh's startled eyes.

"Earth to Raleigh. Earth to Raleigh," she said in a robot's voice. "It's noon and Jerry is going out for coneys. Do you want one?"

"Jerry?" Raleigh glanced around the newspaper office. "Who's Jerry?"

"The new copyboy." Cathy held out a hand, palm up. "If you want a coney, pay up."

"Oh, okay." Raleigh grabbed her purse and withdrew two crumpled dollar bills. "Two with chili only and a small cola." She handed the money to her fellow reporter. "What happened to the other copyboy?"

"He quit two weeks ago. He started college and his class load was too heavy."

"I didn't even know he'd left." Raleigh shook her head, wondering when she'd get back into the mainstream of life again. It wasn't like her not to notice when someone left the newspaper.

"I'll give your order to Jerry," Cathy said. She started to turn away, then stopped to give Raleigh a worried glance. "Are you okay?"

Raleigh forced a smile to her lips. "Sure. I was just thinking about a news story I've got to write this afternoon." When Cathy looked unconvinced, Raleigh added, "I'm fine, Cathy. Really."

"Okay," Cathy said dubiously as she walked slowly from Raleigh's desk.

Raleigh looked back down at the calendar and flipped the pages forward again to March. With a supreme effort, she swiveled her chair around to face her word processor's screen, where she had written the first three lines of a news story hours ago. She sighed, wishing she could write some good news for a change, but the police beat offered few opportunities for that. How long could she keep on reporting burglaries, holdups, rapes and murders? How long before she couldn't stand it any more?

It hadn't been that long ago she'd been overjoyed at becoming the *Tulsa Times*'s first female police reporter. Ever since Curtis's death, however, each story had depressed her more. It seemed as if the whole world was falling apart and there wasn't a thing she could do about it.

Raleigh swallowed hard and placed her fingertips on the keyboard. Mechanically, she began recording the facts on the latest attempted bank robbery in Tulsa.

A light drizzle fell from an overcast sky, and Evan Younger flipped up his coat collar to keep the moisture from inching down the back of his neck. He stuck his weather-reddened hands into the pockets of his pea coat and bent his head into the stiff wind as he weaved among the downtown Tulsa pedestrians. Ducking into an office-building doorway, Evan stamped his boots on the wet pavement and shivered under his wool coat. It had been a long time since he'd braved Tulsa's winter, and his body had lost its resistance to cold weather during those years in Las Vegas and Los Angeles. Evan pulled a pack of cigarettes and a lighter from one of his pockets. He cupped his hands around the lighter's flame, keeping them there for a few moments after the cigarette was lit to warm his palms and fingertips, then stuffed the pack and lighter back into his pocket.

The cigarette dangled from the corner of his mouth as he watched a couple of career women pass by him.

"My legs are freezing!" one of the women said.

"You should have worn slacks today," her companion admonished.

"I would have, but my boss likes me in dresses."

Evan frowned, reading all sorts of things into the snatch of conversation. He looked up and examined the tall buildings through the drizzle, remembering some of them and acquainting himself with others. Some things never change, he thought with a quirk of his lips. Women could pursue careers as long as they dressed to please their bosses. Shaking his head, he laughed inwardly at the twisted irony, thankful that he didn't have to dress for success. People didn't care how a psychologist dressed. People who needed his help were far beyond caring about such trivia.

Peeking around the terra-cotta door facing, Evan looked down the street and spotted a familiar neon light. The sight of it made his mouth water. The Coney Islander! He left the shelter of the doorway and hurried toward the tiny restaurant. It had been ages since he'd sunk his teeth into one of those spicy concoctions. Evan hoped the place hadn't changed hands. A Greek family had owned it before he'd left Tulsa ten years ago, and they had made the best coneys he'd ever put in his mouth.

A smile of gratitude curved his lips as he stepped inside the toasty-warm restaurant. Nothing had changed. Steam coated the street-side window, curling up from a grill covered with hot dogs. A white-haired man, the same one Evan remembered, supervised the grilling of the wieners by rolling them with the flat of his hand so that they cooked uniformly. Evan slipped into line and grabbed a tray. He glanced over his shoulder at the dozen or so school desks lined against the wall, occupied by men in business suits and winter coats who were shoving coneys into their mouths.

"Yes, mister? What can we do for you today?"

Evan snapped to attention, his ears picking up the Greek accent of the waiter. "I'll take four with everything and a carton of milk to go," he answered automatically, amused with himself for slipping into the old routine so effortlessly.

"Four with everything," the man repeated, already spooning steaming chili over the hot dogs. "And the milk is right down there, sir."

"Thanks." Evan inched farther down the bar toward a small, glass-fronted cooler. He withdrew a carton of milk and set it on his tray, then took the paper sack the waiter handed him. He paid for his lunch, deposited the tray and tucked the milk carton into the sack with his coneys. Shouldering his way through the crowded room, he reached the door and headed outside into the cold drizzle. A boy wearing a Will Rogers High School football jacket ran past him into the restaurant, letting a blast of warm air escape and wash over Evan.

The wind seemed to be even colder now. Evan started for his parked car several blocks away, but he paused when he saw an illuminated clock on the face of a building. His gaze lifted to the bold letters above it: The Tulsa Times Daily Newspaper. Someone's shoulder grazed him, and Evan stepped back, removing himself from the stream of scurrying downtown workers. He focused his blue eyes on the eight-story building across the street as he wrestled with indecision.

She worked there, he thought. The one holdout of the Torrence clan. Maybe if he just introduced himself, it would break the ice and she'd want to talk to him. Maybe she didn't want to see him. Evan rounded his shoulders as a raindrop slid down the back of his neck. What the hell? he thought. He checked for traffic, then ran across the street to the building. *Most* people didn't want to see him.

He burst into the foyer, his boots sliding on the tiled floor. A security guard, seated behind a desk in the corner, eyed him, then smiled.

"It's nasty out there today, isn't it?" the guard asked.

"Terrible," Evan agreed as he shook water droplets from his dark hair. "Which floor is the *Times* on?"

"Six." The guard sniffed the air. "Those coneys sure smell good."

"Oh, yeah." Evan pulled the crumpled sack from under his arm, having momentarily forgotten about it. "I hope I didn't smash them to bits."

"They'll still taste good." The guard tipped his head forward. "The elevators are right over there, sir."

"Thanks." Evan returned the man's smile, suddenly aware of how friendly his old hometown was. Smiles were easy to get in Tulsa. He rounded the corner and stood with two other men who were waiting for the elevator.

"Here it comes," one of them said as the elevator reached the lobby and the doors hissed open. "After you." The man stood back, waiting for Evan and the other man to enter first before he took his place inside. "Which floor?"

"Three."

"Six," Evan chimed in.

"I'm going to six, too," the man said, punching the correct buttons. "I work for the *Times*."

"You do?" Evan asked, leaning against the rail as the other man got off on the third floor. "Can you direct me to Raleigh Torrence's office?"

The man chuckled and ran a forefinger across his gray mustache. "I can't direct you to her office, but I can point out her desk for you. Only the high-powered editors have offices."

"I see." Evan shifted the coney sack from one hand to the other. "That'll be fine. Thanks."

"Think nothing of it."

The doors opened at the sixth floor and the man waved at the brunette receptionist. "Good afternoon, Sheila."

"Hi, Bud!" The receptionist smiled warmly. "Be sure and check your box. You've had a lot of messages today."

"Okay, I will." Bud stopped, turning back to Evan. "Raleigh is sitting right over there near that horseshoe-shaped desk. She's the one in the blue sweater with white stripes."

"Yes, I see her. Thanks again."

"No problem." The man headed for a wall of cubbyholes and pulled a stack of pink slips from one of them.

Evan looked back to the woman he'd pointed out. *This* woman didn't dress for a man, success, style or for any other such high-minded consideration. Her sweater was a size too large, cheating Evan out of a peek at whatever curves she might possess, and her black slacks were conventionally cut for comfort, not appearance. Evan scrutinized her from a distance, deciding that she dressed like a woman who had lost weight recently and still couldn't believe it. She was staring at a computer screen, a slight frown pinching the skin between her eyes. Her blond hair was caught by a ribbon at the nape of her neck, allowing the shorter hair around her face to escape and feather softly across her forehead. She wrinkled her nose at something she saw on the screen, and Evan smiled. He liked her nose. It was short-bridged and it tipped up at the end. A pug nose, which always made him think that it was a sign of a pugnacious character. He started across the room toward her, swinging the coney sack nonchalantly as he approached. She glanced up, letting him see her green-gray eyes behind the large, rectangular lenses of her glasses, and the sprinkling of freckles across her cheeks.

"Hello," he said, smiling and hoping he would be smiled at in return. "I'm sorry to interrupt you, but—"

"Oh, thank heavens!" She reached out and snatched the sack from his unresisting fingers. "I'm starved!" She paused, glancing at him again to give him a quick once-over before she opened his sack and thrust one hand inside. "I thought you'd be younger."

Her statement jolted him. What was she? Psychic? How could she have known he was going to drop by when he hadn't even know it until just a few minutes ago? He gathered his senses and cleared his throat.

"I am," he said, watching as she lifted his coneys from the sack.

"You are what?"

"Younger."

Her hazel eyes sought his face again, this time warily, and she slowly took off her glasses and placed them on her desk. "Younger than what? Springtime?" She laughed shortly and removed the Styrofoam top from the coneys. "Oh, I get it. You mean you're younger than me. Well, I don't doubt that. Everyone seems younger than me these days."

He was silent, digesting this revealing statement and happy with himself for coming here to meet her. She was cute, even adorable.

"Wait a minute!" She stared down at the melting cheese on the coneys, then looked up at him a bit accusingly. "These aren't mine."

"I know," he said, laughing a little. "They're mine."

She fitted the top over them again with an impatient sigh. "Well, why did you give them to me?"

"I didn't give them to you. You took them from me," he corrected her gently. "But if you're really starved, you're welcome to them." He smiled, noticing the family resemblance to her sister, Cara, and her brother, Curtis.

"I don't want your coneys," she said, pushing them back into the sack. "Where are mine?"

Before he could answer, her gaze wandered past him and her eyes widened. Evan turned to see what had captured her attention and saw the boy in the Will Rogers football jacket, carrying a large box filled with coney sacks.

"You're Jerry, right?" Raleigh asked sheepishly.

"That's right," the boy answered, handing her one of the sacks. "Here's your lunch." He noticed the other sack on her desk and tossed her a confused look. "Did you go get those? I was supposed to—"

"These aren't mine," Raleigh cut in, then nodded toward Evan. "They're his."

"Oh." Jerry grinned. "Okay."

"Thanks, Jerry." Raleigh reached out and grabbed his sleeve before he could hurry past her. "By the way, I'm Raleigh Torrence. It's nice to have you aboard."

The boy's face reddened slightly. "Thanks, Miss Torrence."

Raleigh shook her head, smiling. "It's Raleigh. We're all on a first-name basis around here."

"Okay. Nice to meet you, Raleigh."

Raleigh released his sleeve, and Jerry headed for another desk. She lifted her gaze to Evan again and handed him his grease-stained sack. "Here's your lunch, Mr...."

Evan took a deep breath and extended his hand. "I'm Younger."

One corner of her mouth pulled sideways, and she lowered her pale brows. "I'm sure you are, but I was asking for identification, not your birth date."

He laughed softly, shaking his head and realizing she was still misunderstanding him. "No, no. I'm Evan Younger." He took her hand, closing his fingers around it and wondering why her hands were colder than his.

"Evan Younger?" Her hand was motionless in his and her eyes weren't as friendly as they'd been moments before. "Dr. Evan Younger, the new police psychologist?"

"That's right. I've been wanting to meet you, Raleigh, so I thought I'd just pop over and—"

"Why?" she asked, snatching her hand from his and tearing open her coney sack with a vengeance.

"Why?" he repeated, confused. "Why what?"

"Why have you been wanting to meet me?"

"Well, I've met the other members of your family and—"

"So?" she challenged, turning frosty hazel eyes on him.

Evan shifted to one foot, impervious to her coolness. "So, you're the missing link. I wanted to meet you. I wanted to talk with you."

"There's nothing to talk about," she said, the words clipped. "There's nothing to say."

Curling his fingers into the paper sack, Evan told himself to keep calm and not take her bait. She wanted him angry, but he was determined to remain friendly. "There is something to say, Raleigh. I wanted to tell you how sorry I am about your brother's death. It was quite a blow."

She pinned him with accusing eyes. "The time for that was at his funeral. He's been dead almost three weeks now."

Feeling his back pressed against an imaginary wall, Evan decided to surrender gracefully on this point. "I'm sorry I didn't attend Curtis's funeral. I sold my house in Las Vegas and I had to fly back that week to sign the final papers." When she made no response to this, he decided to shift the conversation from the past to the present. "Grief is a difficult thing to handle, Raleigh. I thought I might be able to help you in some way."

"Help me?" She snapped the lid off her soft drink and tossed it into the wastebasket beside her desk. "Why didn't you help Curtis? He told me that he talked to you." She tipped back her head, condemning him with unwavering hazel eyes. "Why didn't you help him? He's the one who needed you."

Evan examined the jerky movements of her hands as she peeled the paper off a straw and stuck the straw into the soft drink. She was a bundle of confusion, but she wasn't ready to admit it yet. Not to him, anyway. When she flashed him a cutting glare, he addressed her challenging questions. "Curtis and I just spoke in passing. I hadn't even been hired yet as the police department's counselor. Besides, I'm a psychologist, not a miracle worker. I *did* visit your parents and discuss Curtis with them, but—"

"He shot himself." Her voice was low and her fluttering hands stilled on the desk top. "He shot himself," she repeated, then seemed to shake herself from a clinging nightmare. "I don't need to talk to you. I'm fine."

"I've spoken with the other members of your family and—"

"That's their business," she interrupted, her gaze darting to the clock. "I don't mean to be rude, but I'm on deadline. I can't talk now."

Evan turned sideways to look at the clock, knowing full well she was hours past her deadline. This was an afternoon newspaper, and in order to get the finished product out by two o'clock, all copy had to be in before noon. He decided to let the lie stand as he turned back to her.

"Okay. I'm sorry to interrupt your work. I'll be seeing you."

"Yeah, sure. Goodbye." She swiveled the chair, presenting her back to him.

Evan stared at the blue bow that gathered her blond hair into a curling ponytail. There was so much he wanted to say to her, so much he wanted her to understand, but his timing was lousy. She wasn't ready to listen. She was ignoring her pain; sweeping it under the rug in hopes it wouldn't be there when she peeked underneath again.

With a sigh of defeat, he pivoted and walked toward the bank of elevators. He'd come back, he told himself. He'd give her a while and then he'd come back. Maybe by that time she'd talk to him instead of just snipe at him.

Pushing the Down button, Evan glanced over his shoulder to find that she was looking at him; then her eyes darted away quickly when his gaze touched hers. He wondered what she was thinking. Did she really blame him for her brother's death? The elevator door opened and Evan stepped inside. Before it closed he saw her look at him again, a frown pulling down the corners of her mouth.

I haven't given up on you, Raleigh Torrence, he thought as the elevator descended to the street floor. Don't think you've seen the last of me.

He held up his coney sack, cupping his hand under it and feeling a touch of warmth there. The security guard smiled as Evan approached the desk.

"Here you go," Evan said, placing the sack on the guard's desk. "I've lost my appetite. Enjoy."

"Hey, thanks!" the guard called after him.

Evan waved a hand and pushed open the heavy door. It wasn't drizzling anymore. It was sleeting.

"Who was that *hunk*?" Cathy Carlsbad asked as soon as the elevator doors had closed.

Raleigh picked up her large glasses and pushed them up her nose. "The police department's psychologist." She bit into one of the coneys and took a sip of her cola.

"Oh, yeah." Cathy nodded slowly. "I remember seeing his picture. We ran a story on him the other day."

"I know. I wrote it."

"So you'd already met him before today."

"No." Raleigh sighed and leaned back in her chair. "I wrote the story from a police-department press release. I didn't see any need to interview Dr. Younger."

"What did he want?" Cathy asked, glancing toward the elevator again.

"He dropped by to offer me a miracle cure."

"A cure for what?" Cathy asked, perching on the corner of Raleigh's cluttered desk. "Are you sick or something?"

"No." Raleigh pushed the rest of her lunch back into the sack, no longer able to endure the sight of it. "But he thinks I am." She glanced at the clock again, then rummaged through her purse for her car keys. "I'm going home."

"It's not three yet," Cathy pointed out. "You never leave before three. Are you sure you're not sick?"

"I'm positive." Raleigh beat down the urge to berate Cathy for treating her like an invalid. It wasn't Cathy's fault. Everyone treated her with kid gloves these days, as if she might break into a million pieces at any moment. "I'm just cutting out a little early, that's all. If something comes up, tell them they can reach me at home."

"Okay. See you tomorrow."

"I'm afraid so." Raleigh softened the quip with a smile and went toward the cloakroom for her winter coat. Grant Farris, the *Times* owner and executive editor, was there hanging up his London Fog trench coat.

"Leaving early or do you have an appointment this afternoon?" he inquired as he slicked back his damp, dark hair.

"I have an appointment," Raleigh lied, then thought better of it. "At home."

"Well, you're entitled," Grant said consolingly as he helped her into her overly large coat. "You've been working hard these past few weeks."

"I always work hard," Raleigh pointed out, adjusting the belt.

"I figured you were just losing yourself in your work so that you wouldn't have to think about ... well, your personal problems." Grant rested a hand on her shoulder in a sympathetic way that made Raleigh cringe inside. "I understand, Raleigh. I did the same thing when

Zoe died." He swallowed hard. "I'm still not over it, I guess."

Raleigh removed her glasses slowly and tucked them into her coat pocket. She knew she should say something, but she simply couldn't think of anything appropriate. She'd run out of polite thank-yous and how-kind-of-yous and since her mother had taught her not to say anything if she couldn't say something nice, she certainly couldn't tell him what had leaped into her mind—that she found it difficult to believe he still mourned for his wife, Zoe, since she recalled how flagrantly unfaithful he had been to her. He hadn't even had the decency to hide his indiscretions. Everybody in the newsroom knew of Grant's roving eye and wandering hands. Raleigh flashed him the obligatory smile and left the cloakroom, mindful that he had expected more than that from her.

At the elevator, Raleigh waved at Sheila before stepping into the compartment. She saw Grant watching her with worried eyes before the door closed. At the fourth floor stop, a couple of women from the circulation department joined her, and Raleigh listened as they stabbed their supervisor in the back. Things are tough all over, she thought as she left the elevator on the street floor.

"Calling it a day, Raleigh?" the security guard asked, pausing to throw her a smile before he attacked another coney.

"Yes. See you tomorrow, Joseph." She halted at the door, examined the icy streets and tied her woolen scarf more tightly around her throat before she stepped into the biting sleet and roaring wind.

In like a lion, she thought as she ducked her head and carefully walked to the parking lot two blocks away. She was chilled to the bone when she finally collapsed behind the steering wheel of her battered, mustard-yellow Mustang. She started the engine, letting it idle and warm up while her breath fogged the windshield. Her thoughts tripped back to that awkward scene in the cloakroom with Grant Farris, and she chastised herself for leaving him there with nothing more than a halfhearted smile. He was her boss. She should have been nicer to him. After all, he could fire her just like that!

But he wouldn't, Raleigh thought with a sigh. If the rumors were true, Grant had more important things on his mind. Firing wasn't the issue: laying off people was more like it.

Raleigh switched on the heater, then switched it off again when cold air blasted into her face. Was it true that the newspaper was in financial trouble? she wondered, worry lines creasing her forehead. That was what she kept hearing in journalistic circles. It was a persistent rumor, the kind fueled by people in the know.

It was so hard to imagine Grant Farris broke, Raleigh mused. His family had established the *Times* before statehood and had never been destitute, even during the Dust Bowl and the Great Depression. Grant had married into money, and even though Zoe's illness had been costly, he couldn't have run through a fortune!

On the other hand, the city's other two dailies had been eating into the *Times*'s circulation for several decades. It didn't take a genius to know that afternoon newspapers were folding all across the country and that Tulsa wasn't big enough to support two of them plus a morning paper. Something had to give, Raleigh thought with a worried sigh, and the gossip-mongers all agreed that it was only a matter of time before Grant Farris folded the *Times*.

"As if I didn't have enough on my mind already," Raleigh grumbled, trying the heater again and letting the warm air caress her frozen fingertips.

Raleigh maneuvered the car onto the busy street, her concentration focused on the teeming traffic fighting against nature's elements. Her back tires slipped on the ice-covered street, then caught, and she cursed softly when the traffic light turned amber. Shrugging, she urged the car forward and crossed the intersection on the caution as her muscles tensed. To her left she saw the nondescript cluster of buildings that housed the city-government offices and police department. Six years of covering the police for the *Times* had made her infinitely familiar with those corridors, offices and cells. Of course, she'd been accustomed to them even before that, having visited Curtis there many times.

A red light blinked on ahead of her and Raleigh applied the brakes, never stopping, but rolling slowly and timing the traffic light perfectly. It turned green and she released her brake.

Curtis. He was in her thoughts more now than when he'd been alive. Everything and everyone seemed to remind her of him. Every time she saw a police uniform, she saw Curtis. During every visit to the police station she expected to bump into him. The other day she'd been interviewing a police officer about a string of burglaries in the Brookside area when she'd heard a man laugh, a hiccuping sort of laugh that had brought tears of joy to her eyes. But it hadn't been Curtis.

The officer with her had seemed to understand her abrupt seesaw from elation to despair, and had laid a comforting hand on hers, which had made her all the more embarrassed.

"Curtis is dead," she murmured viciously to herself. "Dead!"

A horn blared and Raleigh slammed on her brakes instinctively. The Mustang fishtailed, and Raleigh shut her eyes and readied herself for a collision. When nothing happened, she opened her eyes to find that she was in the middle of an intersection and other drivers were waiting impatiently for her to get out of their way. She hit the accelerator, only then realizing that the engine had died. Frantic, Raleigh started the car again and eased the Mustang across the intersection. She inched it toward the curb, steered it into a parking space and killed the engine.

Shaking, she covered her face with her hands. "Why did you do it, Curtis?" she asked wearily. "Didn't you know how much I loved you?"

Evan propped his feet up on his desk and opened the file marked "Torrence, Curtis E., Sergeant." Pasted to the inside cover was a typical mug shot of a man with a thick neck, a shock of blond hair and a stern expression that contradicted the gentleness in his hazel eyes. He held little resemblance to the disturbed police officer Evan had met in the corridor right outside this office.

Staring at the photograph, Evan recalled that snowy, gray day when he'd talked briefly with Curtis Torrence. Evan had been given a quick tour of the police station after another round of interviews for the job of counselor. He'd felt pretty good that day, thinking he had the job in the bag even though twenty others had applied for it. It was his third callback, and he had spoken with the mayor and the chief of police this time. They had seemed impressed with him.

He'd heard of Curtis Torrence, of course. Curtis was one of the reasons the city of Tulsa had decided it needed a counselor on the police department staff. An outstanding officer who covered the skid-row beat, Curtis was nevertheless having problems. He was an alcoholic and a two-time loser in the marriage arena. The chief had told Evan that something had to be done about Curtis, but he'd offered no solutions. *That* would be Evan's bailiwick, if he got the job.

The chief had taken Evan to see the office he might call his own within the next few weeks, but the office was locked and the chief had left Evan standing in the corridor while he'd gone to fetch the keys. That was when Curtis had sauntered up. Well, sauntered was the wrong word, Evan thought as the memory became clearer. Staggered would be a better description. Curtis had been three sheets to the wind.

Curtis had run his hand continually through his light-blond hair, mussing it and making it stand up in places. His gaze had darted around the corridor, lightly touching this, glancing off that. He'd never looked Evan directly in the eyes....

"Are you one of the guys up for the counselor job?" Curtis had asked, his words slurring together.

"That's right. I'm Evan Younger." Evan had stuck out his hand and had shaken Curtis's. "And you're—"

"One of your future problems." Curtis had grinned, and in that moment he had looked boyish and bewildered, as if he'd emerged from his alcoholic stupor long enough to wonder how he had gotten into such a mess. "Curtis Torrence. I guess you've heard about me? I'm the one they don't know what to do with."

"Oh, yes. Nice to meet you."

"Captain McDowell says I should make an appointment with whoever gets the counselor job." Curtis had shrugged, dismissing the notion. "He means well, but..."

"But what?" Evan had pressed. "Do you and Captain McDowell talk about your drinking problem?"

"Drinking isn't the problem," Curtis had said with surprising clarity.

"Well, at least you understand that much," Evan had said, trying unsuccessfully to capture Curtis's eye. "What *is* the problem, Curtis? Would you like to go somewhere later and talk about it? Maybe we could find a way to eliminate the problem."

Curtis had laughed then, a hiccuping kind of laugh that was full of nervous energy. "That's a crock and you know it!" Slamming his fist into his other palm, he had drawn a deep breath. "You can't change anything. None of us can! *That's* the problem."

Realizing that they were getting nowhere fast, Evan had written his home phone number on one of his old business cards. "Curtis, let me give you my home number. If you want, you can call me up and we'll go out and lift a few."

"Thanks." He'd taken the card, glanced at it and stuck it in his wallet. "Welcome to the zoo, doc."

Blinking away the memory, Evan flipped through the folder to find the personal effects list. His card was listed among the things found in Curtis's wallet on the night of his death.

That brief meeting had disturbed Evan; so much so that he'd phoned Edgar and Dixie Torrence and discussed Curtis with them. They had been at their wits' end, and Evan's heart had gone out to them. The news of Curtis's death had been a vicious blow to Evan, and when he'd returned to Tulsa after taking care of loose ends in Las Vegas, he had paid a courtesy call on the Torrences. Cara had been there and a cousin, Hess, but Raleigh had been noticeably absent. The Torrences had seemed appreciative of Evan's concern, but Evan had felt crushing defeat. It went with the job, he supposed, even though he hadn't been given the counselor position at that time. Only after Captain Roger McDowell's funeral had the city of Tulsa finally appointed Evan as the police department counselor. To Evan, it was like applying a bandage to an open wound.

Well, doc, you get the job! Have everything straightened out in a couple of days, okay? We've lost two good men, and we don't want to lose any more now that you're here. Can't you wave a magic wand and make everything all better?

Evan sighed wearily. At least Curtis Torrence had had enough sense to know that deeply rooted problems couldn't disappear overnight.

Turning to the back of the file, Evan found the sheet of paper that bothered him the most. He stared at a copy of Curtis Torrence's suicide letter, then forced himself to read it again:

To Whom It May Concern,

I hope this letter doesn't hurt anyone. That's not my intention. I just want to set a few things straight. You see, I'm tired. Very tired. I thought I could make a difference, but I ended up just a burden to the people I love and to the people I care about. It won't be hard to pull the trigger—it will be easy. Much easier than carrying on with this pitiful excuse for living.

If Captain McDowell knew about this, he'd try to talk me out of it. He'd tell me that I can conquer this lust I have for the bottle. I've conquered it before, and I can do it again. But this time, old Cap, I don't want to. It's just not worth it. It's like being on a haunted carousel. I keep grabbing the brass ring, and then something or someone jerks it out of my hand.

My parents will breathe a sigh of relief when they hear about this. They love me, I know that, but I have been a constant worry to them the past few years. I just want them to know that it isn't their fault. It had nothing to do with them.

The Chief will be relieved, too. He doesn't know what to do with me.

Some of the guys on the force—guys like Cody Wakefield—will be sad when they hear about me. Most of them will be glad. They know who they are. They know they made my life miserable. They know they deserted me when I needed them the most. What has happened to humanity? What happened to brotherly love? Don't they know we're all in this together?

My ex-wives will shed a few tears, but they won't be sorry at my passing. They have drained me dry—women tend to do that to me—and they cast me aside long ago.

As for Cara and Raleigh, I know they won't understand, and I know they'll carry this around with them. Please, I beg of them, don't. You had nothing to do with my decision. You are both so beautiful. Don't let this ruin your lives. Cara will bounce back, but Raleigh will be hurt the most. Raleigh, you're just going to have to face the fact that your big brother was a weakling. You always said I was strong, but you're the strong one. Be strong for me. Raleigh always saw me as a knight on a white charger, but I fell off that noble steed a long time ago.

The windmills still beckon me, as they did Don Quixote, but I no longer have the strength to fight them. So, I'm doing what all my fellow officers have kept telling me to do. When I came to you guys and told you I needed help, you all told me I was going to have to help myself. You told me I had to take care of myself.

I'm following your advice, guys. I'm taking care of myself. Finally.

Curtis Torrence

Evan closed his eyes again, his gut churning at the waste of it all. The penmanship on the last page of the letter was shaky, as if the writer had been in a hurry to finish it.

Opening his eyes, Evan glanced down at another sheet of paper in the file. Curtis Torrence had been awarded the honor of Police Officer of the Year two months before he'd shot himself. He had received the award for his work, on and off duty, in the small section of Tulsa known as skid row. Curtis had worked with the bums, the drunks, the prostitutes. He had called attention to their needs and their sicknesses. He had forced the city to recognize them and do something about them. And Curtis Torrence had become one of them, Evan thought with a grimace. He had become an alcoholic, receiving a cure only to backslide into a bottle of whiskey a few months later.

Reading the police report on the suicide, Evan shuddered as the scenario gathered strength in his imagination. After completing his shift near midnight on Sunday, Curtis had driven to an all-night restaurant near downtown where policemen stopped for coffee breaks. He had talked to a couple of fellow officers there, and they had shared a cup of coffee and a few laughs. Then Curtis had left the restaurant and gone to his squad car parked at the back of the building. He had written his suicide note, placed his police revolver to his temple and pulled the trigger. He had been found an hour later by the two officers he had joked with earlier. They'd heard the gunshot but had decided it was a car backfiring. Curtis had been pronounced dead on arrival at St. John Medical Center.

Evan glanced at the suicide letter again. There was a touch of poetry in the scrawled words. It revealed a man with a soft heart, maybe even a bruised heart.

And Curtis had singled out Raleigh, Evan noted, recalling that the other family members he'd talked with had done the same thing. Mr. and Mrs. Torrence and Cara had all praised Raleigh for "holding up so well, and keeping a calm head." That's what bothered Evan. Raleigh was a lot like Curtis. She kept things inside, things that should be released.

He had hoped he'd find a well-adjusted woman today at the *Times*, but his hopes had been dashed. Raleigh was fooling herself. She hadn't accepted Curtis's suicide. That had become apparent when she'd accused Evan of not helping her brother. Raleigh was looking for logic in a situation that was totally illogical. Curtis had been right about his little sister. She was the one who had been hurt the most by his suicide.

Evan closed the folder with a heavy sigh. He couldn't help Curtis now, but he could damn well help Raleigh. And he would, whether she liked it or not.

Chapter Two

Another deadline passed in a flurry of shouted orders from the editors, hasty rewrites by the reporters and frantic phone calls to double-check information.

Raleigh fell back in her office chair, removed her glasses and ran a hand across her eyes in weary relief. Wishing she could kick off her shoes and prop her stocking feet on the desk, she smiled and opted instead for a cup of hot tea. She took her china cup and saucer to the employee canteen at the back of the huge newsroom and filled the delicate cup with hot water. Dipping a tea bag in and out of the steaming water, Raleigh reflected on the story she had just finished.

Changes were brewing in the police department, subtle changes that made Raleigh wonder if the impact of Curtis's suicide was responsible for a new attitude among the policemen. Several Tulsa policemen had formed "the God squad," as they called it, and were recruiting other officers to their fold. They met every morning at the East Precinct for a half hour of brotherhood and prayer before they separated to their squad cars, and on each car's dashboard was a Bible.

Had Curtis's final cry been heard? Raleigh wondered as she added a spoonful of creamer to her tea. Were the policemen finally realizing that it was easier to cope with the stress of their jobs together, instead of going it alone?

"Raleigh?"

Raleigh turned toward Mike Allison, who was standing half in and half out of the canteen. "Yes, Mike?"

"Grant's having an editorial meeting, and he wants you in on it."

"Me?" Raleigh asked, surprised by the request. She was never invited into the inner circle. "Why does he want me in there?"

Mike shrugged and began backing out of the doorway. "Beats me. We're waiting for you."

"Okay, I'm coming." Raleigh paused to stir her tea, wondering why Grant Farris wanted her to sit in on a meeting normally reserved for the editors. Had she bungled a story? Had she misquoted someone? Her lips stretched into a grim line as she carried her tea toward the bank of executive offices that took up the east side of the newsroom.

The conference room, where meetings took place each day following the final deadline, was tastefully decorated in muted shades of brown and ivory. It had a definite masculine stamp to it, and Raleigh noted with an inner twinge of discomfort that she was the only female in the room. Paul Rondyke, the city editor, gave her a warm smile and patted the couch cushion next to him as Raleigh entered.

"Here she is," Paul said. "Have a seat, hon."

"Thanks." Raleigh tipped her head and smiled to the other men as Grant cleared his throat for attention.

"Now that Raleigh's here, I guess we can proceed," Grant said with a flourish of importance.

The other editors shuffled through papers and held pens, ready to take notes if needed.

"Raleigh, I asked you to sit in on this part of the meeting because we're going to discuss the Rendell case," Grant explained, giving her a fleeting glance. "Since you've covered that on the police end, I thought you should hear the discussion."

"Oh, I see," Raleigh murmured, but she didn't see. The Rendell case? Why were they going over that? Howard Rendell had faced charges for murdering his wife and an Arrowhead Country Club golf pro, but the jury had failed to reach a verdict. Rendell was a free man. They'd run a story yesterday summing everything up. What else could be done? Staring at her teacup, which seemed so out of place amid the pipes, cigars and smell of aftershave, Raleigh told herself she should have brought a notebook and pen with her. This wasn't a tea party!

"Let's not beat around the bush," Grant said, capturing the wandering attention in the room. He unbuttoned his expensively tailored jacket and leaned back in his executive's chair. "I'm extremely disappointed in the lack of coverage on the Rendell case."

Blank stares greeted his assessment, and Raleigh hid her own budding smile. Was he kidding or what? What was there left to cover? Beside her, Paul stirred restlessly and tapped the eraser end of his pencil against his knee.

"Rendell is a free man until further notice, Grant," Paul said hesitantly. "I don't quite follow—"

"Yes, but what about the failure of justice?" Grant demanded, placing both hands flat on his desk and leaning forward. "The jury let that murderer go scot-free, and we need to run an editorial about this gross irresponsibility!"

The men stared at their notepads as an uncomfortable silence settled in the room. Raleigh sighed heavily, drawing Grant's dark gaze. He arched his brows as if challenging her to comment.

"I think you're beating a dead horse, Grant," Raleigh said, accepting his mute challenge. "A man is innocent until proved guilty, so why should the *Times* point the finger at the jury just because they couldn't reach a decision? Hung juries aren't *that* uncommon. The jurors needed a preponderance of the evidence and they didn't get it."

"Exactly!" Grant catapulted from his chair. "The jurors can't be blamed, but the district attorney's office should be called on the carpet!"

"The D.A.'s office?" Raleigh shook her head and noticed that she wasn't alone. Mike Allison scratched the top of his head where his hair was thinning and threw Paul Rondyke a baffled look.

"Yes, the D.A.'s office," Grant repeated. "The district attorney appointed to the case showed total incompetence. If a *man* had been handling it, instead of that fluffy-headed—"

"Wait just a minute." Raleigh sat up straighter and met Grant's scowling regard with bold determination. "Are you suggesting that the *Times* attack the assigned D.A. just because she happens to be female?" Raleigh could feel the tension emanating from the editors, but she couldn't let this pass. "Because if you are, I must tell you that I don't want to be employed by a newspaper that would practice such blatant sex discrimination."

Fury settled in Grant's dark eyes, and his lips stretched into a tense line, but Raleigh felt neither remorse nor fear at his reaction. He could fire her right this instant, she thought, and it wouldn't make the slightest bit of difference to her. She just didn't care, and that made her realize how tiresome her work had become and what a coward she was for not going out and seeking new challenges. Hardly aware of the others who sat tensely around her, Raleigh sipped her tea and waited for Grant to release her from the chains of employment.

"Raleigh, you've misunderstood me," Grant said with a mirthless chuckle. Some of the anger left his handsome face as he shoved his hands into his trouser pockets. "I didn't mean to imply that I have found fault with Liann McDowell just because she's female." His lips curved in an indulgent smile and he chuckled again, his gaze moving from Raleigh to the others in the room. "You should know by now that I adore women! I'm even smitten with you." His dark-brown eyes swiveled to her, glimmering with masculine innuendos that made Raleigh's skin crawl.

Grasping the bit of fluff and nonsense Grant had offered, the other men laughed heartily, and a couple of them poked elbows at each other and winked knowingly. Raleigh refused to join in the jocularity, preferring to stare Grant Farris down. She felt a moment of triumph when he looked away, no longer able to withstand her smoking glare.

"I'm not going to argue about this." Grant swung one leg back and forth and stared at the nameplate on his desk that declared he was the owner and publisher of the *Times*. "I want heavy coverage on the Rendell hung jury, and that's that."

The editors jotted down his instruction, and Raleigh finished off her tea. If she lived to be a hundred, she'd never understand some of the decisions made on this newspaper. She couldn't help but wonder what ax Grant was grinding with this new directive. Had Rendell snubbed Grant at a social gathering? It was probably something like that—some trivial affront that had made Grant want to keep Rendell in the glare of the public spotlight. In many ways, Grant Farris was an immature man, a spoiled rich kid who'd never completely grown up.

Mike Allison tapped his pen against his notepad. "Grant, about this pari-mutuel betting issue coming up in Creek County..."

"Yes, what about it?"

"Well, do you want the paper to be for or against it? The question will go before the people in a few weeks and—"

"I don't care which stand we take. I'll leave that to your editorial department."

Mike's eyes reflected his surprise, and he glanced at Paul. The city editor shrugged and shook his head in a show of confusion.

"Is there a problem, Mike?" Grant asked, having noted the silent exchange.

Mike ran a finger around his shirt collar. "You were so strongly in favor of the pari-mutuel question in Okmulgee County that I just assumed you would have a preference this time." When he received no comment from Grant, Mike added, "The *Times* pushed for approval in Okmulgee County, and the people voted it in there. I just thought—"

"That was different," Grant interrupted, waving a hand to dismiss the subject. "I don't care what happens in Creek County." Grant returned his attention to Raleigh. "You know Cody Wakefield pretty well, don't you?"

The abrupt question threw her off guard, and Raleigh could only nod. How did Cody Wakefield fit into this?

"I thought so." Grant stood up and rocked back on his heels. "He'd be a good news source."

Raleigh nodded again. "He always has been. He's one of the police officers I can always depend on."

"Good. Buddy up to him and get an insider's look at the progression of the Rendell case. I think something's going on that we're not being told about."

Raleigh arched her brows. "Do you know something I don't?"

Grant's lips twisted in a cunning smile. "Just do as I say, Raleigh. Wakefield is your friend. A good reporter knows how to use that sort of thing."

Raleigh held back the words that burned in her mind. How dare he ask her to use her friendship with Cody? She decided to let it pass, but she had no intention of following Grant's advice. The reason Cody was honest with her was because he trusted her, and she wasn't going to betray that trust.

Grant fingered the chain dangling across his vest and pulled out his pocket watch. He flipped open the lid to check the time, and a snatch of "Happy Days Are Here Again" floated into the room.

Raleigh cringed inwardly, recalling when Grant had opened that gold watch at her brother's funeral and let those chiming notes escape. The cheery tune had cut through Raleigh, and she'd barely kept herself from snatching the watch out of his hand and grinding it into the freshly turned dirt with the heel of her shoe.

"That's all for today, gentlemen." Grant's dark gaze lifted briefly to Raleigh and he grinned. "And gentle-woman."

Ignoring the insipid remark, Raleigh stood up and escaped from the stifling atmosphere. She far preferred the buzzing activity of the newsroom, and she hoped she wouldn't be invited into the inner circle again.

She headed to the canteen for another cup of tea, all the while dissecting the meeting and the undercurrent of confusion. She couldn't blame the editors for not challenging Grant's policies. They had families to support and times were shaky, at best. Everyone had heard rumors of the newspaper's financial woes, and most of the staff preferred to cling to their jobs and not tempt fate.

Although Grant had never been a great executive editor, he hadn't been completely negligent, either. However, the meeting had changed Raleigh's mind about her boss. Was the financial pressure getting to Grant and muddling his thinking? One minute he was enthusiastically endorsing pari-mutuel betting in Okmulgee County, and the next he was indifferent to the same issue in Creek County. Was he so cloistered in his own high-echelon life that he failed to understand how crucial each county vote was to Oklahoma's future?

It had been a major step for the state to approve county-option pari-mutuel betting and it would have a profound effect on the coffers of each county. The *Times* might be losing subscribers to the other two dailies, but it still had an obligation to keep its remaining readers informed and enlightened on this topic.

Raleigh sighed in frustration as she took a sip of her tea. Grant was losing it. He was concerned about dead issues like the Howard Rendell case and totally unconcerned about the real problems facing the state. Instead of reporting the news, Grant was creating it—the first step toward disaster in the communications field.

The door to the canteen opened, and Raleigh turned to see Grant approaching her.

"Here you are," he said, smiling.

"Is there another meeting I'm supposed to sit in on?" Her flippancy didn't faze his beaming smile.

"I was wondering if you'd like to go out to lunch with me. You've worked here for. . ."

"Almost ten years," Raleigh supplied.

"Ten years, and I've never taken you out to lunch." He stepped back, waiting for her to lead the way.

Raleigh stood firm. "Thanks, but I've lost my appetite."

Grant laughed, throwing his head back a little so that Raleigh could admire his profile. "That's one of the things I've always liked about you. You never give an inch, do you? Even when you're courting disaster. Are you upset about my suggestion that you buddy up to Cody?"

"I don't believe in the buddy system, Grant." Raleigh eased herself into one of the canteen chairs and set her cup and saucer on the small table. "What I'm really concerned about is the talk I keep hearing that the *Times* is a sinking ship. One of the reporters called it the *Titanic Times* the other day."

Grant's indulgent smile died. "If you'd do your job and stop spreading gossip, I wouldn't have to keep giving you instructions on how to get information from your sources! That's one thing I can't abide about you women staffers. You spend most of your time in here trading bits of gossip and—"

"The staff members who are gossiping about losing their jobs when the newspaper folds are mostly male,"

Raleigh informed him. "Is the paper in the crimson column, Grant? I think we have a right to know if we're going to be in the unemployment line next month."

"That's ridiculous," Grant said with a snort. "Every afternoon paper is having a little trouble these days, but the *Times* isn't folding. I don't want you carrying that tale, do you hear me?" He pointed a menacing finger at her. "You just stick close to Wakefield and do your job."

"Why?" Raleigh ignored the inner voice that was telling her to tread softly. "Why are you so interested in Cody?"

"Because he's fooling around with the district attorney, that's why!" Grant placed his hands on the table and leaned into Raleigh's face. "Are you so dense that you don't see that as a little suspicious? Talk about strange bedfellows! The investigating officer of the Rendell case is sleeping with the D.A. assigned to the case!"

"So what? Are we a newspaper or a cheap tabloid?" Raleigh pointed out, just barely remaining civil. "Since when is the newspaper interested in the private, intimate lives of people? I don't see anything suspicious about a man falling in love with a woman. If we're going to start a sex scandal, then be prepared to have the spotlight directed closer to home, Grant."

She knew she'd overstepped the boundaries of good sense when Grant's eyes took on a mean brilliance.

"Just what are you implying, Raleigh?" His voice was as cold and bone-chilling as a March wind.

"Forget it," Raleigh murmured, sensing that he knew she was referring to his own scandalous bedroom romps. "I just think we should get our priorities straight around here."

"So do I." Grant pivoted and headed for the door. "And if you can't cover your beat adequately, then I'll find someone who can. You just worry about *your* priorities, Miss Torrence. I asked our library to bring up the file on Rendell for you. It's on your desk, and I would strongly suggest that you look it over."

The swinging door closed behind Grant, and Raleigh let out her breath in a hiss. How long could she work for a man who was losing his grip on what was right and what was wrong? He had come far short of convincing her that all was well with the *Times* financially and Raleigh acknowledged an itch to go while the going was good. But it was a cruel world out there, she cautioned herself. Newspaper jobs were at a premium, and she had heard through the grapevine that the other newspapers weren't hiring new employees.

Feeling like a fly caught in a web, Raleigh stood up and poured the rest of her tea down the sink drain. Grant could fire her, but she was not going to use her friendship with Cody Wakefield in a dishonest way. If Cody had anything on the Rendell case, he would tell her.

Raleigh pushed through the canteen door, then stopped in her tracks when she saw the police psychologist hovering near her desk. Not him again! she thought with a burst of frustration. Why was he hounding her? Was he so thick-headed that he hadn't gotten her crystal-clear message that she didn't want to see him again?

She wrestled with indecision as one part of her mind told her to face him and another told her to duck back into the canteen and hide. He was standing by her desk, his head tilted to one side as he read something lying there. The Rendell file, no doubt, Raleigh thought as she took in his pea jacket and faded jeans. It occurred to her that he didn't fit her image of a psychologist. For one thing, he was too young. He should have white hair and a trimmed beard, she thought, not a tumble of curly brown hair and a clean-shaven face that revealed two deep dimples grooving his lean cheeks. And why wasn't he dressed in a suit and tie? Didn't he know that a pea jacket and jeans were inappropriate for a trained psychologist?

Recalling Cathy Carlsbad's description of Evan Younger a few weeks ago, Raleigh grudgingly admitted it was accurate. He was a hunk, whatever that was. Tall and lean, he had a friendly smile and easygoing demeanor, both of which he was trying out now on Cathy.

Raleigh realized too late that he was asking after her whereabouts, and she had no time to hide as Cathy pointed in her direction. Evan followed her pointing finger with his blue-eyed gaze, and his smile widened when he spotted Raleigh. Heaving a resigned sigh, Raleigh forced herself forward to greet him. As she neared him, she noticed the sack that he held aloft and smiled, feeling her disgruntled mood dissipate.

"Coneys," she said, taking the sack from him.

"This time they *are* for you. I hope you haven't already eaten lunch."

"No, I haven't." Raleigh slid into her desk chair and opened the sack. The aroma of spicy chili wafted up to her, and she realized she hadn't lost her appetite after all. "I would think you'd have more important duties than to deliver coneys."

"Oh, I do, but I'm on my lunch hour." He sat down in the chair beside her desk. "This Howard Rendell trial is big news. Just exactly what was he accused of?" He tapped his fingers on the thick file bearing that name, and Raleigh noticed he wore no wedding band.

"Have you been living in a cave or what?" she asked, then realized he was a newcomer to Tulsa. "Oh, you weren't here when all this stuff came down, were you?"

"No, I guess not." Evan relaxed in the chair and opened his coat to reveal a bulky white sweater beneath. "The name rings a bell, but I can't place him."

Raleigh tasted one of the coneys and opened the soft drink Evan had also provided. "It's a long story."

Evan checked his watch. "I've got half an hour, so talk fast."

Raleigh smiled and eyed him warily. "Do you really want to hear about this?"

Evan's lips twitched into a grin. "I'm hanging on your every word."

Deciding that she'd much rather talk of Howard Rendell than of herself or Curtis, Raleigh took him up on his tongue-in-cheek request. "Okay, you asked for it. Howard Rendell is what we refer to in this business as a prominent Tulsa citizen. He owns an oil company here, and he was married to and divorced from Victoria Rendell. His ex-wife was murdered along with her lover, a playboy type who was a golf pro at Arrowhead Country Club."

"Ah! The plot thickens." Evan grinned, waiting for her to finish one of the coneys and continue. "Rendell was charged with the murders."

"He was, but the jury failed to reach a decision and the case against him has been dismissed."

"So?" Evan glanced at the file. "Do you still suspect him?"

Raleigh shrugged and reached for a paper napkin. "It's not my job to accuse or condone. I just report the facts."

"Why are you looking through his file?"

"I'm not." Raleigh pushed the file to one side. "I wrote most of those stories. I don't need to read them again."

"I don't understand."

"Join the club." Raleigh removed the other coney from the sack and sighed. "Look, it's been a long day. I appreciate the gesture, but I'm really not in the mood to chat." She looked at him fully for the first time. "I know why you're here and you're wasting your time."

Evan smiled and stood up. "It's my time to waste, Raleigh, but I have no right to waste yours." He stuck his hand in his coat pocket and withdrew a cellophane-wrapped peppermint candy, which he tossed onto her desk. "Here. Sweeten up your life a little, Torrence."

She glanced down at the candy, and when she glanced back up she found that he was strolling toward the elevators. Raleigh shook her head, confused by his parting gesture.

"Goodbye," she called after him. He raised a hand in response but didn't turn around.

Collapsing onto the couch, Raleigh picked up the classified section of the *Times* and scanned the help-wanted column. The weight of the day sapped the remaining energy from her as she kicked off her slippers and relaxed against the soft cushions. After thawing a frozen dinner, she'd forced herself to eat part of the bland green beans, roast beef, starchy mashed potatoes and soggy brownie. She remembered when food had been a major event in her life, and she wondered if she should get a checkup. Granted her loss of appetite had whittled her pudgy frame down from a size sixteen to a size nine, but it wasn't like her to walk past the frozen dessert section in the grocery store without so much as a glance! She had a sweet concoction in the freezer right now, and it had been there since last summer.

Last summer? It occurred to her that her disinterest in food coincided with an uneasy conversation she'd had with Curtis last summer. Had he planted the seeds of discontent within her then? Had she realized that day that all was not what it seemed with Curtis?

She recalled their conversation on a humid, August night when they'd taken a stroll through Woodward Park after seeing a film about a young girl with a terminal disease. It had depressed both of them, and they'd walked in a suffocating silence for a long while before Curtis had finally broken through it as if coming up for air.

"I wish they'd make a movie about someone with a terminal disease of the mind or of the spirit."

Raleigh had glanced sideways at him and was momentarily transfixed by the way the moonlight spilled through the tree branches and created a halo around his blond head. "You mean a movie about mental illness? They've done that."

"No, not mental illness." He looked up at the sky, and the milky light bathed his face. "It's hard to explain. It's like a cancer of the soul, eating away at you and taking little pieces until there's hardly anything left to hold on to."

"I'm not following you." Raleigh stopped, touched his sleeve and made him turn toward her. "I wish we'd seen a comedy tonight. It's such a lovely evening, and I can't enjoy it because of that stupid—"

"Raleigh, you're not listening to me." His voice was ragged, his expression desperate. "Why doesn't anyone ever listen to me?"

Surprised and guilt-ridden, she'd grasped his upper arms. "I'm sorry, Curtis. I'm listening, but I just don't understand."

"How could you?" His expression had softened with love. "How could you understand my jabbering? You with your solid, shining spirit. You see obstacles so clearly and you just...just jump over them or climb over them, but you get over them, don't you?"

"So do you."

"No." He ducked his head and gently removed himself from her reach. "I get stuck. I can't find a way around them, so I sit down and let the disease take me again."

"What disease?" A burst of panic seized her, and suddenly the night seemed black indeed. "Are you sick, Curtis?"

"No." He laughed at her stricken expression. "Not physically. I'm just lost, honey. I guess I always have been."

"Curtis, don't talk like that. You're scaring me."

"Am I?" His eyes were luminous in the moonlight, making them unreadable. "I don't want to do that." In the blink of an eye, the melancholy disappeared and he smiled radiantly, making the shadows recede. "How about a double-dip fudge-ripple ice cream cone?"

"Okay."

But she hadn't been able to finish the cone—a first in the life of Raleigh Torrence. It was as if whatever had been eating at Curtis had infected her, too. She found herself studying him closely, but gleaning nothing from him. All seemed well with Curtis, but Raleigh had been conscious of a shadow across his soul. His smile was beautiful, but not completely genuine. His mood was light, but practiced. Something was amiss with her brother, and it had made her feel edgy and nervous. She felt like Chicken Little, waiting for a crack in the blue sky.

The sky had fallen all right, but it had been the roar of a gun that had started the avalanche.

Anxious to escape the weight of all that had come before, Raleigh reached for another section of the paper and read the editorial condemning the D.A.'s office for botching the Rendell case. What Grant wants, Grant gets, even if it means stopping the presses and shoving in this bit of yellow journalism. The paper had hit the streets an hour later than usual because of Grant's insistence that this editorial run immediately. Raleigh glanced over it again, then threw the newspaper aside. *That* should go over like a lead balloon at City Hall and the police department, she thought with a sigh. Thanks for making my job easier, Grant, dear.

Her stomach muscles tightened into a cramp, and she placed a hand on her forehead. Was she sick or just heartsick? Would she ever be able to get through a day without missing Curtis?

On impulse, she dialed her sister's home number, but Cara didn't answer. Dejected, Raleigh slammed down the receiver and flopped back onto the couch. Cara was probably teaching an aerobics class this evening, or she was at some faculty function at the university. Lord knows Cara keeps herself busy, Raleigh thought. If she's not teaching sociology at the University of Tulsa, then she's working out at the gym or making others work up a sweat through aerobics.

Placing her hands across her stomach, Raleigh told herself it wouldn't hurt if she indulged in a bit of exercise, but then she quickly dismissed the notion. One health nut in the family was enough, she told herself. Cara expended enough energy to excuse the entire Torrence clan.

Cara had always been a little dynamo, Raleigh reflected. Her thoughts strayed to her childhood days, when Cara and Curtis had been her playmates. Life had

been so simple then; summery days spent playing cow-
boys and Indians in front of the grocery store her parents had owned until a few years ago, when an inner-city
expressway had taken it.

Those had been golden days, Raleigh mused, letting
her thoughts drift gently back to that dreamy time again.
Cara had entertained them with back flips and somer-
saults, displaying her athletic prowess and boundless energy, while Curtis had hypnotized his sisters with tall tales
he'd made up on the spur of the moment. Many nights
had been spent huddled on the floor of Curtis's bedroom while he spoke in a hushed whisper and told them
of far-off lands, knights in shining armor, beautiful
maidens, and dragons that breathed tongues of flame.

Relatives had predicted that Curtis would become a
writer, but Raleigh had been the one to pursue that goal.
While Curtis had possessed the makings of a writer, he'd
lacked the necessary discipline and ambition. Raleigh
couldn't remember Curtis ever being on time for anything, so writing deadlines would have been out of the
question. If he'd been more focused and more disci-
plined, would he have been happier as a writer? Raleigh
wondered. Would that have made a difference in his life?
Even as a boy, Curtis had seemed slightly out of step with
the pace of life. He and melancholy had always gone
hand in hand—close, uneasy friends who needed each
other, but didn't trust that mutual need.

Raleigh shook her head, dislodging the memories that
had become tinged with sadness. If Curtis's problems had
started back in his childhood, there would have been
nothing Raleigh could have done about them. She had
been a child then, too, and unmindful of the darker areas
of the human spirit. Cara was always onto her about
shouldering everyone's problems. Even when they were

kids, Raleigh had been the peacemaker, quick to settle fights between Cara and Curtis. The youngest of the children, she had developed an aversion to disharmony early in life.

Smiling, she remembered an autumn day in her seventh year when her father had bought them all a cotton candy at the Tulsa State Fair. Curtis had tried to snatch a bite off Cara's and, in the process, had dropped his own sugary cone to the ground. Edgar Torrence had refused to buy Curtis another, telling him he'd gotten what he deserved, but Raleigh couldn't stand to see Curtis cry. She had given him her own cotton candy and her father had bought her another after giving her a lecture about being too softhearted.

As the memories washed over her, Raleigh closed her eyes and wished for those simpler days when they'd all been together. It had been lovely then, a long span of cloudless skies with not a hint of rain to mar the horizon.

Dropping into a half-conscious state, Raleigh felt the tension ease from her body. The newspaper slipped from her lap and she removed her glasses, turned onto her side and curved her body into the fetal position as her thoughts moved toward dreams.

The rapping of knuckles against her front door made her surface from the dream state with a jerk. She sat up and rubbed her eyes, irritated by the intrusion. Her first impulse was to not answer the door, but then she thought better of it. It might be Cara. Her sister stopped by every once in a while in the evenings.

Pushing herself up from the couch, Raleigh threaded her way across the cluttered living room to the door. She unlatched it and threw it open—only to wish she hadn't when Evan Younger delivered one of his engaging smiles.

Chapter Three

Raleigh leaned against the open door and lifted one dark blond brow in inquiry. "Yes?"

Evan held up a round package. "You ordered a Canadian bacon with extra cheese and a six-pack?"

"No," she replied solemnly, resisting the impulse to smile. "No, I did not."

Checking the top of the package, Evan scowled. "It says right here that this was ordered for Raleigh Torrence. Are you Miss Torrence?"

"I'm *Ms*. Torrence, but I didn't order a pizza and I hate beer." She realized she was enjoying this exchange and couldn't help but laugh softly when Evan glared at her in mock exasperation.

"*Ms*. Torrence, I'm freezing my tush off out here. Can't I come in, please?"

"You should have phoned first." Receiving a frustrated sigh from him at this, Raleigh ended the game and stepped back to let him enter. "Okay, okay. Come on in."

He hurried in, paused to negotiate the room and its supply of scattered newspapers and throw pillows, and placed the pizza on top of the magazines that littered the coffee table.

"You hate beer?"

"I despise it." Raleigh lifted the wrapped pizza, shoved the magazines aside and set the pizza down again. "You'll get grease stains on my magazines."

Evan glanced at them and chuckled. "Most of those are several months old. Haven't you read them yet?"

"Not all of them." She tilted up her chin and tightened the belt of her robe when his gaze moved slowly over her. She wished she still had on her work clothes: she had the distinct feeling that Evan Younger had X-ray vision and could tell she wore nothing but lacy panties beneath the robe. "I've already eaten dinner."

"One piece of pizza," Evan cajoled, waving a slice beneath her nose. "It won't kill you."

"I know why you're here and it isn't to feed me." She crossed her arms and watched as he tore one of the beer cans from its cardboard holder. The game was irritating her now. Did he think she was born yesterday? He was here to counsel her, not to socialize.

"I'm here because I hate to eat alone and I knew you'd welcome me into your..." His gaze swept the small living area. "Your hovel."

"Hovel?" Raleigh viewed the room with new eyes. It *was* cluttered and tiny, but it was hers! "That's a fine how-do-you-do!"

He smiled at this and relaxed on the couch. "When I first drove up I thought you might live in that house in front."

"That mansion?" Raleigh shook her head. "On a reporter's salary? Be real."

"Sit down and wrap your gums around a slice of pizza." He cocked his head to one side, indicating the cushion next to him. "I checked the address again and saw the 'R.R.' after it. Does that stand for rear residence?"

"Yes. This used to be the servants' quarters."

"I see." He fixed her with an impatient glare, waiting until Raleigh had reluctantly sat down in the chair across from him. Shrugging off the distance she had pointedly put between them, he went on. "Then I saw this garage apartment, but it looks bigger on the outside." He looked at the scattered newspapers, and one corner of his mouth twitched into a lopsided smirk. "Maid's day off?"

"If you're uncomfortable here, you can leave."

He held up one hand in surrender. "I'll be a good boy. Don't throw me out. At least let me finish off this pizza first."

"Make it snappy."

He picked up a paper napkin and placed a slice of pizza on it. Leaning forward, he extended the offering to her. "Can't you be nice to me for just a few hours? Would that really put a cramp in your style, Groucho?"

Raleigh examined his innocent expression for a few moments and felt a smile begin to tease her lips. He was hard to resist, and he damn well knew it. With a self-derisive sigh, Raleigh let her guard down and accepted the pizza.

"Is this a professional visit, Dr. Younger?"

He fell back against the couch again and balanced the beer can on his belt buckle. "If the mountain won't come to Muhammad, Muhammad must come to the mountain."

"You should work on your charm, doctor. Women don't enjoy being likened to mountains."

"Sorry." His lips curved into a teasing smile. "How long has it been since you dropped all that weight?"

Her head snapped back as if she'd been slapped, and for several moments she was speechless. How did he know—? "What makes you think I used to be a chubbette?"

Evan chuckled and raised a napkin to his mouth to keep from propelling food in her direction. "Chubbette? Did you coin that description?"

Raleigh shook her head. "It's a common tag among us fatties."

"Former fatties," he corrected.

"How did you know I'd lost weight?"

He waved a hand that encompassed her from head to toe. "The way you dress. Your mind hasn't caught up with your body."

Raleigh tipped her head to one side in confusion. "Run that past me again, please."

"You're still using clothes as a camouflage," he explained. "Your mind is still telling you that you're fat, and you're not anymore. Take that robe, for instance."

Instinctively, Raleigh pulled the lapels of her chemise robe together at her throat. "What's wrong with my robe?"

"Apart from the fact that it has seen better days, it's about four sizes too large for you."

Raleigh looked down at the snagged threads. *He doesn't pull any punches,* she thought.

"Each time I've seen you at the office, you've been dressed as if you have something to hide." His dark brows wiggled comically above eyes that were the same shade as his faded denim slacks. "You've got nothing to hide, Ms. Torrence."

"Someday you're going to make a great dirty old man." She smiled to take the edge from her words. "Well, you've managed to insult my housekeeping and my clothes. What's next on the agenda?"

"Eat your pizza."

Raleigh glanced at the triangle of flaky crust and melted cheese. "Every time I see you, you force food on me. I'm not sure you're the type of friend a former fattie needs."

"We're making progress." He beamed triumphantly. "You just called me your friend."

"Did I?" Raleigh lifted one shoulder. "A slip of the tongue." She bit into the pizza and found it much tastier than her frozen dinner. "You should get out and meet other people."

"Most of my friends are married or they've moved away from Tulsa."

"You've lived here before?"

"Sure." He grinned proudly. "You're looking at a graduate of Webster High School. Where did you go to school?"

"Central. The *old* Central High."

"Yes. I noticed the school is an office building now."

"That's progress."

"It didn't bother you that your alma mater was moved to another part of the city?"

Raleigh plucked a piece of Canadian bacon from the clinging cheese and popped it into her mouth. "I was raised on the edge of downtown. My parents owned a mom-and-pop grocery store for years before the Crosstown Expressway was built. I've watched downtown Tulsa grow and swallow up neighborhoods. I'm used to it.'' She glanced at him, trying to guess his age. "What year did you graduate?"

A sly smile raced across his lips. "I'll save you the trouble of subtraction. I'm twenty-eight." His gaze touched hers. "How old are you?"

Raleigh swallowed hard, forcing a bit of pizza down her tight throat. "Older." She looked away from him, recalling how she'd misinterpreted his introduction at their first meeting. Had it been a specter of things to come?

"Are you ashamed of your age?" Evan challenged.

Her eyes snapped back at him. "No, I'm not ashamed!" She huffed out a breath, stared at him defiantly and said, "I'm thirty-two."

"Does it bother you that I'm younger than you?"

"No." She stared at the half-eaten slice of pizza. "Why should it?"

"Have you ever dated a younger man?"

"No." Raleigh met his gaze. "I don't want to."

"Why not?" he asked, chuckling softly.

Tossing the rest of the pizza slice back onto the table, Raleigh shrugged her shoulders and folded her arms protectively across her breasts. "It's a waste of time."

"How do you figure that?" He was still chuckling under his breath.

"I want stability and ... maturity in a man," Raleigh answered, uneasy with the turn of conversation. Why didn't he just drop it?

"And a younger man can't offer you those things? Is that it?"

"Yes." She pushed her hands into her robe's pockets and tilted back her head to stare at the high ceiling. "I don't want to take someone in to raise."

"Well, that's the stupidest thing I've ever heard." He tipped up the can and took a long swallow of the beer. "Maturity comes with experience, not years." He finished off the beer and smiled. "Get dressed and we'll take a stroll under the stars."

"No, thanks."

"It'll be fun," he insisted. "I haven't been up here on Reservoir Hill since the night I tried to score with Julie Davenport. Did you ever park up here when you were in high school?"

"No. We always went to Swan Lake."

"I've parked there, too."

"A regular back-seat Casanova, right?"

"Right." He looked pleased with himself. "Go on. Put something warm on. It's downright chilly out there tonight."

"Look." Raleigh stood and glared down at him, tired of this cat-and-mouse game. "I know you think I need my head examined and you'd like to do the examination, but I'm tired and I'm going to bed. You're going to have to take that stroll by yourself."

"What?" He rose to his feet, spreading out his hands to indicate the remains of the pizza and beer. "I buy you all this and *this* is what I get as a reward?"

"You've got to be kidding!" she flared, only to cool down quickly when she saw the humor lurking in the corners of his wide mouth. "You *are* kidding, aren't you?"

"Yes." He smiled; a charming smile that reached out to her and held her in a warm grasp. "Don't make me walk alone, Raleigh. Ten minutes," he implored with an undercurrent of desperation. "Just give me ten minutes. It'll be good for you. You need to get out more."

"What I don't need is for a *stranger* to tell me what I need!" She turned her back on him, afraid of his magnetism and what it was doing to her. "You don't know me. You don't know what I need."

"And you won't let me get to know you, will you?"

Her whole body tensed when his hands grasped her upper arms from behind. She wanted to twist away from him, but she didn't...she couldn't. Oh, why hadn't Cara dropped by tonight? Why had she answered the door? *Why did Curtis pull that trigger?*

"Raleigh—" he breathed her name and his warm breath caressed the tip of her ear "—won't you be my friend? I need a friend right now."

She sagged wearily and stepped from the light touch of his hands. She knew his game plan. He didn't need a friend. He was just practicing reverse psychology. The refusal formed on her lips, but something in Evan's expression kept her from voicing it. He was offering her his friendship, and she discovered that she didn't really want to reject his gift. "Okay, okay. I'll get dressed."

"You won't regret it," he called after her as she moved toward her bedroom.

She didn't respond to his promise. She was already regretting her submission. Delving through her bedroom closet, Raleigh pushed aside the clothes she'd been able to wear a year ago and reached for a recently purchased pair of jeans and a bouclé-knit pullover sweater of wine, black and autumn gold. As she dressed she thought of the man—the younger man—who waited for her in the other room. A simple walk couldn't hurt anything, she told herself. She wasn't dating him. She was just... just...taking a stroll under the stars with him.

"Oh, God!" Raleigh whispered with a hint of panic. Whom was she kidding? Certainly not herself. Evan

Younger was good-looking, fun-loving and intelligent. Any woman in her right mind wouldn't think of him in a platonic way! *That* would be a terrible waste of chemistry—something with which he was loaded.

Acting on a streak of rebellion, she pulled on garishly striped warm-ups over the lower part of her jeaned legs and stuck her feet in a pair of battered, frayed tennis shoes. She would not dress for him! If he didn't like her clothes, tough!

Raleigh sat for a few quiet moments on the bed and stared at the orange strings that laced up her tennis shoes. She reflected on her previous image of Mister Right. Ever since adolescence, she had been attracted to older men and had never entertained the notion of going out with anyone younger than she.

"I'm not going out with him," she whispered fiercely, and stood up with a new resolve. "It's an innocent little walk, for crying out loud!"

He was zipping up his black leather jacket when she re-entered the living room. His gaze measured her and his brows met in a slight frown.

"Is something wrong?" Raleigh asked innocently. She picked up her glasses and slipped them on, and Evan's face became clearer across the room.

A tender smile pushed aside his scowl. "No, I was just concerned that you might not be warm enough in that." He paused, his gaze moving slowly over her face. "You look like a studious street urchin with those glasses on." He opened the front door and stood back to let her go first.

Raleigh had been expecting disapproval from him; caught off guard, she found herself floundering under his gentle regard. Her movements were uncharacteristically jerky as she crossed to the coffee table and retrieved her keys. She tucked them into her back pocket and stepped around Evan to the wooden landing outside. He closed the door behind them and extended a hand for her to descend the steep flight of steps first.

Her porch light cut through the shadows and Raleigh took the steps at a bouncing jog. A mischievous breeze pushed leaves across the lawn and dried the moisture from last summer's grass. Raleigh stopped at the bottom of the steps and waited for Evan to join her.

"Let's walk toward the reservoir," he suggested, cupping his hand around her elbow and setting a brisk pace down the driveway. He examined the large brick house with its wedgwood-blue trim as they passed. "Who lives here?"

"Mrs. Trolley. She's my landlady."

"She lives here all by herself?"

"Yes. Just her and her cats." Raleigh paused and mentally counted the feline population. "She has twelve cats, I think."

"It must smell pretty rank in there."

Raleigh laughed. "It's not so bad. In fact, I think the cats are cleaner than Mrs. Trolley."

"How long have you lived in this apartment?"

"Six years. I like this neighborhood. It's quiet and stately."

"And old," he added. "And we both know how you feel about old things."

She ignored his teasing remark, preferring to study the mist around the street lights and the echo created by the click of his boot heels against the pavement. In the distance she could see the blinking lights on the antenna that sat at the crest of Reservoir Hill. But none of these things was as clear to her as the touch of Evan's hand against her elbow. His flesh seemed to burn a hole in her sweater, and her thoughts kept circling back to his reference to back-seat rendezvous. A vision of two bodies wedged on a narrow seat haunted her until she was desperate to escape the flashing images of fogged car windows, groping hands and wet kisses.

"Did you score with Julie Davenport?" she asked, startling herself.

"No. Julie only scored with guys from *this* side of the river." He laughed softly and pressed his fingertips deeper into her skin. "Instead of being from the wrong side of the tracks, I was born on the wrong side of the Arkansas River."

"A river rat," Raleigh whispered, using a tag she hadn't heard since her high-school days.

"Exactly."

She looked up at him and caught his scowl. "It's not like that anymore. River Parks has joined the east and west sides of Tulsa."

"I've noticed a change in attitudes. People in West Tulsa used to say they were from Redfork, but they don't anymore. At Christmas my mother would say she was going into Tulsa to shop, as if we didn't already live in Tulsa."

"Well, we easterners have accepted you westerners," Raleigh assured him. "Redfork used to be a city unto itself, but it's part of Tulsa now."

"That's good news."

"You could probably score with Julie now."

His gaze met hers briefly. "I'm not interested now."

Their rapid gait had brought them to the final climb toward the hill's crest, and Raleigh pressed forward. At the top, she stopped to view the panorama of lights and dark shapes. She looked down at the tawny grass that grew over the top of the water reservoir. This mound of earth used to store the city's entire water supply, but Tulsa had outgrown it. Raleigh lifted her gaze to the canvas of multi-colored lights and picked out sections of Tulsa: the heart of the city, with its jagged skyline; a stretch of darkness that was Woodward Park; the scattered illumination of southeast suburbia. Tulsa oozed across the landscape until earth and sky appeared to meet and end.

"My, my," Evan breathed beside her as he took in the sprawling splendor. "What a view! Tulsa never looked so good."

"Did you miss it?" Raleigh asked, tipping back her head to study his profile against the backdrop of a starry night.

"I didn't think so until just now."

"Where were you living?"

"Las Vegas, and before that, Los Angeles."

"Really? You must be experiencing a culture shock."

He smiled and nodded. "You bet. Those cities are vastly different from Tulsa. Here, you can stop a guy on the street and ask directions and he won't just give you directions, he'll offer to *take* you there to make sure you get where you're going."

Raleigh laughed at the truth in his statement. "We're a friendly bunch all right." A wickedly cold breeze passed over her, and she crossed her arms and tucked her hands in the folds of her sweater.

"Here," Evan said, taking his hand from her elbow to unzip his jacket. "Wear this. You're shivering."

"No, that's okay."

"Don't be silly. Slip into it." He took off the jacket and held it out, waiting for her to push her arms into the sleeves. "I'll be fine. I'm warm-blooded."

I don't doubt that. The statement remained unspoken, but Raleigh acknowledged the direction she was headed in as she snuggled into the leather jacket, which smelled decidedly male.

"I've got a great idea." Evan stared out at the blanket of fallen stars. "Why don't I pick you up tomorrow night and we'll have dinner somewhere and then we can tour River Parks? I haven't really explored that place yet, and you can be my guide." He glanced at her but quickly returned his attention to the twilight vista. "Doesn't that sound like fun?"

"I don't know...." Raleigh looked down at her shoes and tried to quiet the little voice in her head that kept saying, *Tell him yes, stupid!*

"I'll come by around seven. Okay...? Raleigh, are you still with me?"

"Yes," she said, answering his last question.

"Good. Seven it is."

"No, I mean..." She turned startled eyes on him, and her denial melted under the heat of his gaze. "Seven?"

"Seven," he repeated.

Returning to the safety of the breathtaking view, she nodded. "Seven."

"Ready to walk back?"

"Yes." She breathed a sigh of relief and started back down the hill with Evan close at her side. He seemed content to just walk silently, and she was thankful for that. Had she really agreed to go out on a date with him? she asked herself. How had he tricked her into that? Okay, she'd go out with him just this once. Just this one time.

"This is my car."

Raleigh jerked to a stop and stared at the dark-colored Corvette. "Nice wheels."

Evan laughed and reached for the door handle. "Would you like me to walk you back up to your apartment?"

"No, that's okay." She waited for him to get into the car, and when he didn't, she looked up into his face. He was smiling, his gaze moving pointedly from her face to her sleeve. "Oh! Your jacket!" She removed it quickly and handed it to him. "I'm sorry."

"That's all right." He was still chuckling softly as if he found her flustered state amusing. "I'll see you tomorrow night."

"Tomorrow night?" She blinked at him while her mind ran around in circles. Was he going to kiss her or what? Should she offer her hand to him?

"Dinner and River Parks?" he prodded her fleeting memory.

"Oh, yes!" She laughed at herself and stepped back from the car. "Right. Seven o'clock."

He folded himself behind the steering wheel and closed the door. "Good night, Raleigh. Sweet dreams."

She waved one hand, smiling blankly as the car zipped forward to be swallowed up by the night.

Shaking herself mentally, Raleigh closed her eyes for a few moments. What was it about that man that made her feel like an inexperienced sixteen-year-old? she asked herself.

"Evan Younger," she whispered, opening her eyes to the deserted street. "Who invited you into my life?"

The first part of the evening had gone off without a hitch, much to Raleigh's surprise. Walking along the pedestrian bridge that spanned the Arkansas River and connected East Tulsa with West Tulsa, she sent up a silent prayer that the remainder of her time with Evan would transpire harmlessly. Even the weather had cleared. It had been raining when Evan had picked her up, and the showers had increased while they'd dined at The Chalkboard Restaurant, but just as they were preparing to leave the rain had stopped.

"New dress?" Evan asked, walking beside her.

Raleigh jumped slightly, then smiled and nodded. "Yes. I . . . I bought it recently." Like this morning, she added mentally.

"It's nice."

"Thanks." She glanced down at the bold red-and-black-striped dress with its tight black stockinged sleeves and belted waist. A year ago she would not even have looked at this dress, much less have tried it on. Stripes were taboo for chubbettes. But Evan had been right, she was a *former* chubbette. A smile teased the corners of her mouth. For the first time in her life, she knew she looked positively *chic*. Feeling as brash and daring as her outfit, Raleigh reached out and tugged the sleeve of Evan's tweed jacket with its leather-patched elbows. "New jacket?"

He grinned. "No, but I haven't worn this in a few months. I dusted it off just for you."

"You look like a young college professor," she observed, keeping hold of his sleeve and making him turn toward her so that she could examine him carefully. His style of dress connoted a man who preferred comfort and a classic style: charcoal-gray corduroy slacks, argyle sweater, open-throated twill shirt, tweed jacket. "Ralph Lauren would be proud of you."

Evan held his jacket open and looked down at his wool sweater. "Do you think so?"

"Without a doubt." It seemed natural to tuck her hand in the crook of his arm and continue their stroll along the bridge. They squeezed to one side as three hell-bent teenagers raced past them. "It's almost eleven o'clock. Those kids should be at home."

"Were you always home by eleven?"

She smiled up at him. "Always. I had a good reputation as a teenager."

"Oh?" His hand covered hers. "And how's your reputation now?"

"Sterling," she answered without hesitation, tossing him a saucy grin.

He seemed momentarily enchanted by her smile, and Raleigh felt a flutter of feminine allure; then he tore his gaze from hers and nodded ahead of him.

"What's that? Some kind of theater?"

Raleigh followed his gaze to the semicircle of escalating bleachers. "Yes, I guess so. I think they have concerts and stuff here."

"Let's sit down for a while," he suggested, pulling her toward the center of one of the concrete bleachers. He sat down, propping his elbows on the row behind him, and sighed expansively as he tipped back his head to examine the sky. "Did you enjoy your dinner?"

"Yes, it was scrumptious." Raleigh sat beside him. "Is The Chalkboard one of your favorite hangouts?"

He chuckled. "That was the first time I've been there. I asked some of the policemen to suggest a nice restaurant, and The Chalkboard was on each list. Actually, this is my first evening out since I moved back to Tulsa."

"I guess you've been busy settling in and getting used to your new job." Raleigh adopted his lazy posture and watched a cloud skirt past the crescent moon. "What kind of work were you doing before coming here?"

"I was operating a clinic for chronic gamblers in Las Vegas, and before that I was a counselor at a halfway house for runaways in Los Angeles."

"And now you're counseling policemen."

"And their families," Evan said pointedly.

Here it comes, Raleigh thought, turning her face away from him. She found herself staring at a young couple in the murky shadows a few feet away. The teenagers were entwined, their mouths clinging hungrily, their rapid breathing filling the silence.

The girl tore her mouth from the boy's. "Ronnie...oh, Ronnie!"

Raleigh looked away, embarrassed by the panting passion.

"Ain't love grand?" Evan asked in a lazy drawl.

Raleigh frowned and stared at the toes of her black patent-leather pumps. "They don't know what they're doing."

"They know what they're doing," Evan corrected. "They just don't know where it's leading." He leaned sideways until his shoulder pressed into hers. "Wanna neck, cutie?"

Raleigh laughed, relieved that he wasn't trying to psychoanalyze her. She nudged him in the ribs with her elbow. "Stop it."

"We could go back to my car, if you like it private."

"You don't have a back seat," she reminded him, still smiling.

"That leaves your place or mine."

She looked at him sharply and saw that he was only half kidding. "It's getting late. We'd better go."

"Are you worried that I might tarnish your reputation?"

"No. I'm worried that I won't be able to crawl out of bed at five-thirty and make it to work by six-thirty." She stood up and started to step over his extended feet.

"Five-thirty!" He grabbed her wrist. "You get up at five-thirty?"

"I sure do. My first deadline is at ten o'clock, and my final one is at eleven-thirty." She laughed at his stricken expression. "It's not so bad. My workday ends at three." She wrapped her other hand around his wrist and pulled. "Come on. It's getting chilly out here."

"Okay." He lumbered to his feet, then yawned and stretched his arms above his head as he drew a deep breath. "Ummm. Smell that."

Raleigh sniffed the air. "What?"

"That clean, fresh smell that comes right behind the rain. It's the scent of new beginnings." He took her hand and walked beside her toward the bridge. "Do you like your job?"

Raleigh chose her words carefully. "I used to."

"You don't like it now?"

"I'm bored, I guess." She glanced over the bridge at the whirlpooling water and felt an eddying restlessness. "I've covered the police beat since I was twenty-six. It's time to move on to something else, but I can't think of any other beat I would want to cover."

"Maybe it's time to do something else besides writing for a newspaper," Evan suggested.

"Maybe." Raleigh shrugged, and the restlessness churned within her. "But I can't think of anything else I could do."

"You look like a smart cookie to me. I bet you could do anything you set your mind to." He let go of her hand and leaned back against the railing to light a cigarette.

Crumpling the empty pack in his hand, he sighed and tossed it into a trash receptacle. "Uh-oh."

"Last pack?" Raleigh asked.

"The last *cigarette*. I'm quitting after this one." He examined the lighted cigarette as if it were a treasure. "I've been thinking about quitting for a few months. Now is as good a time as any, I guess."

"Just like that? Do you think you can kick the habit that easily?"

A rueful smile curved his mouth. "I didn't say it would be easy. I just said I was quitting after this one." His eyes searched hers. "It's a matter of setting your mind to it."

"Are we talking about smoking or job hunting?" Raleigh settled against the rail next to him. The Arkansas was a wide swatch of rolling black velvet stretching to the horizon.

"Both. I've done a lot of things that I never thought I could do."

"Like what?"

"Oh, like waiting tables, selling shoes . . . I was a carnival barker one summer."

"You're kidding." She looked sideways to take in his profile.

"Nope." He sucked in a breath. "Step right up, ladies and gentlemen. You won't believe your eyes. Here he is—the amazing, mind-boggling Herbie, the human pretzel!"

Raleigh laughed at his singsong voice. "What else have you done?"

"I've been a lifeguard, a photographer's assistant, and—oh, yes!—I was a strip-tease artist for one week."

"*You* were a male stripper!" She pushed herself from the rail and faced him.

"For one week," he repeated with a grin.

"One week? Did you get fired?"

"No. I was stripping because . . . well, it was all part of my research."

"Ha! Research. That's a good one."

"No, really." He was chuckling under his breath as if even *he* found it a little absurd. "I was working on my master's—'Fantasies and Realities of Exhibitionism'—and I put myself on exhibit for one week." He whistled softly. "What a week!"

"Were you successful?"

A hint of pride glimmered in his eyes. "I made over four hundred dollars one night in tips."

"Four hundred?" She stared at him, aghast. "Was this a straight or gay strip joint?"

"Straight. For women only." He seemed momentarily annoyed by her question, then he smiled. "I'll have to show you my act sometime."

"Hmmm." She turned away from his mischievous grin and started toward the other end of the bridge. He slipped an arm about her shoulders, and Raleigh fitted her arm about his waist before her mind registered the action. What was she doing? She looked up into his face and saw a pleased expression in his eyes.

"You ought to think about changing jobs if you're bored," he said quietly. "What would you like to be, other than a journalist?"

She pondered the question for a few moments, then shrugged. "What everyone would like to be, I guess."

"What's that?"

"Happy." His fingers curled into her shoulder, causing her to look up again and be caught in his probing gaze. She heard herself talking, surprised at the honesty spilling forth. "Sometimes that's the hardest thing to be."

He stopped and turned her around to face him. "Raleigh, I wish I could make you happy." His voice was soft and gentle, drawing from her a rush of yearning that expanded her heart until it was painful. "I'd like nothing better than to scatter smiles all over you."

He dipped his head a fraction, and Raleigh instinctively tipped up her chin. His lips were warm and soft, brushing across hers and then settling like a butterfly on a blossom. He added pressure by sliding a hand up to the back of her head and moving his lips against hers until she opened her mouth a little. His lips touched her teeth and grew moist and pliant, no longer taking, just waiting. She knew he was waiting for the touch of her tongue on his, but the acute longing she felt scared her. Raleigh wedged a hand between her body and his and pushed away from him.

"I don't want to do this," she murmured as she ran one hand through her hair distractedly. "I shouldn't have agreed to this."

"To what?" His hand caught one of hers. "A simple dinner date—"

"A date." Raleigh snatched her hand from his. "I shouldn't be dating you. We're ... you're ... I'm ..."

"I'm twenty-eight and you're thirty-two."

She spun to face him, surprised that he had managed to read her mind so easily. "That's right. I don't want to date a younger man. I know some women really like it, but it's not for me. It makes me ... uncomfortable."

"*That's* not what makes you uncomfortable. You're uncomfortable because you want me and you know that I want you."

"Oh, shush!" She plastered her hands to her ears, saw his grin and whirled from the truth of it all. Practically running along the bridge, she headed for the parked

Corvette across the street and was breathless when she reached it. She grabbed the door handle and tugged. It was locked. Looking back, she saw Evan walking slowly across the street toward her, keys in hand.

She could do nothing but wait for him to fit the key in the lock. The bolt shot back and Raleigh opened the door, only to have it slammed shut again by Evan.

"What are you—" The words died in her throat as his lips claimed hers in a crushing kiss.

Raleigh pushed at his shoulders. His arms tightened around her waist. The earth tipped to one side, overturning all her good intentions. She met his thrusting tongue with her own. Wet flesh met wet flesh. Hot breath mingled with hot breath. And Raleigh learned the meaning of animal attraction.

His curling hair was vibrant silk under her fingers. Raleigh pulled his head down until his mouth was hard against hers. His hands found the curve of her buttocks, and he moved her closer until the lower part of her body cradled his stirring passion. Crazed desire bolted through her, and Raleigh opened her mouth wider to the slick friction of his tongue. He tore his mouth from hers and breathed incoherent words into her ear as his lips and tongue explored the length of her neck.

Raleigh forced his lips back to hers, her fingers curling into his hair, her fingernails scraping against his scalp. He moved forward, making her step back against the cold metal of the car. His hands came up to cup her breasts and knead them with a rough urgency, and Raleigh felt her nipples pucker against the stiff lace of her bra. She pushed her hands up under his sweater and realized she was desperate to touch him, to feel him, to make—

"—love to you at my place." His disjointed words wedged into her mind. "Get in the car."

Headlights bounced over them, blinding them momentarily. Raleigh blinked, her eyes focused and she drew a shaky breath. Evan was looking at her in a way that made her aware of how close she was to becoming his lover.

His mouth tipped up into a smile that was warm, but strained. "There goes your reputation."

She found no humor in his remark. Turning, she groped for the door handle, jerked open the door and collapsed into the bucket seat. He closed the door behind her and walked around the car to the other side.

Evan slipped behind the steering wheel, and Raleigh covered her mouth and chin with a hand that trembled slightly. Her thoughts tumbled to the panting teenagers in the park, and she realized she was breathing rapidly. Panting, even. She closed her eyes for a moment, sick with the realization that she had so blatantly revealed her weakness for Evan Younger. She shouldn't have agreed to this. She should have known he would pierce her inadequate armor.

"My place?"

She removed her hand from her lips and turned her head to meet his shining eyes. "I'm not staying with you tonight, Evan."

He slid his arm across the back of the seat and his fingertips touched her shoulder. "Raleigh . . ."

"No." The word dropped like a stone from her lips. Raleigh shook her head and looked out the side window. "No." She felt his burning gaze, could see his scowling regard in her mind's eye, but none of it penetrated her resolve. "I don't want to see you again. I've set my mind to this, and you can't change it."

"Damn!"

Raleigh flinched from the explosive anger in his voice. He started the engine, and the car shot forward.

Chapter Four

"So what's your problem?" Cara Torrence asked, fixing a look of concentration on her face.

Raleigh sighed and realized she had made confetti out of her paper napkin. "So, the problem is I don't want to see him anymore."

It was Cara's turn to sigh as she swept the confetti from the table into the palm of her hand and took it to the plastic trash can in the corner of Dixie Torrence's kitchen. "I thought you said you hadn't seen Evan Younger in almost a week and that you told him you didn't want to see him again—ever."

"That's right."

Cara returned to the kitchen chair and sat down with a fluid grace. "So where's the problem?"

Raleigh took a breath to speak, but in the face of Cara's logic, there was nothing to say. She looked into her sister's hazel eyes and her mind went blank. Cara smiled and slid a hand across the kitchen table to grasp one of Raleigh's.

"First, I think we need to pinpoint your problem. Your problem isn't that you *aren't* seeing Even, it's that you *aren't* seeing Evan. Right?"

Raleigh nodded, then shook her head quickly. "I haven't the slightest idea what you just said, Cara."

"Okay." Cara tried again. "You aren't seeing Evan, right?"

"Right." Raleigh concentrated hard, determined to follow Cara's explanation this time.

"But you're whining around here because you aren't seeing Evan, right?"

"I wasn't aware that I was whining!" Raleigh pulled her hand from Cara's. "I was just asking for some sisterly advice!"

"Okay, okay." Cara laughed lightly, a pleasing, purring sound. "The way I see it, you *want* to see Evan. *That's* your problem." She sat back, stretching out her long, slim legs and folding her hands across her firm, flat stomach. "Right?"

"Wrong." Raleigh selected another paper napkin from the holder on the table and began shredding it. "I don't want to see him."

"Raleigh!" Cara flung up her hands in exasperation. "Wake up! You're attracted to the man. 'Fess up to it and jump on his bones!"

Raleigh glared at her older sister as she stood up. "Sometimes you scare me, Cara."

Cara followed her to the coffee maker and stuck her cup next to Raleigh's for a refill. "You want me to be serious?"

"Please." Raleigh filled Cara's cup, then her own. "And do it before Mother comes in here. I don't want to discuss this in front of her or Dad."

Cara's eyes glimmered with catlike zeal. "Our little secret, is it?"

"Yes."

"I get the picture." Cara carried her cup to the table and sat down again. "My serious advice to you is to call the good doctor up and ask him out."

"I can't do that!" Raleigh frowned into her cup. "I told him to get lost. I can't just call him up and—"

"Of course you can! Who made up the rule that men have to call women? Where is it written that a woman can't approach a man first? Since when can't—"

"Cara, please?" Raleigh interrupted gently. "When it comes to women's rights, I'm in your corner, remember?"

"Sorry." A self-derisive smile tugged at Cara's full-lipped mouth. "Sometimes I get carried away."

"You're telling me?" Raleigh smiled, then joined Cara in a bout of giggles.

"What's so funny?" Dixie Torrence asked as she entered the cozy kitchen. "I'm not complaining, mind you. It's nice to hear laughter in this house again."

"We're talking about Raleigh and this—" Cara flinched as Raleigh's foot slammed into her shin under the table. "Women's rights, Mom. We're talking about women's rights." Cara's hazel eyes blazed at Raleigh as she bent to rub her shin.

"And you're laughing? Usually you two are dead serious when you latch onto that subject." Dixie poured herself a cup of coffee and joined them at the table.

The noon sun spilled bright light over Dixie's face, and Raleigh was struck by the web of lines evident in her mother's cheeks and neck. She's getting old, Raleigh thought with a jolt as her gaze moved to Dixie's fading blond hair. She could remember when her mother's hair had been flaxen, and it hadn't been that long ago. Curtis's death had added years to her looks in just a few weeks, Raleigh thought.

"Raleigh, your dad and I were just talking about how skinny you are. You don't look well." Dixie pursed her lips in concern. "Have you had a checkup recently?"

"Mother, Raleigh is not skinny, she's svelte." Cara's smile was full of pride. "I think she looks terrific!"

Raleigh started to defend her new figure, but her mother spoke up first.

"She doesn't have your metabolism, Cara. Raleigh takes after my side of the family—"

"The plump side," Raleigh interrupted with a grin.

Dixie laughed and her blue eyes twinkled. "Well, yes, I guess that's right. Anyway, it's not healthy for you to be too thin. Cara takes after your father's side—"

"The svelte side," Raleigh cut in.

"And Raleigh has joined our side," Cara said with a laugh, then sobered quickly. "Leave her alone, Mother. She's far from being malnourished. She's even got a younger man chasing after her these days."

"Cara, you promised!"

"Really? Who is he, dear?" Dixie asked, her eyes alight with interest. "Do we know him?"

Raleigh's eyes narrowed to smoking slits, making Cara avert her gaze nervously.

"I'm sorry," Cara murmured. "It just slipped out."

"Tell me about him, Raleigh," Dixie urged. "How much younger is he?"

Feeling like a cornered animal, Raleigh looked down at the napkin she had mutilated. The silence was deafening.

"Dixie!" Edgar Torrence's voice floated in from the direction of the living room. "Where's my new fishing rod and reel? I want to show it to the girls."

"Be right there, hon." Dixie pushed her plump frame from the chair and sighed. "He's probably tearing up the closet. I'll be right back." She hurried from the room to save the contents of the hall closet.

"That was real sisterly of you, Cara."

"I said I was sorry. You know I'm the worst at keeping secrets. Remember, I used to spill the beans every Christmas."

At the memory, Raleigh's irritation began to wane. "We all learned to *act* surprised, didn't we?"

"I don't think Mom and Dad ever caught on that we knew what was in the packages before we opened them." Cara laughed and shook her head, lost in her own memories. "Those were the days." Without thinking, Cara swept Raleigh's latest pile of confetti from the table and took it over to the trash can. When she turned, her hazel eyes met Raleigh's and held them.

"Do you miss him, Cara?" Raleigh asked in a husky voice that revealed her innermost feelings.

"Of course I do, but life goes on." Cara shrugged her narrow shoulders and plucked a bit of lint from her turquoise leotard top.

"I think of him so much. I keep wondering why—"

"Stop wondering." Cara gave Raleigh a stern look. "It won't do you any good to torture yourself over Curtis's suicide. He asked us in his letter that we not allow this to ruin our lives. We should honor that request."

"Here it is, girls." Edgar Torrence stopped beside Cara and held up a blue rod and reel. "Isn't it a beauty?"

Cara eyed it critically, then wrapped one hand around the pole. "Dad, can I borrow this? It would go perfectly with an evening gown I have my eye on."

Edgar looked befuddled for a moment, but he joined in on the joke with Cara, Raleigh and Dixie when they broke into merry laughter. He ran a hand over his balding head, then hooked an arm about Cara's neck.

"You stinker! Making fun of your old man, huh?"

Cara hugged him around the waist and planted a kiss on his lean cheek. "You're such an easy target, Dad."

"I told him you girls didn't give a hoot about seeing a fishing rod, but he wouldn't listen." Dixie clucked her tongue and began opening kitchen cabinets. "What do y'all want for lunch?"

Raleigh glanced at her watch. "Mom, I can't stay for lunch."

"What?" Edgar leaned his rod against the wall and surveyed his youngest child through his thick eyeglasses. "You need to eat, baby girl. You're getting too skinny."

"I'm going to eat, Dad." Raleigh stood on tiptoe and kissed the end of Edgar's nose. "I have to go to the annual *Tulsa Times* Spring Fling. It's a company picnic at Mohawk Park."

"Oh, that's different." Edgar framed her face with his large hands. "You're looking peaked, Raleigh. You want to talk about it?"

Raleigh could feel the concern emanating from her family, but she couldn't voice the helplessness and guilt she had felt since Curtis's death. They were all struggling to get past the grief, and she knew she couldn't drag it all out in the open again. She conjured up her most dazzling smile and stepped back from her father's tender touch.

"As a matter of fact, I'm feeling fantastic! Would you believe that I actually bought a *striped* dress a few weeks ago? You're just going to have to get used to having *two* slim daughters, Dad."

Edgar didn't look convinced, but Dixie bought it.

"A striped dress?" Dixie asked with a touch of longing. "It's been a while since I wore anything striped."

"Well, you could," Edgar said, moving over to his wife of thirty-seven years and giving her an affectionate hug. "You're still my little doll, Dixie Lou."

Raleigh turned and moved into the dining room. Her mother's giggles floated out to her and she smiled.

"Raleigh?" Cara stepped in front of her and placed her hands on her sister's shoulders. "*Are* you okay?"

"Yes!" Raleigh lifted her hands to cover Cara's. "What is this? Pick on Raleigh Day?"

Cara placed her forehead against Raleigh's and stared deeply into her eyes. "Call him. You could use a little fun and games, and he sounds like he's fun and we both know he's game."

"He's four years younger than me!"

"So what? You don't have to marry him." Cara leaned back and sighed. "I don't think marriage is what it's cracked up to be, anyway."

Their father's low murmurings reached them, followed by their mother's pleased giggles.

"How can you say that when we have parents who are still mad for each other?" Raleigh asked.

Cara dropped her hands and tucked them in the back pockets of her jeans. She started for the front door, and Raleigh fell into step beside her. "They're the lucky ones, sis. We can't all be that lucky.'' Cara opened the front door for Raleigh. ''Have fun at the picnic.''

Raleigh paused, examining the beauty of her sister's lionesque features. ''You've always been lucky, Cara. Don't give up.''

Impulsively, Cara kissed Raleigh on the cheek, then gave her a playful slap on the rump. ''Will you get out of here?''

''I'm going. I'm going!'' Raleigh laughed and hurried outside to her car.

Once behind the wheel, Raleigh paused to look at the house where Dixie and Edgar Torrence lived, a house she had never called home. Her home had been the apartment above the Torrence grocery store. When the building had been razed, the Torrences had bought this house near Owen Park in an older section of Tulsa, but Raleigh had been in college and living in her own apartment by then.

Raleigh started the car and drove past the place where her family home had once been before she headed for Mohawk Park.

Evan Younger wanted a cigarette badly. He drummed his fingers on the desk top and ground his teeth together as the need consumed him. Glancing at the calendar, he counted backward. Almost a week without a cigarette. Why did it seem like months? He wasn't going to blow it now! He could get past this burning need.

Lacing his hands behind his head, he leaned back and tried to get his mind off his addiction. His gaze fell to the two theater tickets on his desk, and he frowned. Why had he bought those? Did he really think that Raleigh would— A familiar figure passed by Evan's office door, and he shot forward, his hand outstretched as if he were grabbing for a lifeline.

"Cody! Hey, Wakefield!"

Cody Wakefield backed up until Evan could see him again. "Did you call me?"

"Yes." Evan was surprised to find that he was standing. He looked at his own beseeching hand and stuck it into his pocket, embarrassed by the obvious desperation he was displaying. "Got a minute?"

"Sure." Cody entered the office. "I just got off my shift. What's up?"

What's up? That's a good question, Evan thought with an inner laugh. I was hoping you could answer that question, Cody old boy. Could you wave a magic wand and make me better, please? "Have a seat." He motioned to one of the office chairs. "I'm not keeping you from anything, am I?"

"No, not really. I was just going to meet some guys. We're all going drag racing tomorrow."

"Oh, really?" Evan smiled and sat in a chair near Cody. "You're a drag racer, are you?"

"Sort of. I just dabble in it."

"I might come to see how you make out tomorrow."

"Why not? If I win, I'll buy you a beer."

Evan stared at his laced hands, feeling like a fool for inviting Cody Wakefield into his office. Cody checked his watch, and Evan knew it was unfair to keep him here when the man obviously wanted to wrap his hands around a beer and jaw with his friends.

"What are you doing here on a Saturday?"

Evan shrugged. "I just dropped by to finish arranging my files. I think I'm finally organized now."

"Is there something specific I can help you with, Evan?" Cody unbuttoned his jacket and relaxed.

"You know Raleigh Torrence pretty well, don't you?" There! It was out.

Cody's wise blue eyes widened as if he'd never expected to discuss Raleigh with Evan. "Yes. We're friends."

Evan's lungs burned, and he wondered if giving up smoking was going to kill him. Unable to sit still, he stood and moved around his desk to shuffle papers and rearrange pencils and pens in the holder there.

"Evan, do you want to talk about Raleigh Torrence? Are you seeing each other or something?"

Sinking into the chair behind his desk, Evan puffed out a frustrated sigh. "To tell you the truth, Cody, I don't know what I want." He tried to laugh, but it was a vain effort. "Go on. I'm sorry I delayed you." Evan flipped one hand in a shooing motion, but Cody didn't move.

"Who does a psychologist talk to when he has a problem?" An understanding smile softened Cody's features.

"A friend, if he's got a good one."

"You do." Cody hooked his thumbs in his belt. "What do you want to know?"

Evan laughed harshly. "Everything."

"Well, I don't know everything about the lady in question. Raleigh is an awfully private person about some things. How long have you been seeing her?"

"I'm not seeing her at present. She's giving me a hard time."

"Oh, I see." Cody gave him a knowing wink. "It's those hard-to-get ones that drive you crazy. I know the feeling."

Evan tossed Cody a sympathetic glance, then looked out his office window at the other office window facing him across the way. It was a view that left much to be desired. "Tell me what you know about her."

"I know that she was close to Curtis and that she took it hard when he died."

"Yes, I'd gathered that. Has she been dating anyone recently?" When Cody didn't answer immediately, Evan turned his head to look at him.

"I'm not sure about that...." Cody ran a hand through his blond hair. "To tell you the truth, I don't know much about Raleigh's personal life. When we talk it's usually about police business. She's never mentioned any man in her life, but I'm not sure she'd discuss that sort of thing with me. Like I said, she's pretty closemouthed about herself." Cody paused as if he didn't quite know how to say what he wanted to say. "You know, she's lost a lot of weight. I always thought she was a cutie, but most guys, I guess, don't pay much attention to plump women. I *have* noticed that some of the guys around here are looking at her—*really* looking at her—for the first time lately."

Evan nodded and felt guilt cut through him. Yes, we're all guilty of judging people by the size of the clothing they wear, he thought. We should be ashamed. From the corner of his eyes, he saw Cody check his watch again. The guys were waiting. "Well, I won't keep you any longer." Evan stood and offered his hand. "You probably think I'm nuts asking you these questions."

Cody straightened from the chair and shook Evan's hand. "Sorry I wasn't much help. I hope things work out between you and Raleigh. I imagine she could use all the friends she can get right now."

"Oh? Why do you say that?"

Cody buttoned his jacket and started for the door. "She just seems uptight lately. I think she must be under a lot of pressure." He turned and gave a short, choppy wave. "I hear that the *Times* is on the verge of collapse, so Raleigh is probably worried about her job. Hang in there, doc.''

"Thanks, Cody. Good luck in the race tomorrow.''

"Thanks. I have a feeling I'll need it.''

Evan dropped back into the chair and pondered Cody's analysis of Raleigh Torrence. You didn't have to be a psychologist to know that Raleigh was under pressure, and maybe it was wrong for him to add to that pressure by relentlessly pursuing her.

It wouldn't bother him so much if she were rejecting him just because she had some stupid notion that dating younger men was like eating green bananas. But it went beyond that. She was rejecting him because he was the police-department psychologist and he was too close to her pain. Why didn't she just accept his friendship and use it? He certainly wouldn't object to being used by the likes of Raleigh Torrence.

A bitter taste coated his tongue, and Evan realized he was chewing on the eraser end of a pencil. He threw it down and catapulted from the chair and out into the corridor. With purposeful strides, he made a beeline to the vending machine and dropped five coins into it. He pulled the lever under his favorite brand, and a pack of cigarettes slipped from the machine like Lucifer slipping from heaven to hell. Evan grasped the pack, tore it open and withdrew one of the cigarettes. He placed it between his lips, the tip of his tongue touched the filter and his stomach lurched. Evan plucked the cigarette from his mouth and threw it and the pack into the trash can.

"I don't need these," he mumbled irritably. "I need her, damn it!"

Raleigh selected a spot under the shade of an elm and settled there. The first tender blades of green grass provided a soft carpet, and she leaned against the tree's gnarled trunk, arranging her plate of food and soft drink next to her. Paul Rondyke sat Indian-fashion on one side of her and Mike Allison sprawled on the other.

Mohawk Park was alive with families, friends and teenagers who were taking advantage of this first breath of spring. Fifty or sixty *Times* employees had staked their claim near a shelter. Some of them were roasting marshmallows and wieners on a grill, but most were gathered into friendly circles. The scent of burning wood and charcoal permeated the air, and bits of conversation and spurts of laughter could be heard.

Raleigh turned her attention to her picnic lunch as the sun warmed her shoulders and back. Is spring finally here? she wondered. Are the gray days over?

"Will you look at that?" Mike nodded to where Grant Farris was busy roasting marshmallows. "He's the only one who seems to enjoy these company picnics."

"If you ask me, I think it would have been better for us if Grant had saved the money he spent on this shindig and put it back into the newspaper. From what I hear, the coffers could use it," Paul said.

Munching on a chicken wing, Raleigh watched Grant offer a hot marshmallow to Sheila. The receptionist fluttered her false eyelashes demurely before she accepted the offering. Grant had dispensed with his usual tailored suit for jeans and a western-cut shirt today, and Raleigh couldn't help but think it was his way of "getting down" to the level of his employees.

"Uh-oh. Sheila had better watch out." Mike propped himself up on one elbow and selected a dill pickle from his paper plate. "She might be Grant's next trophy."

"Do you really think the newspaper is teetering on the edge of disaster?" Raleigh asked, returning to the earlier mention of financial ruin.

Mike nodded. "If we're still publishing at the end of the year, I'll be flabbergasted."

"If I were young like you two, I'd be checking out other employment," Paul said. "I'm only six months away from retiring, so I'm just going to stick it out." Paul glanced in Grant's direction and laughed softly. "Sheila's no dummy. She's just getting on the boss's good side."

Raleigh opened her soft drink, not interested in Grant and Sheila's casual dalliance.

"I don't see how that guy can make goo-goo eyes when he's got his financial problems." Mike sat up and began eating his picnic lunch with relish. "Betsy complained last night that I'm taking her for granted." Mike's mouth twisted into a comical grimace. "It's weird how your job can screw up your personal relationships."

"Grant's always had an eye for the ladies. That'll never change." Paul set his plate to one side and stretched out on the grass. "Ever since I've been at the paper, Grant has always left several phone numbers where he might be reached during emergencies. And all of them, I imagine, are phone numbers of his lady friends."

Paul's observation stirred an old memory in Raleigh, but it was in a far corner of her mind, draped in cobwebs, and she couldn't quite get to it.

"Are you going to play softball with us after we finish eating, Raleigh?" Mike opened a can of beer and foam spewed from it.

"No, I can't stay." She pulled her lower lip between her teeth, knowing that Mike was waiting for a reason. "I'm meeting a friend later. We're going to...to a movie." She glanced at Mike, hoping he couldn't read the lie in her eyes; she had never been good at fabrication.

"I don't blame you. These picnics are never much fun."

"Why didn't you bring Betsy and the kids?" Paul asked.

"Amy has a bad case of diaper rash and Justin is fighting a head cold. Betsy stayed at home with them. Why didn't you bring your wife?"

Paul shrugged. "She shares your opinion of these Spring Flings. She decided she'd much rather stay home and read one of those romance novels she dotes on." Paul laughed softly. "She reads five or six of those books every week."

"So does Betsy." Mike frowned slightly. "I think those books give her weird ideas about how I *should* act. She keeps saying she wishes I was romantic like those guys in the books."

Raleigh poked Mike's shoulder with her fist. "Better listen to her, Mike. It wouldn't kill you to send her roses every so often, would it?"

"You know how much roses cost these days?" Mike shook his head. "If the paper folds, I'll be lucky to afford food for the kids."

The conversation was dropping into the doldrums, and Raleigh shifted uneasily. "I'm going to walk off some of this food, guys. I'll see you later."

She stood up, swept bits of grass from the back of her jeans and sauntered toward a deserted baseball diamond, which would be the focus of interest when the softball game commenced. Raleigh began walking to first base, then headed for second. Her thoughts returned persistently to her sister's suggestion that she phone Evan. Cara just didn't understand the circumstances,

Raleigh told herself, then wondered if *she* fully understood why she was afraid to see Evan Younger again.

Her thoughts skipped crazily to the first time she'd ridden the roller coaster at Bell's Amusement Park. The experience had been partly wonderful and partly terrifying, and she hadn't been able to ride it again that day. Curtis, Cara and Hess had taken several trips on the roller coaster, but once was enough for Raleigh. Still, she could remember standing beside the ticket booth and watching her sister, brother and cousin swoop and climb. She'd wanted to be with them, but she just couldn't force herself to endure another ride.

She felt the same sort of fear with Evan Younger. He was partly wonderful and partly terrifying. He made her dreams of meeting an older man who would cherish and pamper her seem stupid and illogical. He'd stormed her flimsy defenses and driven right to her heart. He attracted her the way a fish is attracted to a bit of bait suspended on a shiny, sharp hook. If she accepted the lure, could she escape the hook? Was it possible to deepen their acquaintance without becoming emotionally involved with him?

He said he wanted to be her friend, but he wanted more than that . . . and to be truthful, so did she.

Raleigh found that she had rounded third base and was headed for home plate. She broke into a jog and jumped on the dusty bag, but she felt no exhilaration at reaching her destination. She wasn't safe. During the past year she had learned that life could shower you with sorrow at a moment's notice. No one was safe.

She stood on the lumpy, dirty cushion and crossed her arms against her chest in a protective gesture. Friendship meant sharing, and she couldn't share certain things with anyone right now—at least not until she was comfortable with those things herself.

A year ago she'd been a plump, carefree young woman who doted on her big brother. Curtis had been her substitute for a steady male companion, and she'd adored his company. In his eyes, she wasn't a chubbette. She was Raleigh, simply Raleigh. He had made her feel loved and appreciated. They'd both been lonely and craving companionship. Curtis had struck out twice in the marriage department, and he'd had so much love to give and no one to give it to. Raleigh had given up trying to attract a worthy male. She had resigned herself to being every man's buddy and no man's lover. She and Curtis had shared so much... Or had they? She had seen Curtis on his last afternoon in this world. He had joked with her, promised to see a movie with her sometime in the next week. *He had seemed fine!*

Raleigh closed her eyes, refusing to give in to the sobs clutching at her throat. She was a different woman now, and not only in the physical sense. Sorrow had slapped her hard across the face, and she was still stinging from the attack.

No. She couldn't call Evan. She couldn't see Evan. She had to sort out all this mumbo jumbo. She had to get to know herself again. She had to bury the past... and Curtis. She certainly didn't need to add another puzzle to her life.

Puzzle?

Her eyes flew open as a jagged piece of memory fit neatly beside its companion.

"Victoria Rendell!" As the deceased woman's name slipped from her lips, Raleigh felt a rush of adrenaline.

When Paul had mentioned all those telephone numbers Grant left for emergencies, it had jogged Raleigh's memory, but not enough. Now she had it! It was one of those freak tricks of the mind, like when you go to bed with a problem only to start awake with the solution.

She had needed Grant one morning before deadline, and Paul had given her a number to call. Victoria Rendell had answered the telephone and then passed it on to Grant.

What had Grant been doing at Victoria Rendell's house at six o'clock in the morning? Raleigh wondered. It just didn't jibe. Raleigh pivoted and started walking toward her car. Should she mention this to Cody? Did he already know about it? Should she talk to Grant about it first?

"You're not leaving, are you?"

Raleigh looked up into Grant Farris's tanned face, and her heart began to pound. "Uh...well...yes, I'm leaving." She swallowed nervously, chiding herself for breaking out into goose-flesh at the sight of her boss.

"We're just getting ready to play softball, and I wanted you to be on my team." Grant gave her his best lady-killer smile.

"Sorry. I've made other plans for the afternoon." She started to walk past him, but Grant reached out and grabbed her arm. Raleigh flinched and looked sideways into his dark eyes.

"Have you talked to Cody yet?"

"Cody?" An unreasonable panic surged through her. "About what?"

Grant frowned. "About the Rendell case!"

"The Rendell case?"

Releasing her, Grant gave her a stern glare. "I asked you to feel out Cody about any further investigation on the case. Remember?"

"Oh!" Raleigh laughed, and her panic subsided. "Cody's been out of reach. I . . . I'll talk to him Monday or Tuesday."

"Good. Keep me briefed on it."

"I will." She edged away from him, anxious to be in her car and away from this place. "Bye! It was a great Spring Fling." Raleigh hurried toward her car and breathed a sigh of relief when she had closed the door and locked herself inside.

A crazy laugh tumbled from her. Good grief! She was letting her imagination run wild. So what if Grant had been at Victoria's? It wasn't any big deal. Still, she should probably mention it to Cody. The past week she had spent as little time as possible at the police station for fear of running into Evan, but she knew now that she would have to face him sooner or later. It was inevitable, and she couldn't let it interfere with her work.

She glanced at the digital clock on her dashboard and was surprised to find that it was already four o'clock. The numerals flashed to the date, and Raleigh smiled. It was April Fools' Day.

How appropriate that the Spring Fling should fall on April Fools' Day this year, because if Paul and Mike were correct, this little picnic might just be the *Tulsa Times* staff's Last Supper.

She started the car and headed for home. Half an hour later, she parked her car in Mrs. Trolley's driveway. Four of the Trolley cats rubbed against her legs as she got out of the car, and Raleigh leaned down and stroked each sleek head. Then she straightened, stepped carefully around the purring felines and started for the flight of stairs.

"Hey there, beautiful!"

Raleigh whirled around in the direction of the husky voice. Evan Younger was getting out of his sports car, which blocked the driveway.

"Hello." Raleigh was startled to hear the pleasure in her voice. Just minutes ago she had decided she shouldn't see this man again, and here she was smiling at him and drinking in the sight of his tousled brown hair and sparkling blue eyes. He wore jeans, a blue jean shirt and a black leather jacket. Casual, but very masculine.

"I was hoping to catch you. Are you ready to go?"

"Go?" Raleigh shook her head in confusion. "Go where?"

"My place." His smile took on force, deepening the dimples in the lean cheeks. "Dinner is waiting for you there."

Chapter Five

Evan's attractiveness enveloped Raleigh in a tight but tender grip.

He has such kind eyes, she thought as he closed the distance between them; he looks as if he wouldn't hurt a fly. So kind.

"Well?" He held out one hand to her. "Ready to cruise over to my place? Dinner's getting cold."

Raleigh shook a finger at him. "You're feeding me again. Want me to become a miniblimp again?"

"No." He hooked his finger around hers and tugged. "Come on. Please? I want you to see my home."

No harm in having dinner with him, she told herself. As long as she kept it friendly. Raleigh gave a quick, decisive nod. "Okay. I'd love to see your house, but I just finished eating. I've been to a company picnic."

"Oh, well." Evan shrugged, stepped nearer and draped an arm across her shoulders to lead her toward his car.

"My dinner will beat that picnic food all to heck." He opened the passenger door and handed her in, then closed it behind her.

Evan started the car, and it left the curb with a smooth, powerful roar.

"What if I hadn't been home?" Raleigh asked.

"I would have searched the city for you, of course." He glanced at her and winked. "As it turned out, my timing was perfect."

"You have a house?"

"Yes, in West Tulsa." He braked at the bottom of Reservoir Hill, looked both ways, then accelerated across the intersection. "It was my parents' home, but they gave it to me when they retired to Eureka Springs last year. It's been sitting empty. I thought I might sell it, and then I decided to check into the job situation here. It's all worked out fine. I've moved back to my old stomping ground, secured an interesting job and I'm living in the house I grew up in."

"How do you like your job?"

He seemed to weigh the question for a few moments before he answered. "It's challenging. Being Tulsa's first police counselor has its advantages and disadvantages. I don't have a predecessor, so I have to make up the rules as I go along. Police officers, on a whole, are a pretty macho bunch of guys and they don't like to show weaknesses."

"And talking to a counselor is a weakness," Raleigh added.

"Exactly. It will take a while before I'm accepted. I'll have to gain their confidence, and that can't happen overnight."

"No one expects it to," Raleigh said, trying to make him feel more optimistic.

"Oh?" He gave her a bitter smile. "I get the distinct feeling that some people do expect me to work miracles. I've been reading about policemen to better understand the pressure they're under. It occurred to me that you could help me in that department. You already have their confidence."

"I do?" Startled, Raleigh turned to look at him. "Who says?"

"You are the *Times* first female police reporter. That must have been difficult at first."

"Being a police reporter is difficult, period." Raleigh's thoughts reverted to those first few months as a police reporter. There had been times when she'd been ready to resign. Police departments viewed reporters as a necessary evil, but when that reporter was a woman it was a double whammy.

"You seem to have fared well." Evan steered the car onto the bridge that spanned the Arkansas, and Raleigh looked out over the water. The sun was setting in a show of purple and violet. "The officers seem to respect you."

"That's good to hear."

"I guess they consider you one of their own since your brother was a cop."

Raleigh averted her face and swallowed hard. "I suppose so. I never really thought about it."

"You don't want to talk about it, do you?"

His gentle tone softened her, and she leaned her forehead against the cool glass of the car window. "No. I'd be glad to help you understand cops better, but I don't really want to discuss Curtis. Not yet, anyway."

"Sometimes it helps to talk about it, Raleigh. I won't push you, but I want you to know that I'm a good listener."

"Thanks." A kind of restlessness gnawed within her, and for a moment she longed to tell Evan about the confusion, the pain, the failure. But the moment passed, and the shield came up around her heart again. "I've noticed a change among the police lately."

"What kind of change?"

"The God Squad." Raleigh turned sideways to face Evan. "They're beginning to band together and look for guidance. They used to be independent—being a loner was popular. But not anymore. I hope it means that they are realizing they're in this together and need to help each other."

"Oh, yes." Evan nodded slowly. "The God Squad. Maybe I should talk to those guys. They'll probably be more receptive to me."

"Cody Wakefield is a team player. Do you know him?"

"Yes." Evan smiled, recalling his peculiar chat with the officer. "He's a nice guy. He thinks the world of you."

Raleigh felt the beginnings of a blush. "I like him, too. Anyway, Cody is a good starting place. He opened a lot of doors for me when I first started the police beat. The other officers respect him."

"The officers' families are glad to have me around. Several of the wives have stopped by to welcome me to the department. I wish their husbands were as cordial."

"Wander around the police precinct. Go to the places where they hang out. Make yourself a fixture."

"Is that what you did?" He glanced at her.

"Yes." Raleigh slanted him a smile. "But it will be easier for you. I was conspicuous. Don't be so impatient, Evan. They'll come around when they need you."

"And what about you?" He had braked for a traffic light and his eyes sought hers. "Will you come around when you need me?"

Uneasiness sifted through her and she looked away from his penetrating gaze. "I'm here, aren't I?"

"I guess I'll just have to settle for that and be patient."

The car sped forward, releasing Raleigh from Evan's intense regard. She fell silent, pretending to find the passing scenery fascinating. The temptation to tell Evan all about her unhappiness and confusion was great, but she reminded herself that she didn't know him that well. If she couldn't discuss her feelings about her brother's death with her family, she certainly couldn't talk to him.

The thing that disturbed her most was her failure to sense the depth of Curtis's inner pain. Was she so shallow? So superficial? Was she guilty of the same shortcomings she found so contemptible in others? She had been closer to Curtis than to anyone else in her life, yet she'd blithely accepted his assertions that all was well.

"I live on this street," Evan said, breaking into her thoughts. "It's that house with the hedge all around the front yard."

As Evan turned into the slanting driveway, Raleigh examined the two-story structure. Its lines were clean and the corners were rounded. She looked at Evan, opening her mouth to ask about the design, but he anticipated her.

"It's art deco," he said with a laugh. "I grew up in this house, but it wasn't until I moved back here that it hit me. This is an authentic art-deco house. The restoration society told me that it's considered one of the city's finest showcases now."

"Really?" Raleigh looked back to the house, noting the three blue lines that ran horizontally around the middle. "Did your parents know they lived in a show-case?"

"No." Evan laughed, tipping back his head in enjoyment. "It was just a nice house to us. It's weird how you overlook the familiar. When I turned into this drive a couple of months ago, I saw this place with new eyes. I looked up the original deed at the courthouse. This place was built in the late thirties by a wealthy oilman who had been raised in West Tulsa. At the time it was built, the neighbors complained that it was an eyesore."

Raleigh laughed, shaking her head in irony. "An eyesore? It's beautiful!"

"Come inside. I've been working hard on the interior."

A waist-high hedge enclosed the front yard, and a yard lamp cast a warm glow, illuminating the sidewalk and small porch.

"It looks as if you have plenty of room," Raleigh observed.

"I hope to grow into it." He laughed softly when she tossed him a baffled smile. "I'm not a confirmed bachelor. My bachelor status is temporary—I hope."

"Oh, I see." Raleigh opened the door and scrambled from the car, feeling oddly ill at ease at this revelation.

Evan followed her to the house and opened the front door. He stepped back, swinging the door wide. "After you."

"Age before beauty?" Raleigh asked, laughing when Evan frowned. "It's a joke, doctor."

"Yes, it is. I'm relieved to hear you've finally come to that conclusion."

Raleigh ignored his comment and walked through the front foyer. To her left was a spacious living room that sustained the streamlined art-deco effect. White and silver were the predominant colors, with end tables and coffee tables in blue glass and chrome.

"I'll pour us some wine and then we can have dinner." Evan entered a room to the left of the foyer, and Raleigh followed him into a small but cozy den. "Would you like a tour of the Younger mansion?"

"Yes. So far, I like what I see. Did you decorate it all by yourself?" She took the glass of wine he had poured for her at the portable bar.

"Yes, but my mother helped."

"Did you say that your parents live in Eureka Springs?"

"That's right. I'd like you to meet them someday." His eyes met hers over the rim of his wineglass. "We could take a weekend and drive to Eureka Springs. Have you ever been there?"

"Yes. It's lovely." Raleigh turned away from him and examined a Rubens print on the far wall. Why was he talking family to her, and why did it bother her so much?

She was relieved when he began showing her his house. It was a spacious, dazzling place. Downstairs were the living room, dining room, den, kitchen and bath. Upstairs were an office, three bedrooms and two bathrooms. Evan's bedroom, at the west end, was the largest of the three, with an adjoining bathroom. Raleigh peeked in but didn't cross the threshold. Irrationally, she didn't want to enter this room, which belonged totally to Evan. Giving the queen-size brass bed with its black satin comforter a cursory glance, Raleigh backed away and started for the staircase again.

"You have a lot of rooms to clean, Evan. I hope you have a maid."

"I like housework."

"You do?" She tossed him a wide-eyed glance over her shoulder as she descended the stairs. "I hate it. It seems such a waste of time."

"Your environment has a direct impact on your mood. A clean, orderly, comfortable living space makes for a happier person."

"Are you lecturing me, doctor?" Raleigh paused at the foot of the stairs and looked up at him. "Are you comparing my dwelling to yours and my mood to yours?"

"If the shoe fits..." He softened his missile with a grin and reached out to flick the tip of her nose with his fingertips. "I've wined you, now let me dine you."

"I hope you didn't go to a lot of trouble."

"No, no." He placed the flat of his hand between her shoulders and guided her toward the dining room. "I just threw together a seven-course dinner."

"Evan! You didn't!" Raleigh turned to face him, appalled that he would go to such extremes.

"I didn't." Once again, he placed his hand on her shoulders and directed her to the dining room. "We're having good, old-fashioned beef stew, corn bread and blackberry cobbler for dessert."

"My, my!" Raleigh sniffed the air, catching the aroma of the savory stew. "It smells wonderful." She paused to appreciate the table settings before she took her seat.

"I love to cook." Evan stood behind her chair and leaned down until his lips were near her ear. "Go ahead, say it."

"Say what?" Raleigh stiffened, staring straight ahead and not really knowing what was coming next, but preparing herself for it anyway.

"I'll make someone a great husband." His breath fanned the side of her face, and she caught the heady scent of wine.

"If the shoe fits..."

He laughed and straightened up, taking the chair near hers. Lifting his wineglass, he waited for her to honor his toast. "To the immediate future." He clicked his glass against hers.

Raleigh felt a stiff smile touch her lips before she sipped the fruity wine. Evan ladled thick stew into a bowl and set it before her. Raleigh tasted it, then smiled again when she caught his eye.

"It's delicious, of course," she said, telling him what he was waiting to hear.

"My mother always told me that the way to a woman's heart is through her stomach."

"I think you've got that a little turned around," Raleigh told him, accepting a square of golden cornbread.

"Oh?" Evan paused, fixing an innocent expression on his face. "The way to a woman's stomach is through her heart?"

Raleigh laughed, quickly covering her mouth with her napkin. "You're crazy!"

Evan chuckled, holding her gaze with his. "And you're beautiful."

"No, I'm not." The denial rose instantly to her lips.

"Raleigh, don't argue with the chef until *after* you've finished dinner." He leaned closer to enjoy her blooming smile. "I was told by members of your family that you are clever, witty and have a bawdy sense of humor. Why are you withholding those fine qualities from me?"

"I wasn't aware I was withholding them." Raleigh glanced at him through her lashes, realizing only then that she had been moody around him. But then she'd been moody for several weeks now. Ever since Curtis...

"You have been," Evan charged, his voice low and intimate. "But we're changing all of that tonight. We're going to have fun, you and I. After dinner we're going to cut the rug while I sing a sweet song in your ear, and then we're going to have a go at the three T's.''

This time she looked at him fully. "The three T's?"

"Tickle, tease and tantalize. My favorite game. I hope you're a good sport." He glanced at her bowl of stew. "You aren't eating."

She smiled and forced herself to concentrate on the meal he'd prepared. Throughout the ensuing silence Raleigh mulled over his agenda for the evening. It had been so long since she'd relaxed enough to devote herself just to having a good time. The past weeks had drained her, and for what? She was still as confused and restless as she had been when she'd heard of Curtis's suicide. No one and nothing had been able to alleviate her pain and self-doubt. She glanced at Evan and felt a smile curve her lips. At least not until now.

Glancing again at the man seated next to her, Raleigh felt that wanton yearning surface. The good doctor had prescribed the three T's. She'd be a fool not to follow his medical advice.

"Finished?" When Raleigh nodded, Evan reached for her bowl and whisked it from the table. "Good. I'll just pop these in the dishwasher and meet you in the living room."

"Okay. Can I help?"

"Yes. Pick out a record we can slow-dance to. The albums are in a rack beside the stereo." He shouldered open the swinging door and disappeared into the kitchen.

Following his orders, Raleigh located the stereo in the living room and looked through his wide assortment of music. She narrowed down the possibilities and finally selected a Nat King Cole album. She placed the record on the stereo and switched on the equipment. Music flowed from two large speakers, filling the room with romance. Raleigh closed her eyes, enjoying the light touch on the piano and the lush sound of violins.

"A wise choice," Evan said, entering the room.

Raleigh opened her eyes and smiled. "I'm glad you approve." She glanced around the neat, picture-perfect room and sighed. "Evan, do you really disapprove of the way I live? My apartment, I mean."

"If you like it, who am I to complain?" He walked over and adjusted the tenor on the stereo.

"It's just that...well, no one sees it except for me and my family. I guess I've gotten used to it and...cleaning house seems such a waste when I'm the only one there."

"I used to be like that."

"Really?" she asked, pleased that he understood.

"Yes, until one day..." He paused and shook his head as a pained expression crossed his face.

"What happened?"

"Oh, I was so embarrassed!" He ran a hand through his hair and sighed. "My apartment was the pits. I was living in L.A. at the time. And who should drop by un-announced?"

"Who?" Raleigh asked, thoroughly hooked.

"That month's Miss Centerfold." His eyes widened. "She waltzed right in and my place was a pigpen. I hadn't cleaned it in weeks."

"Miss Centerfold?" Raleigh frowned good-naturedly. "That must have been terrible." She looked away from his dancing eyes. "I should have known you'd go for that type. What was her name?"

"I never kiss and tell. I liked her a lot at first," he admitted, carrying on the farce. "But she turned me off when she made such blatant demands for my body. It was pathetic!"

Raleigh turned to face him, a smile playing at the corners of her mouth. "Her behavior or your body?"

He gasped as if he'd been wounded, then shook a finger at her as he approached. "There's that wit. I knew I'd find it eventually." He stopped in front of her and looked down at his shoes. "Could I ask a big favor of you?"

"That depends on the favor."

When he lifted his eyes, she saw that he was perfectly serious. "Would you teach me to dance?"

"You can't dance?" She watched him shake his head slowly, but still she found it impossible to believe. "You told me you were a stripper. They have to dance."

"Fast-dance...by themselves, yes, but I've never been able to slow-dance. Won't you try to teach me?" He held up one hand and placed the other lightly at her side. "Please?"

"Are you sure you can't slow-dance?"

"I'm positive. Can't you?"

She examined his face, found no deceit or banter there, and decided he was being honest with her. Raleigh placed one hand in his and the other on his shoulder. "Yes, I can. It's simple. I'll lead for now and you follow me. Don't look down at your feet. Look at me."

"With pleasure." He flashed her a grin, then sobered immediately and began to concentrate.

It was similar to pushing a plank around the room at first, but Raleigh persevered. More than once, Evan's foot came down squarely on hers, but she merely kept hauling him about the room as she counted with the music.

"I never dreamed it would be this complex," Evan complained after two songs.

"Well, most men fudge."

"Fudge? How?"

His foot squashed hers and Raleigh sucked in her breath. "Most men just sway from one foot to the other, but I don't call that dancing. I call that wobbling in three-four time."

He laughed, stomped her foot again and grimaced. "Oops, sorry. Your feet keep getting in my way."

"Maybe we should sit one out and catch our breath," Raleigh suggested, wanting desperately to kick off her heels and examine the damage.

"No, just one more song. I think I might be getting the hang of this."

"Okay." Raleigh heaved a sigh and waited for the next song to begin. "Here we go."

"Let me try to lead this time."

Raleigh looked up into his face, thinking it was a dangerous idea, but she decided to be a good sport. "Okay. Go ahead. I'll try to keep my feet out of your way this time."

"Thanks. That will help a lot."

She bit her tongue to keep from telling him bluntly that her feet weren't in his way! All he needed were two left shoes and he'd be fine. His fingers closed tightly around hers and his other hand slid up between her shoulder blades. It was awkward going at first with Evan stumbling slightly and cursing softly under his breath, but then he began smoothing out. Halfway through the song, a miracle occurred. He actually began *floating* across the carpet. Stunned, Raleigh captured his gaze and saw the devil there. She stopped and pulled her hand from his.

"You said you couldn't dance!"

Evan caught her hand and pressed it to the front of his shirt. "April Fool, honey."

She found that she couldn't be angry with him, not when his eyes were sparkling with blue lights. Raleigh acknowledged his smile with one of her own and allowed him to pull her back into his arms. This time, the pretense gone, he began moving to the music with a liquid grace. He didn't fudge.

"You're not mad at me, are you?" he asked.

"No. I'm a good sport." She rested her cheek against his shoulder and closed her eyes, letting Mr. Cole and Dr. Younger have their way with her.

Evan began humming, his breath fanning her ear. Raleigh listened to the song that was playing, but it wasn't familiar to her. She smiled when Evan began singing to her in a husky baritone.

"Love words whispered close to my ear,
Love words that no one else can hear,
Whisper them softly and release me
From my heartbreaking misery.
Darling, talk dirty to me."

Raleigh jerked back, her mouth slightly agape as Evan's laughter rolled over her. "You made that up!" she charged, her own voice laced with laughter.

Evan nodded. "It's kind of catchy, isn't it? It gets you right here." He tapped her hand in the region of his heart.

"It gets me right here." Raleigh shoved a gentle fist into his stomach, but the skin and muscle were so taut there that her fist didn't even make a dent. Surprised, she looked down and realized that Evan Younger was quite a fit specimen. "Do you work out?"

"I've been known to lift a few weights now and then. It's not a religion to me, though."

"Good. I'm not much at exercise, either."

"How did you lose your weight? Didn't you exercise then?"

"No." Raleigh glanced toward the stereo. The record had finished and the machine had shut itself off. "I just stopped eating. The record needs to be turned over."

"That must have been hard to do."

She looked back at him, momentarily confused, then realized that he was still talking about her weight loss. "No, not really. It wasn't a conscious effort. I just got lucky and lost my appetite. The pressures of my job and things like that got to me, and I lost interest in food. Aren't you going to start the record again?"

"No. Let's relax." He gathered her hands in his and pulled her toward the couch. Then he sat down, making her sit next to him. "I hear that the *Times* might be in financial trouble."

Raleigh turned a shoulder into the couch to face him. "Have you heard that, too? Hmmm." She digested this, then shrugged. "I asked Grant Farris about it, but he denied the rumors."

"What do you think? Are the rumors valid?"

"I think they are, but I can't be certain. We didn't get our cost-of-living raises, and those usually come in January. Grant said he'd issue them in June this year, but he didn't sound firm on it."

"Maybe you should scout the job market to be on the safe side."

Raleigh sighed and settled back against the soft cushions. "Maybe you're right." She lapsed into a moody silence, which was broken by the touch of Evan's fingers against the side of her neck. A delicious chill raced through her, and she looked sideways at him. He was staring at her, a gentle smile curving his mouth as he wound a curl of her blond hair around his index finger.

"Will you respect me in the morning?" he whispered.

Raleigh swallowed against the tension clutching her throat. "Is this another practical joke?"

He spread his fingers across her cheek and turned her head to face him. "If it is, then the joke's on me."

"Evan...I..." Looking into the peaceful blue depths of his eyes, Raleigh suddenly wanted nothing more than the pleasure he offered her. She sighed and her lashes fluttered down. "Oh, forget it." She leaned forward, meeting his descending mouth and relinquished her feeble excuses.

A treacherous ache filled her as Evan's mouth claimed hers, and Raleigh acknowledged her own desire. How many times had she dreamed of this moment? How many nights had sleep eluded her while her thoughts turned to the thrill of being wanted by a man, of being held by a man, of being kissed into submission? The moment was here, and she wanted Evan Younger.

Her fingers stole into the dark mass of his hair, and the strands curled around her fingertips. Evan's mouth settled more firmly on hers, rocking back and forth until her lips parted. His tongue outlined her lips twice before moving inside to mingle sensuously with her own. Raleigh's breathing became shallow as she arched her body into his and reveled in the feel of his hands along her back and hips. He was starving for her, and this revelation fueled her hunger for him.

When Evan stood and swept her into his arms, Raleigh felt like Scarlett O'Hara. She laughed softly, loving the man who held her weight so effortlessly. With long strides he carried her up the staircase to his bedroom. Raleigh wrapped her arms around his neck and pressed her face to his throat. He smelled delicious and she tasted him. Evan shivered as if she'd touched a flash point with the tip of her tongue.

He set her on her feet in his bedroom and stepped back, closing the door slowly behind him. His gaze took in her heightened color and shining eyes, then moved lower to where her breasts strained against her blouse. He moved toward her and placed his hand along her flushed cheek.

"Roses have bloomed in your cheeks, Raleigh," he whispered, then placed a kiss on the tip of her nose. "You're beautiful to my eyes." He tipped his head to one side and studied her rapt expression. "Do you believe me?"

Raleigh nodded, so full of her own blooming passion that she could hardly speak. "Yes, I believe you."

"Good, because I mean it. You...are...beautiful."

His words wrapped around her heart, squeezing it with gentle possession. Raleigh turned her face and pressed a kiss into his palm. Her lashes lowered as Evan unbuttoned her blouse with his free hand. He undressed her slowly, exposing soft shoulders, pillowy breasts, the curve of her stomach, slim thighs, a triangle of autumn gold. Sweeping her into his arms again, he walked to the bed and placed her there. His eyes caressed her as he pulled free the snaps on his shirt to expose a bronzed chest made even darker by sable hair.

Raleigh reached out and caught the tails of his shirt to pull him down to her. Her seeking mouth found his, and her body temperature soared. He pulled free of her long enough to shed his clothes with savage urgency, and then his body slid on top of hers, releasing a spectrum of sensory delights. Raleigh was immediately aware of the contrasts: his body was hard where hers was soft, and soft where hers was hard. Her hands explored him with gleeful abandon, tingling under the discovery of flexing muscle and hot, leathery skin. Her lips moved across his shoulder, sucking and nipping until he moved down her body so that he could nuzzle her breasts with his lips and nose. His breath heated her skin, and she moaned in ecstasy when he enclosed one of her nipples in the warm cavern of his mouth; her eyes squeezed shut in exquisite pleasure as he flicked his tongue across her satiny skin. She drove her fingers through his hair and murmured his name in a mindless chant.

Her previous image of herself dissolved under Evan's loving manipulations, and a new image emerged. Suddenly Raleigh felt like the most beautiful, most prized woman in the world, and this elevated self-image brought tears to her eyes. She wanted to thank him, but she was incapable of speech, so she tried to telegraph her gratitude through her hands. She sought him, found him and stroked him. Evan's mouth left her breasts, and he flung his head back, groaning in pleasure. Watching him, Raleigh continued her homage until she could feel the life force throbbing within him.

Evan's lashes lifted slightly to reveal glazed blue pools. His lips formed her name as he spanned her hips with his hands. Gently he guided himself into her. Their union stole her breath; she could only stare up into Evan's face in wide-eyed wonder. A gentle smile curved his mouth, and he leaned closer to her until his forehead rested lightly against hers.

"All aboard for a trip to the moon," he murmured, his voice strained by passion. "Hold on tight."

Raleigh hooked her arms around his neck. "Take me there," she whispered before the stimulating movement of his body made it impossible for her to speak again.

With each thrust, Evan pushed her upward to a shimmering plateau of passion. She imagined herself to be a rocket, blazing a trail through a twilight of flashing blue and violet; pushing aside stars and racing comets as she blasted through space to a disk of milky white. She raced Evan to the moon and reached it first. Her body stilled and then she landed in a shower of writhing pleasure and blinding passion. She gasped Evan's name and pulled his mouth to hers. His lips clung to hers in a trembling embrace as he followed closely with his own fulfillment, sending a violent shudder through him that reverberated inside of her. Two became one, and Raleigh couldn't tell where she ended and he began.

Slowly she floated back to earth, pleasantly relaxed and fulfilled. Evan nuzzled the side of her neck and whispered her name. Raleigh lightly stroked his back with her fingernails, and he purred like a jungle cat. He stayed inside of her, unwilling to break that final, sweet contact. Raleigh held him closer and pressed fervent kisses to the side of his neck. Her tongue caressed the back of his ear, and he shifted, raising his head to look at her.

"We're great together, aren't we?"

Amused by his self-confidence, Raleigh shrugged and fixed a consoling smile on her lips. "It was okay, I guess."

"What?" His eyes widened, and he leaned closer to see her more clearly in the semidarkness. "You're complaining? What more did you want? You should have told me you weren't satisfied. You should have said something—"

Raleigh lifted her head and kissed him. "April Fool."

His indignation died, and he closed his eyes briefly in relief. "That borders on cruelty, Raleigh."

"I'm sorry." She laughed softly and pulled his lips to hers. "Let me kiss it and make it better." Sensuously she moved her mouth over his and felt him stir to life within her. "Oooops! What's happening down there?"

He chuckled and rained kisses over her face. "Kiss it and make it better, honey."

Sun rays lengthened across Evan's face, and Raleigh examined his sleeping form as fear of rejection crowded into her mind.

Rejection was not foreign to her, but that didn't make it any less painful. She turned her face away from him and shut her eyes, feeling waves of bitterness wash over her. She recalled the men she had wanted over the years, wincing at memories of being treated like a pal, a good buddy, a funny friend...but never as a woman. Through high school and college she had dreamed of sharing her love with someone special, but somehow she'd always found herself being a good pal to the men she longed for, listening as they recounted their problems with the women in their lives. It had not been blatant rejection: no, it had been far more subtle—the kind you have to live with all by yourself.

By the time she had graduated from college she'd built a wall around her heart. It had been bruised and battered far too often, and Raleigh had decided she didn't want anyone using it as a punching bag anymore. Her work had become her pleasure, and Curtis had become the man she could lean on, dream with and have heart-to-heart conversations with. She had learned not to expect anything. Expectations were lofty wishes that never came true.

Lately, she'd noticed that some of the police officers were flirting with her. Instead of being flattered, she'd been consumed with bitterness. Where had they been when she'd worn her heart on her sleeve? The same officers who had never given her a second glance were now winking and wolf-whistling. It disgusted her because she knew she was the same person she'd been a year ago. Slimmer, yes, but the same person.

Of course it was different with Evan. He hadn't known her a year ago, so she couldn't accuse him of having a change of heart just because she'd dropped some weight.

Sensing his body so close to hers, Raleigh felt tears burn the back of her eyes. He was everything she had ever dreamed of—gentle, courteous, sensitive, honest and witty. His physical attributes were considerable, too, of course, but Raleigh had learned long ago that beauty is only skin deep. Evan was beautiful throughout.

However, if past experience had taught her anything, it was that expecting Evan to fall in love with her was pure foolishness. The longer she stayed around him and the more she dreamed of a life with him, the harder it would be to release him.

It would be easier to walk away now, instead of watching him bolt and run when he discovered that this was not a casual dalliance for her. He couldn't know now that she wouldn't be here in this bed if she weren't already halfway in love with him. When he realized how deeply she cared for him, he'd vanish from her life.

Rejection. Raleigh opened her eyes and stared blindly at the morning sun spilling into the room. Being rejected by Evan would not bruise her heart; it would break it.

The irony of it made her smile: she hadn't wanted to become involved with Evan because of the age difference, but last night had erased the few years that separated them. No, that was no longer a consideration. He might be younger, but he was her senior in the romance department. She was putty in his hands, defenseless and vulnerable. The walls around her heart strengthened as Raleigh came to a decision: she had to protect herself.

How should she face this morning? Casual was the operative word. No expectations. No promises. No strings. She'd leave with her memories of him, and those would have to warm her during the lonely nights to follow.

A sixth sense stirred within her, and Raleigh turned her head to find that Evan was awake. His gaze moved sleepily over her face and a lazy smile tipped up one corner of his mouth.

"Sunlight becomes you, Miss Torrence," he murmured, and his hand found the soft skin of her stomach under the sheet. "Good morning."

"What time is it?"

He rolled onto his back and peered over his shoulder at the alarm clock. "Eight." He looked at her again. "I suggest we make love, and then I'll prepare a tasty breakfast and then we'll make love again and—"

"I can't." Raleigh slipped from the bed and began grabbing up her clothing from the floor, feeling exposed and awkward. "I've got things to do today."

"It's Sunday." Evan propped himself up on his elbows. "Come back to bed. I've got a surprise for you under the sheet."

Raleigh frowned and headed for the bathroom. "I've got to get dressed. Can I use your shower?" She glanced over her shoulder, caught his brief nod and ducked into the bathroom.

Dumping her clothes on the vanity stool, Raleigh went to the shower and adjusted the spray. She stepped into the cubicle and started to pull the shower curtain closed when she saw Evan standing in the bathroom doorway. He wore nothing but a scowl.

"Why do I feel like a hit-and-run victim?"

Raleigh sighed, wishing he'd play by the rules and leave her alone to shower. "I'm sorry, Evan, but I'm going over to my parents' today." She pulled the shower curtain across and stepped under the stinging spray. The curtain fluttered, and she found herself pressed against the tiled wall by Evan. "Evan, get out!"

"It's my shower." He took the soap from its holder and lathered it. "Allow me."

"Evan, please, I just want to shower and get dressed." She gasped softly when he placed his lathered hands firmly on her shoulders and pushed her rather roughly against the wall.

"Listen to me, Raleigh." The scowl was back in place. "I'm not going to be treated like a one-night stand. I deserve better than that." The water plastered his hair to his head and ran in rivulets down his face. "Just because you're having second thoughts doesn't give you the right to treat me like a hired stud."

Justly chastised, Raleigh bowed her head. "Evan, last night was wonderful, but I need time to myself."

He was quiet and the sound of the shower seemed unnaturally loud. When she looked up, she could see by his contemplative expression that he was having difficulty understanding her request. Abruptly, his hands popped off her shoulders and he stuck them under the spray to wash away the suds.

"Okay, if that's what you want. I'll get dressed and drive you home."

"Thank you."

He bolted from the shower and whipped the curtain back into place. Raleigh turned her face up to the stinging assault and let the water camouflage her tears.

Raleigh slammed the car door and hurried up the driveway to her apartment. Evan dipped his head to watch her through the car window. Anger boiled within him, and he shoved the car into gear and burned rubber away from the curb.

"So much for meaningful relationships," he growled sourly. It seemed that instead of taking one step forward, he had taken one giant step backward.

He cautioned himself not to let his anger make him unreasonable and tried to place himself in Raleigh's shoes. She was feeling insecure, he decided. She'd revealed that by telling him that she needed to be alone. Maybe the pace of their relationship was too fast for her. Although she protested that she was too old for him— God, what rubbish!—Raleigh was a novice when it came to romance. Yes, she was having a bout of insecurity. She'd come around eventually and realize that he hadn't taken her to bed on a whim. Couldn't she guess that by the way he'd romanced her last night? Did she think he went to that much trouble for every woman who made his libido kick up its heels?

It had been a bitter blow when she'd treated last night lightly. Her casual attitude had hurt him more than she'd ever know.

Not wanting to return home, where the memory of her supple body and blazing passion still lingered, Evan drove toward the summit of Reservoir Hill. At the top of the crest he parked the car and got out. Gazing out at the city that was relatively young as cities go, he suddenly felt old and weary. He wondered if he had enough strength to break down the fortress Raleigh had built around herself. There was a treasure trove of lasting love behind the fortress walls, he knew, but now he wondered if he was up to such a challenge.

If he could just get her to open up to him! Evan kicked at a tuft of green grass, taking out his frustration on spring's patchy carpet. She had so much bottled up that he felt she was at the point of exploding. Her family had spoken to him of Raleigh's inner strength, but there was a limit to strength and Raleigh was quickly depleting her supply. He wanted to be there when it all came down on her; when she finally realized that it was too much to bear by herself. The walls would tumble down and she'd be free to begin again. As it stood now, she was clinging to tattered dreams and tarnished memories.

He had hoped that she would feel secure enough with him this morning to talk about Curtis. Yes, Curtis was at the center of it all. Suicide was a heavy cross for the survivors to bear, and there always seemed to be one who buckled under the weight.

"Why did you do this to her, Curtis?" Evan's mouth tensed into a bitter line. Of course, suicide was a totally selfish act. Curtis hadn't been thinking clearly, and he certainly hadn't considered the devastation to his family and friends.

But it's Raleigh's burden, not mine, Evan told himself, and the thought was jarring. He squinted into the sun and examined his desire to share her burden.

"I guess I'm falling in love," he whispered, then shivered. If he believed in such things, he would have to admit that he'd fallen in love with her at first sight; but that was irrational. Like believing in the tooth fairy or Tinker Bell. No, he didn't know the exact moment when his interest in Raleigh Torrence had far exceeded mere attraction. All he knew was that his feelings for her ran deep.

Evan wandered to his car and sat on the hood. He looked out over Tulsa and recalled his decision to put down roots here again. It was a good place to raise a family, and he'd always wanted that in his life. He had never been a loner. Since his first big crush when he was in fifth grade, he had been a one-woman man. His relationships lasted years, not days.

For the past few years he had been looking—searching—for someone special. He had so much to share and his inner timetable told him that it was time to plant seeds and find someone to share in the harvest. He wanted marriage. He wanted children. Most of all, he wanted Raleigh.

The sun washed over him in warm rays, and he began to feel better. His inner equilibrium and strength returned, and an hour later he got back into his car and went home. The memory of Raleigh didn't hurt anymore because Evan meant to scale the fortress walls and take what was his.

He went upstairs and stared at his bed and thought how wonderful it would be to call that bed "ours."

Chapter Six

Grant Farris was heading for the elevator when he suddenly stopped and pivoted toward Raleigh. Catching the action from the corner of her eye, Raleigh held her breath, then let it escape softly in a sigh when Grant started toward her desk. Raleigh looked up, forcing a smile to her lips. She could almost read his mind, and she mentally prepared an answer to the question he was bound to ask.

"Raleigh, have you got anything on the Rendell story yet?"

Pushing aside her notebook, Raleigh fixed a sincere frown on her face. "No. I guess you heard that Cody was in a car accident last weekend."

"Oh, yes, that's right." Grant shoved his hands into his trench coat and matched her frown. "He's out of the hospital, isn't he?"

"Yes, but he hasn't come back to work yet. I visited him yesterday and he said he'd be back to work Monday."

"Did you ask him about the Rendell investigation?"

"No. I wasn't alone with him. Some of his friends and family were there, too, so I didn't want to talk business in front of the others."

"Okay." Grant started to turn away, but he glanced sharply at her. "You *are* going to speak with him on Monday?"

"As soon as I get a chance," Raleigh assured her editor, choosing her words carefully since she had no intention of hounding Cody about Howard Rendell. "Have a nice weekend." She offered a cheery smile, which Grant didn't bother to acknowledge.

After he'd gone, Raleigh fell back in her chair, relieved that the inquisition was over for the time being. The trouble with editors was that they were one-track-minded. They concentrated on a single story and forgot that the reporters were covering a section of news and a number of stories. Grant Farris was a perfect case in point, Raleigh decided. He was stuck on this Rendell story, forgetting—or ignoring—the fact that Raleigh covered crime in the city and that crime was ongoing. She glanced at the stack of notes on her desk, tapping them with her fingertips. There were at least six stories among those notes. Today she had filed ten news stories. She had a drawer filled with possible feature-story ideas that she never seemed to get around to doing. What she needed was two more reporters to help her cover her beat.

"What a day!" Cathy Carlsbad stretched her arms above her head and looked over at Raleigh. "Are we still on for lunch?"

"Sure, I'm starved." Raleigh rolled back her chair to get a better view of the young woman at the next desk. "What are you in the mood for? Chili or hamburgers or Chinese food?" Noticing that she no longer had Cathy's attention, Raleigh looked over her shoulder. Evan Younger stood near the elevators. He raised a hand in greeting, and Raleigh swiveled back to face Cathy. "What's he doing here?"

"I don't know, but I hope he's free for lunch." Cathy smiled and waved merrily. "Here he comes."

Raleigh squared her shoulders and turned to face Evan. He looked casual and approachable in his gold-colored corduroy slacks and matching vest, which was unbuttoned to reveal a brushed-flannel shirt of green-and-gold plaid. Muhammad had come to the mountain once more, Raleigh thought, feeling a twinge of guilt for not answering her phone all week. She had known the calls were from Evan and had stubbornly refused to answer the ringing telephone. There was nothing she could say. He'd want a better explanation of her attitude toward him, and she couldn't give it. What could she say? *Evan, I'm falling in love with you and I can't help myself. I want all of you or nothing at all, and I don't think I'm the woman you want to spend the rest of your life with.* Raleigh laughed to herself. He'd think she was crazy if she told him that. He just *thinks* he wants the truth, Raleigh thought, but he really doesn't.

"Hello, ladies." Evan nodded toward Cathy. "Raleigh, how about having lunch with me?"

Raleigh looked away from his eyes, which told her *I want to talk to you—alone.* She found herself looking at Cathy's swooning expression, and a wonderful idea hit her. She turned back to Evan. "I can't make lunch, Evan, but Cathy would love to go with you. Wouldn't you, Cathy?"

Cathy blinked her big green eyes in confusion. "Why, sure, but I thought you were going to have—"

"I've got to follow up on some stories right now. You and Evan run along and have a good time." Raleigh positioned her fingers on the computer keys. She could feel Evan's eyes burning a hole in her back.

"Raleigh, I wanted to— Raleigh, I'm talking to you."

With a sigh, she swiveled back to face him. "Yes?"

Evan looked away for a moment as if he were reining in his temper. When he looked back at Raleigh she could see anger smoldering in his eyes. "Can you at least take a coffee break?"

"No, I can't right now." Raleigh shrugged. "You should have called first."

"I've been calling you for days and you know it." He shook his head and his gaze fell on Cathy, who was looking decidedly uncomfortable. "It looks as if you're stuck with me, Cathy."

"If you'd rather not . . ." Cathy let the sentence trail off, giving Evan an out.

"No, on the contrary. Are you ready to go?"

"Yes, I'll just get my sweater and I'll meet you at the elevator." Cathy swept her purse off her desk and headed for the coat room.

Evan made no move toward the elevator, and his immobility and tense silence drew Raleigh's attention to him again. He shoved his hands in his trouser pockets and his jaw hardened.

"Raleigh, I'm going to talk to you. We can either talk here where everyone can hear us or we can talk in the canteen; which will it be?"

Staring into his icy blue eyes, Raleigh accepted defeat and stood up. "The canteen." She pivoted sharply and headed for the canteen, excruciatingly aware of her colleagues' curious stares. Pushing open the door, Raleigh went to the center of the room, then turned to face Evan. "Let's make this quick because I've got work to do."

He approached her, keeping his back to the newsroom and shielding her from prying eyes. "I asked *you* to lunch, not Cathy."

"She likes you, Evan."

"I don't need a dating service. It was rude of you to force Cathy on me."

Raleigh lowered her eyes, feeling like a louse for using Cathy as a weapon against Evan. "I know. I just wish you'd—" she lifted her eyes to his again "—pick on somebody your own age. It won't work between us. Can't you see that?"

His self-control snapped and he reached out for her, his fingers biting into her upper arms. "Listen to me," he said in a growling tone. "I'm sick of hearing that crock. Age has nothing to do with us and you know it!" He closed his eyes for a moment, and his hands fell away from her. "I wish you'd drop all these flimsy excuses for rejecting me and be honest with me for once."

"I'm trying to be honest with you." Raleigh collapsed in a chair and stared at her hands clasped in her lap. "Cathy's waiting for you."

"I'm not going to let it end here. If it's going to end, I think I deserve an explanation that makes sense. I'll see you later."

She didn't look up as he left the canteen and made his way through the newsroom to the elevators. He was right, she told herself. She had been acting like a juvenile delinquent. He'd been so patient and kind while she'd thrown one insult after another in his face.

Raleigh pushed herself up from the chair and went back to her desk. She made a mental note to apologize to Cathy for placing her in an uncomfortable position. As the afternoon wore on, she came to a difficult decision, but one that made her feel better about herself. She was going to treat Evan with the respect he deserved. The past few months had taken their toll on her, stripping her of her finer qualities. It was time to rebuild and regain her sense of humor and her sense of decency. By the time Cathy returned to the office after her luncheon with Evan, Raleigh's convictions were firm and she felt better about herself.

"How did it go?" she asked as Cathy dropped her purse onto her desk and sat down.

"He's nice, but I got his message loud and clear." Cathy's mouth twisted into a wry grin.

"Cathy, I'm sorry for foisting you on him. I shouldn't have done that. Forgive me?"

Cathy shrugged and waved a dismissive hand. "That's okay. I understand." She flipped her red hair over her shoulders and smiled. "He likes you, Raleigh, and he's a nice man."

"I know." Raleigh propped her chin in her hands and sighed. "I've been a shrew around him and I'm ashamed of myself."

"You can still repair the damage," Cathy pointed out. "That is, if you want to."

Raleigh nodded slowly. "I want to."

The package on her doorstep was long and flat. Raleigh picked it up and carried it in with her, her curiosity piqued. She shoved the morning newspaper aside and sat on the couch, the package in her lap. Fishing her glasses from her purse, she slipped them on and then lifted the lid off the package. She stared at the items nestled in the tissue paper and laughter bubbled past her lips. She touched each item—a bottle of medicine for iron-poor blood, a package of dried prunes and a pair of support panty hose—before she grasped the card and read the message. "Since you are convinced you're an elderly woman, I thought these might come in handy. Evan, the kid."

"Tenacious," Raleigh murmured as she replaced the lid on the package and set it to one side. Falling back on the couch, she sighed wearily and wished for the peace of mind she'd found in the arms of Evan Younger.

"The problem isn't age," she said as if speaking to the sender of the package instead of to the package itself. "The problem is me."

Had she become such a cynic—such a skeptic—that when something was right she refused to believe it? Curtis had reached that low level. The last few months of his life he had expected nothing, had hoped for nothing and had finally died for nothing.

Raleigh pushed herself up from the couch and looked around. The cluttered atmosphere of her apartment scraped across her senses, and she started grabbing magazines and newspapers in a flurry of impatience.

"This place is a pit," she whispered, angry with herself for dropping into this period of apathy and foul moods. "You deserve better than this, Raleigh Torrence."

A pleased smile curved her lips and a weight lifted from her soul as she began cleaning her apartment and straightening up her life.

It took more than three hours to get her living room and dining room in order. Raleigh collapsed on the couch and decided to attack the bedroom, bath and kitchen tomorrow. Months of neglect couldn't be swept away in a day. She looked around her, pleased with the orderly appearance. The scent of furniture polish permeated the air, and Raleigh breathed it in and felt cleansed. She straightened the scarf on the coffee table and decided that Evan was right: environment did have an effect on a person's outlook.

Glancing at her smudged slacks and blouse, Raleigh pushed herself up from the couch and started for the shower when a knock sounded on her front door. She circled back and opened the door.

"Evan!" She smiled and stepped back to let him in. "I was ho—"

"I know I'm the last person you want to see, but I'll make this quick," he interrupted as he took off his jacket. "I just wanted to clear the air and then I'll be out of your life for—" He stopped abruptly and looked around the tidy room. His brows lifted in surprise as he turned to face her. "For a minute I thought I was in the wrong apartment."

She laughed and took his jacket from him. "I'll hang this in the closet for you."

Evan watched in amazement as she hung up his jacket, then he surveyed the living room again, not quite believing his eyes. He looked back to Raleigh, noting her smudged clothing and flushed face. The sight of the room's tidiness threw him off track for a moment, but he soon recalled his original purpose.

"I'm not staying long. I just wanted to—"

"Sit down," Raleigh interrupted, motioning toward the couch. "Would you like a cup of coffee or a soft drink?"

"No." Evan shook his head, trying to collect his thoughts as he sat on the couch. He glanced at the uncluttered expanse of cushions, still baffled by this abrupt change.

"Are you sure I can't get you a drink or something?"

"No." He looked at her fully and was momentarily taken aback by the friendly light in her eyes and the gentle smile on her lips. "Raleigh, after that scene today I've come to my senses. You're right. I should quit pestering you."

"You haven't been pestering me."

Evan ran a hand over his face, irritated by her interruptions. "Will you just let me say what I have to say, please?"

Raleigh shrugged and sat in the chair opposite him. "Sure. I'm sorry."

"Okay." He paused, trying to remember the speech he had rehearsed on the way over to her apartment. "I realize I've been fighting a losing battle. I thought we could learn to care for each other, but it isn't working out, so I'm conceding defeat." He laughed, more from uneasiness than amusement. "I should be used to rejection by now, but I guess no one ever gets used to it. Anyway, you've made your feelings toward me clear. After that night . . . after we made love, I expected more from you than you were willing to give. I just want you to know that there's no hard feelings." He frowned, perplexed by her disappointed expression.

She looked away from him, her gaze encompassing the room. "I'm going to clean the other rooms tomorrow."

Something about her statement and the look in her eyes triggered Evan's intuition, and all his senses sharpened. "That's good. What prompted all of this?"

"I don't know." Her hands rose and fell back to her lap in a helpless gesture. "I couldn't stand it any longer. You're right about your environment making a difference. I feel better now."

Evan leaned back on the couch, no longer eager to leave her. He studied her carefully and was puzzled by her distracted air and restlessness. They were good signs, and a glimmer of hope warmed his insides. "Am I crazy or have you done a one-hundred-and-eighty-degree turn since this afternoon?"

She half smiled and laced her hands in her lap. "I've been thinking." Her eyes lifted, touched his and lowered again. "I don't like what I've become over the past few months. I've been living like a mole, afraid to face the world." She pulled her lower lip between her teeth and drew a shaky breath. "He's gone and there's nothing I can do about it."

Evan felt his heart hammer against his chest, and relief flooded through him, making him limp. "That's right, Raleigh. Curtis is dead and it's not your fault."

Tears welled in her eyes, and she removed her glasses and wiped the moisture away. "It makes me so angry sometimes, Evan. I thought he trusted me, but he lied to me. He told me he was getting off the booze and that he was piecing his life back together. He told me that everything was just great." She frowned and balled her hands into fists. "He lied to me!"

Evan forced himself to remain seated, although he wanted to take her in his arms. It was hard to watch her struggle with her feelings, but he knew that this battle had to be fought alone.

"He could have talked to me. I would have listened."
A tear rolled down her cheek and she wiped it away.

"But you couldn't have done anything to help him,"
Evan said. "Curtis obviously didn't want to drop his
problems in your lap."

"Why did he do it, Evan? Someone could have helped
him. *You* could have helped him."

The anguish in her voice crumbled his professional resolve, and Evan left the couch and sat on the coffee table facing her. "I don't know why he killed himself. No
one will ever be able to fully understand that because
Curtis took the reason with him." He placed a hand on
her arm, drawing her gaze to his. "I think Curtis was too
idealistic. He should have been a poet or a missionary,
but never a police officer."

"He was a good cop," Raleigh argued.

"He was a good cop," Evan agreed, "but being a cop
wasn't good for him. Your brother wanted to make this
a better place to live, but one person can't do that."

"He expected too much of himself."

"Yes, that's right." Evan smiled, relieved that Raleigh was coming to terms with her brother's frailties.
"When things were bad Curtis blamed himself. He took
the world's faults on his shoulders, and they crushed
him."

Evan shrugged and took her hands in his. "I read his
suicide letter and it said a lot about him." He captured
her gaze and held it. "Raleigh, don't be like Curtis. Don't
blame yourself for things that you have nothing to do
with. No one appointed you your brother's keeper."

"I should have looked closer. I should have been able
to see that he was lying."

"Raleigh, he didn't want you to see. You hero-
worshiped Curtis, and Curtis knew that. He didn't want

to expose his weaknesses to you, and he didn't want you to go through what you've gone through these past two months. In many ways, I think he wrote that last letter just for you. He wanted you to understand that he loved you and that his decision to take his own life had nothing to do with you."

She sighed and gently extracted her hands from his. "You're a good doctor, doctor."

"Thanks." He stood up, deciding that she probably wanted to be alone to think, but as he started for the closet her hand shot out and grabbed his sleeve.

"You're not leaving, are you?"

He looked down into her upturned face, and hope surged through him again. "Do you want me to stay for a few more minutes?"

"Yes." She tugged his sleeve, making him sit back down on the coffee table. "I want to apologize for being so...so mean to you. I haven't been myself lately, and I don't blame you for wanting to get rid of me."

"I didn't say I wanted to get rid of you," he corrected sternly. "I said that I concede."

"What if I don't want to accept your concession?"

"What do you want from me, Raleigh?" Evan held his breath and waited for her answer, hoping that it was one he wanted to hear.

"Another chance?" She leaned forward, her eyes wide with tender appeal. "Earlier you said you should be used to rejection."

"Yes?" he prodded gently, not quite sure where she was headed.

"You've been rejected?"

He smiled at her blatant disbelief. "Of course I have. Everyone has been rejected in one way or another."

"Were you rejected by someone you cared for?"

"Yes." Unable to withstand her intent stare, he looked sideways at the empty fireplace. "If you're asking if I've had my heart broken, the answer is affirmative."

"You've been in love before?"

"That's right." He looked back to her. "Haven't you?"

"Sort of."

Her answer provoked a bemused smile from him. "What does that mean?"

She squirmed uneasily in the chair. "It's always been one-sided for me." A frown clouded her features, and Evan winced at the bitterness he saw in her eyes.

"I'm not interested in one-sided relationships." He curled his fingers under her chin and brought her gaze to his. "I think we should give each other another chance."

She uttered a sound of relief and grasped his hand. "I do, too."

He sensed her hesitancy. "But?"

"But I don't think we should expect too much from each other."

He didn't like the sound of that but decided to argue the point later. He nodded and received a smile from her. "Have you eaten dinner?"

"No, but I'm not hungry."

"We could go someplace and grab a bite . . ." The sentence died on his lips when Raleigh turned her mouth into the palm of his hand and moistened his skin with the tip of her tongue. "I'm not hungry, either."

She laughed, slipped from the chair and knelt on the floor in front of him. Evan dropped to his knees and circled her waist with his arms as his lips sought hers. Her glasses bumped against his nose, and he laughed and drew back from her.

"Let's get rid of these," he said, removing the glasses and placing them on the coffee table. He examined the sultry passion lurking in her green-gold eyes and smiled. "Why, Miss Jones! You're gorgeous!"

She laughed softly, and one hand stole up to the back of his head. "Kiss me, you fool."

He sensed a commitment in her that had been missing the last time he'd held her in his arms. His mouth took hers, and he was surprised when she wound her arms about his neck and ran the tip of her tongue across his lips. He could feel the building in his loins, and he shifted from his cramped position on the hard floor.

"Raleigh," he said, standing, "let's go to your bedroom."

"No!" She shook her head and seemed genuinely alarmed. "It's a mess in there. Let's stay here."

He laughed and grabbed her hands to haul her to her feet. "I don't care how it looks. There's a bed in there and that's all I'm concerned with." When she still held back, he took matters into his own hands and lifted her into his arms. "You're adorable. Did you know that?"

"No." She smiled and kissed the tip of his nose. "But I'm glad you think so."

He carried her into the bedroom and set her on her feet. She hurried to the bed and swept the clothes and books scattered there to the floor.

"I told you it was a mess in here."

"Come here." He fell across the bed and held out his arms to her. "As far as I'm concerned, I'm in heaven."

A sly smile touched her lips, and her hands moved to slowly unbutton her blouse. Evan propped himself up on his elbows, his attention riveted to the revealing spectacle. He mirrored her, unbuttoning his own shirt and shrugging out of it; but she had a head start, and by the time he started to unfasten his jeans, Raleigh had shed her clothing. She sat on his stomach and brushed his hands aside.

"Let me," she whispered, and the snap at his waistband gave way, followed by the scrape of the zipper.

He grinned, enjoying this brazen side of her, and lifted his hips so that she could push the jeans and shorts down his legs. She stood and tugged them off his feet, then flipped them nonchalantly over her shoulder. A mischievous grin curved her mouth and her eyes sparkled.

"Why, Mr. Jones! You're gorgeous!"

Impatience blew through him like a hot wind, and he sat up, hooked an arm around her waist and pulled her down to him. She responded to his urgent kisses with an abandon that made him want her all the more. Her tongue parried with his, and her kisses were wet and clinging. Tearing her mouth from his, she moved down his body and rained kisses across his chest and stomach. Evan closed his eyes as passion pulsated through his body. Her hands circled him, and he felt himself expand and quiver.

"Raleigh... Raleigh..." He pulled his lower lip between his teeth as the pressure built until he thought he would explode.

She stroked him with languid caresses, then her feathery fingertips tingled the skin between his thighs, causing him to catch his breath in a strangled moan.

A moist warmth consumed him, and his eyes flew open in surprise. Raleigh shifted her body more comfortably on his and looked down into his face. Her expression was a study in self-absorption. She tipped her head back until her blond hair curled around her shoulders and shut her eyes tightly as she began to move upon him. The movement, while slight, triggered a violent reaction from

Evan. His body writhed beneath hers and his hands clutched her hips. She leaned back on stiffened arms, and her hands spread across his thighs for balance. Evan guided her into a slow, grinding tempo that soon increased to a blistering pace.

Her body shuddered and her panting breath gave way to a long sigh. Watching her pleasure sparked his own. He cupped her breasts in his hands, and the hard centers pressed against his palms. She opened her eyes, glazed now with passion, and sent him a lazy smile. Feasting on her beauty, Evan caressed her breasts, then traced the curve of her waist. He curled his body until his lips could sandwich one pebbly nipple, and he tugged gently on it. Her skin was soft and honey-colored. Evan nuzzled the sides of her breasts, and she whispered his name with a reverence that made him shiver with pleasure. He sat up straighter and pushed her back, careful not to slip from her and lose the fiery connection of their bodies.

He nuzzled her breasts, flicking his tongue across them until they were moist and straining. His fingers explored the curve of her stomach and the velvety smoothness of her thighs, and he couldn't help but wonder about the fools who had passed her up. Thinking of them made him all the more anxious to please her and make up for their rejection of the sweet gifts she had offered.

Placing a lingering kiss on her full lips, Evan smiled into her eyes and she smiled back.

"You're everything I've ever dreamed of," he murmured.

"You don't have to say those things to me," she said, and a sadness flickered in her eyes.

Evan drove his hands through her hair and held her gaze with his. "I meant it, Raleigh. You're special. Very special."

Her eyes misted before her lashes lowered to hide the emotion from him. Evan kissed her eyelids, then let his lips slide down her cheek to the pulse beneath her ear. He began moving inside of her again, and her legs came up to cradle his hips. He started to close his eyes, but the myriad emotions racing across Raleigh's face mesmerized him. Her enjoyment heightened his own, and he felt himself soar to the point of explosion.

His release was an avalanche of mindless desire; dimly he heard himself cry Raleigh's name, but he was barely aware of speaking. Floating slowly back to earth, he leaned forward and kissed Raleigh's moist lips, which seemed incredibly tender beneath his mouth, like velvety rosebud petals. His heart swelled with a feeling so poignant that it made him ache with a need to share it. He rolled onto his back and brought Raleigh with him so that she was draped across his chest. He ran the back of his fingers along her cheek, and she opened her eyes and sighed softly.

"Raleigh?"

"Yes?" She pushed his hair back from his temples in a lovingly familiar way that made him tighten his arms around her.

"I'm glad you gave me another chance," he whispered, wondering if she had any idea of how profoundly she affected him.

"So am I." Her fingers delved through the hair on his chest. "I love being with you, Evan. I really do."

He grasped her hand and brought it to his lips. He had been so close to losing her that it terrified him. A surge of desperation seized him, and he smoothed her hand along his cheek and held it there.

"You're still going to be here in the morning, aren't you?"

She seemed surprised at his burst of emotion. "I live here," she reminded him gently.

"But you're still going to like me in the morning, aren't you?" It surprised him that he needed her reassurance so desperately, but he couldn't face another morning like that last one, when she had treated him with such casual disregard.

Her lips touched his. "I've never stopped liking you, Evan."

"But this meant something to you, didn't it?"

Her eyes searched his features, and she frowned slightly. "Of course it meant something. It was wonderful. You're wonderful." She smiled and placed a brief, hard kiss on his mouth. "*We're* wonderful."

He tightened his arms around her. "Hold me close, sweetheart."

Her arms came around him, and she rubbed her cheek against his shoulder. "I feel better than I have in months."

Evan closed his eyes, confident that she was sincere and would be in his arms when he opened his eyes again. "So do I," he whispered. "In fact, I can't remember ever feeling this good."

Raleigh stowed the last of the dirty dishes into the dishwasher and switched it on, then turned to watch Evan break eggs into a frying pan.

"You know, if we lose our jobs, we could hire out as a maid and butler."

Evan chuckled and sprinkled pepper over the eggs. "That's an idea." He replaced the pepper shaker and sent her a tender smile. "Why don't you take a shower and get dressed while I finish making breakfast?"

"That's a great idea." Raleigh started to leave the kitchen, then paused to place a kiss between Evan's shoulder blades before she made her way to the bedroom.

She stood on the threshold and surveyed the tidy bedroom. Leaning a shoulder against the door frame, she smiled and recalled how she and Evan had bounded from bed earlier that morning and had torn through the room like a couple of tornadoes. Cleaning house had never been so much fun, she reflected with a contented sigh. She headed for the bathroom, removing her robe and tossing it on the bed as she passed by.

As she showered she let her thoughts circle around Evan and the way he had changed her life. Last night, while he'd slept peacefully, she had realized that she was deeply in love with him. This morning when they had made love again, she'd wanted to tell him how much he meant to her, but had been too afraid to voice her deepest feelings.

Raleigh turned her face up to let the warm water flow across her eyelids and into her mouth. She recalled her initial misgivings about Evan and wondered if she had known even then that he would be easy to love. It was hard to believe that a woman had cast Evan Younger aside.

"She must have been nuts," Raleigh said to herself as she stepped from the shower. "Incurably insane." She grabbed a towel and dried herself, then reached for her panties and bra.

"Breakfast is ready."

Raleigh looked up to see Evan crossing the bedroom. She fastened her bra and reached for her jeans. "I'm almost dressed."

"So I see." His eyes danced with delight. "Need any help?"

"I think I can manage. I've been dressing myself for years." She pushed her legs into the jeans and pulled them up over her hips.

"What do you want to do today?" He picked up her blouse and handed it to her.

"Nothing." She grinned and slipped into the cotton shirt. "Why don't we just spend the day together—alone."

"Sounds perfect." He pulled her to him and dropped a kiss on her lips. "Why don't we do that tomorrow, too? We could make this a weekend to remember."

"It already is." Raleigh stepped around him, grasping one of his hands and pulling him with her. "Let's eat. I'm starved."

"I don't believe it. Have you regained your appetite?"

She threw him a sly wink over her shoulder. "In more ways than one, I think."

Sitting at the dining-room table, she sniffed the aroma of scrambled eggs, sausage, biscuits and coffee. "Mmmm, I'm so glad you can cook."

"Didn't your mother ever take you aside and instruct you on the fine art of scrambling eggs?" Evan asked as he took his seat across from her.

"She tried, bless her heart." Raleigh shrugged. "I was a tomboy and I had no desire to spend my time over a hot stove." She helped herself to a generous portion of the eggs. "I decided that my dad had the right idea."

Evan chuckled and dropped a sausage pattie onto her plate. "What was that?"

"I decided that I'd rather work and come home to supper already on the table."

Evan poured coffee into her cup, a thoughtful expression on his face. "What about your desire to settle down with an older man?"

Raleigh shrugged. "I guess I was hoping my older man would be rich and have a staff of maids and chefs."

Evan stirred his coffee and frowned. "Have you ever wondered why you dreamed of marrying an older man?"

"No, but I have a feeling you're going to tell me why."

He grinned. "Indulge me."

"Okay." She resigned herself to the lecture.

"It's because an older man wouldn't expect much from you. He wouldn't make the demands on you that a younger man would."

Raleigh spread melting butter on a biscuit and considered his theory. "What kind of demands would a younger man make?"

"He'd demand something more than a secure, comfortable relationship. A younger man wants passion and—"

"Lust," Raleigh supplied with a smile as she bit into the biscuit.

"There's nothing wrong with a little lust." Evan picked up his napkin and wiped a drop of butter from the corner of her mouth. "If it's good enough for presidents, it's good enough for me."

Raleigh giggled and popped the rest of the biscuit into her mouth. "Are you trying to sell me on a younger man?"

"I think I already have." He spooned strawberry jam onto a wedge of biscuit and offered it to her. "Do you really feel that much older than me?"

"I didn't last night." She opened her mouth and received the biscuit.

"You know, in many ways I'm the more experienced."

She lifted her brows in a haughty challenge. "Is that so?"

Evan smiled and pushed back his chair. "Come over here and sit in my lap."

"I haven't finished my breakfast," Raleigh complained.

"Come here, woman!"

She laughed at his show of superiority and went to him. His arms circled her waist and his mouth searched out the skin at her throat. He lifted his gaze to hers, and Raleigh saw that he was no longer teasing.

"How many lovers have you had before me?"

She swallowed the lump in her throat and opted for a white lie. "Hundreds."

"Hundreds?" he asked, not bothering to hide his disbelief.

"That's right. How many lovers have you had?"

He glanced up. "Let me see . . . about a dozen, give or take a few."

Raleigh pushed her fist into his shoulder. "That's not fair. You're telling the truth." She smoothed her hands along the width of his shoulders and sighed. "Does it matter how many?"

"No." He kissed her chin and moved his hands up her back. "What does matter is that the other women I've known can't hold a candle to you."

"Oh, Evan." Raleigh stood up, unable to accept his honesty. "You shouldn't say things like that."

"Why not?"

"Because I'm not ready to hear them."

"Would you rather that I lie?"

"No." She went back to her chair and took a sip of her coffee. "I just think it's better if we don't say things that . . . well, will be hard to forget."

"Do you think we could ever forget each other?" He sighed and fell back in his chair. "I hate to break the news to you, but we've progressed past the stage of platonic friendship. We're involved with each other, Raleigh."

"I know." Raleigh picked up the newspaper, needing a diversion from Evan's intense glare, and her attention was arrested by a story on the front page. "Oh, damn!"

"What?"

"There's a story in here about a possible break in the Rendell murder case. They've scooped me and I'm going to catch hell from Grant about this." She jumped slightly when Evan slammed his hands down on the table and shot up from his chair. Raleigh lowered the paper and watched him stride angrily from the room. "Where are you going?"

"What do you care?" he growled.

"Evan, don't be that way." Raleigh scrambled from her chair and followed him into the living room. He switched on the television and fell into the chair in front of the set, staring moodily at a Donald Duck cartoon. "Evan, don't pout."

"Don't patronize me." His eyes singed her.

She dropped the newspaper and sat in his lap. "Evan, I'm sorry. I just . . . let's not run headlong into this." She fingered the buttons on his shirt and realized that she was going to have to level with him. "I've been disappointed and hurt in the past. Give me time to get over that, okay?"

"I'm not your past, I'm your present."

"I know, and I'm so glad you're here with me." She kissed his forehead, then the dimples in his cheeks. "I'm just unsteady. I've never felt like this before about anyone."

His mouth curved into a slow smile. "Was that so hard to say, Raleigh?" He brought her lips to his. "See what a little honesty will get you?" He covered her mouth with his—and his tongue stroked hers with rough passion. "Turn off the television and make love to me right here."

"Here?" Raleigh felt her eyes widen, and when he shifted beneath her, she realized he was serious.

He gave her a push and unbuttoned his shirt. "Right here."

Raleigh stood up, backing toward the television and turning it off as Evan unbuckled his belt and unfastened his jeans. Passion spiraled through her, making her knees weak and her heart pound. She unzipped her jeans and shook her head, baffled by the way he could transform her into a quivering mass of longing.

"I've never met anyone like you before."

His smile was slow and sure. "And you never will again." His gaze moved over her body as she tossed her jeans aside, then he reached for her and dragged her back into his lap. He rubbed against her and grinned with devilish delight. "Take me, I'm all yours."

Raleigh framed his face in her hands and settled her mouth confidently on his as he filled her with a love so powerful it shook her soul.

Chapter Seven

Standing just outside Evan's office, Raleigh peeked around the door facing, and her heart skipped a beat. The purely feminine reaction to the sight of him sent a mixture of emotions swirling through her, making her all too aware that she was in love with him. Still, one part of her cowered from the possessive feeling, warning her not to depend on Evan too much. Nothing is forever, the little voice in her head cautioned. Don't build castles in the sky.

A tender smile touched her mouth as she studied him, unnoticed. He was seated at his desk, his profile to her, as he thumbed through a thick file folder. The afternoon sun spilled in through the window, picking out the chestnut strands amid the darker brown mass of his hair. His feet were propped on his desk, his chair tipped precariously backward. The jacket of his navy-blue suit was draped over the back of the chair, and he'd rolled up the sleeves of his white dress shirt. His striped tie was askew, pulled to one side for more comfort. The desk radio blasted a top ten hit into the room, and one of Evan's black loafers moved to the beat.

He pursed his lips in concentration and his dimples deepened. Raleigh took a deep breath as his attractiveness reached out to her. In her mind's eye she could see him as he had looked yesterday morning when she'd awakened to find that he had left the bed and was standing by the window. The venetian blinds had been open causing thin bars of light to fall across his nude body. Then, as now, Raleigh had wanted to pinch herself. His body had the symmetry of those statues of Greek gods that depicted every woman's fantasy of masculine grace. Sensing her intent scrutiny, he'd turned his head to look at her and his eyes had seemed uncommonly blue in the morning sunlight. He'd shifted his weight to one foot, making the sinewy muscles in his thigh and calf flex in a sensuous display and provoking a sexual longing in Raleigh that had made her frighteningly aware of how much she wanted him and how close she was to needing him in her life.

Blinking away the memory, Raleigh stepped into the office and rapped her knuckles on the open door. Evan jumped slightly, swinging his feet off his desk and rising to his feet. He smiled and dropped the folder to his desk, then unconsciously straightened his tie.

"Hello, beautiful." He turned down the radio and held out his hands to her.

"Am I interrupting?" Raleigh asked, placing her hands in his and leaning over his desk to receive his quick, hard kiss. "I just thought I'd drop by for a coffee break."

"I'm glad you did." He glanced at his watch. "I thought you'd be through for the day. It's after three."

"I stopped by to talk to Cody about the story that appeared in the morning newspaper this weekend."

"The one on the Rendell case?" Evan asked as he poured her a cup of coffee. "This coffee smells strong. Do you want me to make a new pot?"

"No, that's okay." She reached for the cup. "Do you have any creamer?"

"I'm out of it."

"No problem." Raleigh sat in the chair across from his desk. "Are you sure I'm not bothering you?"

"I'm sure. Did Grant give you a hard time about getting scooped by the competition?"

Raleigh rolled her eyes dramatically. "Did he ever! Cody Wakefield has some explaining to do. It isn't like him to leak information and play favorites with the newspapers. I'm hoping he has a good explanation for this mess."

"I'm sure he does." Evan sat on the edge of his desk and flicked down his shirt sleeves. "Do you want to come over to my place for dinner tonight?"

Using the coffee as a diversion, Raleigh argued with herself while Evan waited impatiently for her answer. The weekend had been glorious, but this morning a battle had raged within her. She wanted to give herself up to the circumstances and enjoy every minute she could in Evan's company, but she didn't trust these wanton urges. There were places within her that were still tender, reminding her that the closer she got to Evan, the harder it would be on her if things didn't work out and he ended the relationship.

"Would you rather go out to dinner?" Evan prodded, folding his arms across his chest and giving her a smile that tugged at her heart.

"Evan, I've got some things to work on tonight," she said hesitantly, feeling as if he knew she was lying. "Do you mind?"

He shrugged, and the smile slipped from his lips. "No, I understand. You're not tired of me already, are you?"

"No, of course not." She laughed and placed a hand on his knee. "I just have to work on some stories, and you'll distract me if we're together."

"I'm a distraction?" His laughter took the edge from his words. "That's not the same as a nuisance, is it?"

"No, it's not." Raleigh held up a hand as a familiar voice floated from the radio. "Turn that up, will you?"

"Sure." Evan reached behind him and turned up the volume. "Who is that?"

"Our illustrious governor," she said, listening as Andrew Mathison launched into a speech on why he hadn't appointed a racing commission yet. The political double-talk brought a frown to her face, and she counted herself lucky that she wasn't covering politics. The governor promised to appoint a commission after he had "investigated each angle carefully," and then refused to take questions from the reporters. Raleigh puffed out an exasperated sigh and flicked one hand in dismissal. "Turn it off, please."

"You don't like our governor, I take it." Evan switched off the radio and grinned at her.

"I've never been impressed with him. He's too wishy-washy. I like decision makers, and the only decision Andrew Mathison has ever made was to become governor. That speech he just gave should be entered in the world book of records as being the most poorly written one in history. Does he really think people are so stupid that they can't see through his excuses? He'd better hire a new speech writer or he's going to lose the next election.''

"Do you think you could write a better speech?"

"I *know* I could." Raleigh placed the empty coffee cup on the desk beside Evan.

"Have you ever thought about becoming involved in that sort of thing? I bet you'd be good at it."

She started to dismiss this idea but found herself intrigued by the proposal. A political speech writer. Heaven knows there's room for improvement in the area, she thought.

"Well?" Evan leaned forward and captured her attention. "From the expression on your face I think the idea interests you."

"It's certainly an alternative," Raleigh said as she stood up. "I'd never thought about it before, but it has possibilities.''

"Would you like to work for Mathison?"

Raleigh's eyes widened in shock. "Mathison? Not on your life!" Then she smiled slyly. "But I have a few friends in the political arena who could tell me if anyone is looking for a speech writer. Who knows? Donnelly Wakefield might even need a talented, enthusiastic writer.''

Evan snapped his fingers. "That's right! I've met Cody's brother. He's a nice guy. He'll give Mathison a run for his money in the governor's race. Do you know Donnelly?''

"Only in passing." Raleigh pushed aside some papers on Evan's desk and sat next to him. "I know I could get behind him, though. Donnelly isn't afraid to take stands and make decisions. He wouldn't be dragging his feet on this racing commission if he were governor now.''

Evan stretched out his legs and crossed his ankles. He nudged Raleigh's shoulder. "What's all this controversy on the racing commission?"

"A commission needs to be appointed so that it can govern the type and number of tracks in the state. Horse racing is big business, and everyone is flocking here for a piece of the action; but Mathison doesn't want to tread on any financial backers' toes, so he's putting off appointing a commission until after the governor's election."

"He's hedging his bets," Evan said.

"Yes, at the expense of the state. While he's looking out for number one, tracks are being built all over the state." Raleigh stood up and wandered aimlessly around the office, her mind wrestling with the political sand trap. "Horse racing can be good for Oklahoma or bad. A few well-run tracks can add to the state coffers, but too many tracks could be disastrous. All these fly-by-nighters could ruin the state's reputation and put off the people we need to attract here to make the horse-racing business solid."

When Evan didn't comment after a few seconds, Raleigh stopped pacing and faced his amused smile. She smiled back and planted her hands at her hips.

"What's so funny?"

Evan pushed himself from the desk and came over to her, his hands resting on her shoulders. "Raleigh, I think *you* could run for office and win."

"Me?" Raleigh shook her head and laughed off the idea. "I prefer to remain behind the scenes."

"Why don't you ask Cody if his brother would be interested in a topnotch speech writer?" Evan pulled her close, and his lips grazed her forehead. "It couldn't hurt, and you did tell me that you wanted out of the newspaper business."

Raleigh closed her eyes, wrapped her arms about his waist and leaned against him. It felt wonderful to lean on someone again, she thought, then pushed herself abruptly from his arms. How easy it was to put herself in his hands and lose herself in him!

Evan's brows met in a scowl. "It was just a suggestion, honey," he said, placing his hands on her shoulders again. "I'm not dictating to you."

"I know. It's not that...." Raleigh shook her head and added a lightness to her voice. "It's a great idea." She hitched the strap of her purse onto her shoulder. "I've got to find Cody. Thanks for the coffee."

"I'll call you tonight." Evan kissed her temple. "And I'll miss you tonight."

Managing a shaky smile, Raleigh moved away from him and gave a short wave as she left his office. She ran a hand over her face, feeling flustered and upset for no apparent reason. As she walked from Evan's office toward the detective division, she mulled over Evan's advice and decided that it wouldn't hurt to approach Cody about the possibility of being hired by his brother. She admired Donnelly Wakefield and wanted him to be the victor in the upcoming election. After being dressed down earlier today by Grant concerning her "inability to get the job done," she found the prospect of leaving the *Times* for greener pastures was even more appealing.

Several of the detectives looked up and greeted her as she entered the large room filled with desks and filing cabinets. Cody's desk was in a far corner, and as Raleigh approached, Cody ended a telephone call and greeted her with a wide grin.

"Hi, Raleigh." He stood up and his blue eyes swept her from head to foot. "Is that a new dress? It looks great on you."

Raleigh glanced down at the peach-colored, shirtwaist dress she had recently added to her wardrobe. "Yes, thanks. How are you doing?" She sat in the chair beside his desk and eyed the cast on his left arm. "Is that a souvenir from the car wreck?"

"Yes, but I'm fine," Cody assured her as he took his seat again. "I bet I know why you're here." He fell back in his chair and looked at her as if he'd been caught with his hand in the cookie jar. "You saw that story in the morning paper about the Rendell case, right?"

"It was hard to miss." Raleigh pulled her notebook and pen from her purse. "Was it true? Have you found another angle in the case?"

"Off the record?"

Raleigh stiffened, surprised that Cody would make such a request. "Cody, you know I don't like to go off the record," she admonished gently. "I need something I can print."

Cody shrugged, a determined look on his face. "Then I can't tell you anything."

"Why not? You told my competitor about the case."

"No, I didn't." Cody frowned and ran a hand through his blond hair. "I don't know how that information was leaked, but I didn't talk to the press about this. It's confidential."

"Why?" She studied Cody carefully, noticing an uncharacteristic show of nerves when he shifted uncomfortably in his chair, then tugged irritably at his tie's knot. He was on to something and she had to know what it was, but she could tell by the firm set of his jaw that it would have to be on his terms.

"This could be something and it could be nothing," Cody said with a sigh. "It's touchy right now, and I can't take a chance of having it blow up in my face before I have time to really investigate it." His blue eyes were stony. "Either we go off the record or you'll have to fish."

It was Raleigh's turn to sigh heavily. "Okay." She gritted her teeth and hoped she wouldn't regret this decision. There was nothing worse than being told something important—something that should be reported—and not being able to use it, especially when Grant Farris expected her to file a story today. "Off the record."

Cody relaxed and the dark scowl lifted from his face. "We've turned up something peculiar about Victoria Rendell." He stared pointedly at the pen and notebook Raleigh held and didn't continue until she'd put them back into her purse. "It seems she purchased a parcel of land in Okmulgee County before she died. She left it to her daughter, but her daughter doesn't know anything about it."

"So?" Raleigh shook her head, unable to see the importance of this revelation.

Cody shrugged his broad shoulders, momentarily drawing Raleigh's attention to the gun and holster under his left arm. "So, it's a long shot, but it deserves investigation. I've been trying to contact the former owner of the property to find out why Victoria bought the land, but I haven't been able to reach him. It just seems strange that she would buy land out there."

Her competitors had printed a story about a break in the case on such flimsy information? Raleigh shook her head, amazed at the lack of integrity. "Are you sure you're telling me everything, Cody? I mean, this doesn't break the case open, and that's what our competitors reported. They made it sound as if you were ready to arrest someone."

"They exaggerated. I wish I was near an arrest. I'd like nothing better than to solve this case, believe me, but I don't have anything concrete. It's just a hunch ... a nibble. In a case like this you have to follow up every discrepancy, no matter how trivial."

"I wish we could wrap this one up, too." Raleigh propped an elbow on his desk and rested her chin in her hand. She glanced at Cody and smiled. "Have you seen your brother lately?"

"Donnelly?" Cody seemed taken aback by her question, then he smiled. "I thought you were dating Evan Younger."

Catching his drift, Raleigh flushed. "No, that's not what I'm talking about. Granted, Donnelly is an attractive man, but I'm not interested in him that way."

Cody grinned, as if enjoying her embarrassment. "In what way are you interested in him?"

"In a professional way." Raleigh picked up a paper clip from the desk and focused her attention on it. "I was listening to Governor Mathison on the radio a few minutes ago, and it occurred to me that your brother might need a good writer on his staff." She glanced at Cody and saw that she had his interest. "A good speech writer can mean the difference between success and failure on the campaign trail, you know."

Cody leaned forward to catch her wandering gaze. "I didn't know you were seeking other employment."

Raleigh tossed the paper clip back on the desk and adopted an indifferent pose. "Lately, I've been thinking that I should look for something else. I guess you've heard the rumor that the *Times* is in financial trouble?"

"I've heard." Cody nodded slowly. "The last time I talked with Donnelly he did mention that he was looking for a press agent. Why don't you send your résumé to him?''

''Really?'' Hearing the exuberance in her voice, Raleigh forced a calmer tone. ''Would you write me a letter of recommendation?''

Cody laughed and teased her with his eyes. ''You're really serious about this, aren't you?''

''It means a lot to me, Cody.''

He was silent for a few moments as he studied her carefully. ''Okay. Sure I'll write you a letter of recommendation. I want my brother to win, and I can't think of a better person to have on his team than you.''

''Oh, Cody!'' Raleigh seized his hand and gave it an affectionate squeeze. ''You're a doll.''

Cody smiled and settled back in his chair, a thoughtful expression on his face. ''And you're getting back into the swing of things, aren't you? It's about time, Raleigh. I was beginning to worry about you.''

''Why? I'm fine.''

Cody shook a finger at her in a playful way. ''Has Evan Younger put that sparkle in your eyes?''

''No.'' Raleigh stood up, uneasy with the conversation. ''You have. I'll work on the résumé and get it to Donnelly by next week.''

''Okay, and I'll get the reference letter to you in a few days.'' Cody stood up and shoved his hands into his pockets. ''Was I out of line with that comment about Evan?''

Raleigh laughed nervously, unwilling to talk about Evan to Cody, but anxious not to make Cody feel as if he'd committed a social blunder. ''No, of course not.'' She wrinkled her nose playfully and popped him in the shoulder with her fist. ''I couldn't help but notice that

Liann was at your place when I visited you after the accident."

Cody smiled and looked down at his desk shyly. "We're seeing each other again."

"Good for you." Raleigh gathered up her purse. "I've got to check with some of the other guys before I leave. You'll contact me if anything breaks with this Rendell case?"

"You'll be the first reporter I call," Cody promised.

"Okay. See you later." Raleigh threw him a smile over her shoulder and left the detective division.

She checked in with a few other police sources and was about to leave the station when she remembered that bit of information she had intended sharing with Cody about Grant being at Victoria Rendell's house. She debated with herself, thinking that it really wasn't worth mentioning, then decided that Cody should be the one to judge whether or not the information was worthless. He'd said that he wanted to investigate every possibility, however trivial.

Raleigh headed back to the detective department, only to find that Cody wasn't at his desk. She stopped at Ben Leonard's desk instead.

"Ben, do you know where Cody is? Has he already left for the day?"

Ben shook his head and pointed toward an office in the back of the room. "He's talking to somebody in there. It shouldn't take long if you want to wait."

"Thanks, I will."

"I hear you're seeing our resident shrink," Ben said, giving her a toothy grin.

Raleigh shied away from his desk without answering. It was disturbing to realize she was part of the gossip among these men, but she told herself she shouldn't be surprised. She'd covered this beat too long not to have found out that police officers make it their business to know everything about everyone. They probably already knew that she was in love with Evan, even though she'd only made the discovery herself a couple of days ago.

Sitting in the chair right outside the office Ben had indicated, Raleigh kept her gaze averted from Cody's fellow officer, not wanting to give him any encouragement to continue his questioning. After a few minutes, she breathed a sigh of relief when Ben left his desk and started foraging through a file cabinet.

It was a new experience to be the center of speculation, she thought with a little thrill. While she didn't exactly enjoy knowing that tongues were wagging about her and Evan, it was still exciting. She'd never been linked romantically with a man before, and while it had its drawbacks, it was a wonderful feeling.

So why was she fighting it? she asked herself. Why couldn't she just give in to the feeling and enjoy the experience? Why did one part of her resist the temptation to fall head over heels in love for the first time in her life?

Cody's voice floated into earshot, slicing through her inner struggle. She glanced sideways and saw that the door to the office was ajar, letting the conversation within spill out.

Raleigh's inborn curiosity surfaced, and she couldn't help but tune in to the voices. Leaning sideways a little, she was able to hear Cody's voice clearly.

"Thanks for coming by, Mr. Green," Cody was saying.

"I'm just sorry I put you to so much trouble," said the other man in a voice raspy with age. "You see, I took some of the money I got from that land and bought a motor home. Me and the wife have been traveling around the country the past few months. Just got back into town yesterday and my daughter said you had been around asking for me."

"Do you know what Victoria Rendell intended to do with the land she bought from you?" Cody asked.

"Why, sure. She and her friend were going to build a racetrack on it."

"A racetrack?"

Raleigh smiled, having mouthed the same question.

"That's right," Mr. Green said with a chuckle. "If you ask me, she was putting the cart before the horse."

"Why do you say that?"

"Pari-mutuel betting hadn't been passed in Okmulgee County at the time she bought the land. Of course, it *was* passed later, but at the time I thought she was taking quite a chance. I told her as much, but her friend said he wasn't worried. He seemed pretty cocksure that it would pass. In fact..." Mr. Green paused, making Raleigh hold her breath and listen intently. "I believe he said he would make sure it would pass."

"Who was she with? Did she introduce him to you?"

"Nope, never did get around to introductions. She kept calling him by his last name, though."

"What was that?"

"Can't recall."

Raleigh let her breath out slowly and slumped in disappointment.

"Is this the man? Look at the photo carefully."

Raleigh closed her eyes, wishing she could study the photograph Cody has given him. Who was it? Howard Rendell?

"Nope, it wasn't him. I saw this guy's picture in the paper. He was the one who was killed with her, wasn't he?"

Johnny Stratton, Raleigh thought.

"Yes. His name was Johnny Stratton. Are you sure he wasn't the man with Victoria?"

"Positive."

"Can you describe the man for me?"

Raleigh strained to hear Green's answer.

"To tell you the truth, I didn't pay that much attention to him. I know *that* guy isn't him, but I can't really describe the fella. He was older than that Stratton guy, more Mrs. Rendell's age. Nice-enough looking fella."

"Do you remember anything different about him? Anything that would single him out?"

Raleigh opened her eyes and found herself staring at Ben. Nervously she looked away and pretended to study the Wanted posters on the far wall. She shouldn't be listening to this, she thought with a sense of guilt, but she *had* to listen now.

Mr. Green chuckled. "I wish I could help you, but I don't remember much about him. Mrs. Rendell did the talking and she was pretty enough to keep my interest, if you know what I mean."

"Yes, I understand."

"Let me think here a minute."

Raleigh's eyes burned, and she blinked and looked away from the posters to stare at her hands clasped tightly in her lap. She should get up and walk away from this room, she told herself. This was eavesdropping, and Cody would be livid if he knew she was out here listening to this confidential interrogation.

"I did like his watch," Mr. Green said, and Raleigh snapped to attention.

"His watch?" Cody asked. "You mean a wrist-watch?"

"No, one of those fancy pocket watches. It was the kind that plays a song when you open it."

"Do you remember which song it played?" Cody asked, and his voice was pitched higher with excitement.

Raleigh felt her heart slow, then kick into overdrive, sending blood pulsing through her veins. One corner of her mind played out a scene from her recent past. Curtis's funeral. Grant opening his watch and letting that song escape, a song that was so out of place at a funeral.

"It played 'Happy Days Are Here Again,'" Mr. Green said. "I always liked that song."

Raleigh felt as if she'd just been punched in the stomach; she closed her eyes, and someone called her name, and she opened her eyes and smiled inanely at a passing detective. She realized he had complimented her on her outfit, and she murmured, "Thank you," while her mind scrambled furiously in another direction. Grant Farris, Grant Farris, Grant Farris! Her mind screamed the name as she stood up, unaware that she was moving, and started forward. She bumped into someone, blinked and stared wide-eyed, at the man in bib overalls and a plaid shirt. Big, rough hands steadied her.

"Whoa, little lady!" The man chuckled good-naturedly and dropped his hands.

"Mr. Green," Raleigh murmured, and the sound of her voice broke through her dazed state. She gasped, realizing that she had shown her hand. Mr. Green seemed taken aback by her recognition of him, and Raleigh moved away, anxious to leave the station.

"Wait just a minute, Raleigh," Cody Wakefield said, and grabbed her forearm to hold her in place. "Thanks for your help, Mr. Green. You'll come back in tomorrow to look at those other pictures?''

"I'll do it." Mr. Green touched his forehead and his gaze encompassed Raleigh before he turned and ambled across the room.

Cody's hand tightened on Raleigh's arm, and she looked at him, flinching when she saw the accusing glint in his eyes.

"Come in here a minute, Raleigh. We need to talk." Cody pulled her into the office and pushed her into a chair. "You heard that, didn't you? How much did you hear?"

Raleigh tried to swallow, but her mouth felt as if it were stuffed with cotton. "Can I have a glass of water?"

"Sure, I'll get you one." Cody headed for the door but turned back to face her. "You're not going anywhere, are you?"

"What?" Raleigh asked, then shook her head in annoyance. "Of course not. I just need a drink."

"Okay."

Raleigh slumped in the chair after Cody had gone and tried to regain her equilibrium, but it was a difficult task. She remembered the company picnic and how edgy she'd been around Grant after she recalled that he'd been with Victoria Rendell. She'd never heard their names linked, but she felt certain now that they had been lovers. They had purchased land together in Okmulgee County for a racetrack, but someone had murdered Victoria and Johnny Stratton. A clammy chill worked its way up Raleigh's spine, and she sat up straighter to fight off the feeling. Could Grant have cold-bloodedly murdered Victoria and Johnny? For what? Had he caught them in bed together and pulled the trigger in a lover's rage?

"Here we go," Cody said as he entered the cramped office and handed her a paper cup of water. He sat behind the metal desk and leaned forward. "How much did you hear?"

Raleigh drank the water in four long gulps, then crumpled the cup and tossed it into the trash can. "All of it."

"You can't print it, Raleigh," Cody said in a voice that brooked no argument.

"I wasn't even thinking of printing it," Raleigh told him with a touch of injured pride. "Not unless you gave me permission by issuing an official statement, and you're not going to do that, are you?"

"No, not now...not yet." Cody stared moodily at the plaster cast on his arm, and Raleigh sensed that he was gathering his own thoughts. "Grant carries a watch like that, doesn't he?"

"Yes." Raleigh leaned forward, anxious now to tell him of her discovery. "I came back to tell you that I remembered something about Victoria and Grant."

"What?" Cody's eyes sparked with interest.

"He always leaves numbers where he can be reached in case of an emergency at the newspaper. One time I called one of those numbers—it was early in the morning, just after sunup—and Victoria Rendell answered the phone. She passed it to Grant, and he sounded as if he'd just woken up. I didn't think anything about it at the time—"

"But you do now," Cody said with a slight smile. He fell back in the chair, a thoughtful expression on his face. "Sounds as if they were lovers, doesn't it?"

"Yes, it does, and they sure kept a lid on it. Usually, I suspect who Grant is seeing, but I never thought that he and Victoria..." Her voice trailed off as the significance of the situation rocked her. "I can't imagine them together."

"We're going to have to keep a lid on this," Cody warned sternly.

"But Cody, I've got to file a story eventually," Raleigh argued. "It will leak out and I don't want egg on my face again."

Cody held up a hand to silence her, and his face settled into hard lines. "Not yet, Raleigh." He stood up and came around the desk to where she was sitting. Dropping to his haunches, he took her hands within his and lowered his voice to a conspiratorial tone. "Green is coming back tomorrow to look at some more pictures, and Grant's picture will be among them. If he makes a positive identification, I'll notify you and you can run something on this." A wry smile tilted up the corners of his mouth. "That is, if your publisher will let you print a story that implicates him in a double murder."

"Oh, my gosh!" Raleigh tore one of her hands from Cody's and held it to her mouth. "I never thought about that!"

"I think you're right, Raleigh," Cody said with a disarming grin. "Maybe this *is* a good time to look for other employment."

Raleigh chewed nervously on her lower lip and looked away from Cody's amused expression. "We'll have to print it. We can't ignore it and let the other papers have a field day."

Cody squeezed her hand and drew her attention back to him. "Keep this quiet. We can't blow this now, Raleigh. We're sitting on dynamite. You understand that don't you?"

"Yes, I understand." She nodded and felt that clammy chill again. "Grant has always given me the willies, but now..." She swallowed hard. "Why would he kill them? Jealousy, do you think?"

"First things first," Cody cautioned. "We have to get a positive identification from Green, and then we'll work on a motive."

Raleigh pushed her hair back distractedly. "I'm sorry I eavesdropped, Cody, but I was sort of a sitting duck out there."

"No harm done, unless you let any of this slip."

She ran a finger across her lips, zipping them. "My lips are sealed."

"Good. I know I can trust you." He stood, pulling her to her feet with him. "I'll be in touch as soon as I know something."

"Promise?" Cody placed a hand over his heart. "You can drop by tomorrow and I'll fill you in *and* give you that letter of recommendation."

"Thanks, I'll do that." Raleigh picked up her purse and left the room. She waved to Cody and gave him a friendly smile, then hurried from the detective division. She still felt dazed, as if she'd been awakened from a terrible nightmare and one part of her mind was still clinging to it.

She decided to leave the station from the back entrance so that she wouldn't have to pass Evan's office and risk the chance of running into him. She couldn't even tell him about this, and she knew she would give herself away: right now she was a jumble of nerves, and she needed to go somewhere and think this out.

Walking through the underground parking lot, Raleigh felt that clammy fear again. Grant had been hounding her about this Rendell case. He'd been livid when Howard Rendell had been set free. Grant had wanted a conviction, Raleigh realized suddenly. Did he want Howard Rendell to go to prison so that the case would be closed and he would be off the hook?

And Grant had pushed the pari-mutuel betting issue in Okmulgee County, Raleigh recalled with a mild start. He hadn't cared about the other counties, just Okmulgee County.

It was all falling into place, and Raleigh was relieved not to have to return to the newspaper office until tomorrow. By then, she hoped, she could face Grant without cowering in fear or suspicion. Was she really afraid of Grant? she wondered as she got into her car and locked the door.

Her gaze flitted nervously around her at the dark shadows of the parking lot. If Grant Farris had murdered two people, she answered herself, he could kill again.

Raleigh started the car and drove quickly from the shadows into the sunlight.

Dropping into the office chair, Raleigh examined Cody Wakefield's face but could find no answer there.

"Well?" she asked, and her voice cracked on the word. "Did Green identify Grant?"

Cody ran a hand over his face. "Yes."

"Oh, no!" Raleigh slumped in the chair and brought her hands to her mouth for a moment.

"Are you okay?" Cody asked, touching her knee.

"Yes...no...I'm okay." Raleigh shook her head and lowered her hands. "I just didn't want to hear that." She tried to laugh but could only manage a shaky giggle. "My boss is a murderer. I thought all I had to worry about was the *Times* financial woes, and now this!" Her lips twisted into a semblance of a smile. "Do you have that letter of recommendation? I'm going to need it."

Cody chuckled and flicked a piece of paper across the desk to her. "There it is, as promised."

"I don't know how I'm going to handle this story, or if Grant will let me handle it." Raleigh picked up the paper and glanced at it. "Thanks, Cody."

"You're welcome. But Raleigh, you can't print anything about Grant yet."

"Why not? You've got a positive identification."

"Yes, but I need to follow up on this before we put out an arrest warrant. I can't have you printing anything until I've got something more tangible to go on."

"But Grant was with Victoria," Raleigh argued.

"So what? So he bought some land with Victoria. That's no reason to kill her. Don't you see?" Cody asked, and his eyes begged her to listen to his reasoning. "I can't issue a warrant just because Grant and Victoria were lovers and bought land together for a future racetrack."

Raleigh drew a deep breath and expelled it in a sigh. "Yes, I see your point. I guess I've tried and convicted him in my head."

"Do you think he could kill someone?"

"I don't know," she said on a note of exasperation, and her hands fluttered helplessly in her lap. "All I know is that I'm doing my best to avoid him. Every time I see him, I head the other way."

"For heaven's sake, don't tip him off, Raleigh!" Cody's eyes widened apprehensively. "He's not stupid, you know."

"I know." She frowned as she folded Cody's letter and placed it in her notebook. "Just hurry and follow up your leads. This business is making me a nervous wreck."

"It's not doing my nerves any good, either," Cody admitted. "I'd like to concentrate on marrying Liann, but I can't get this business out of my mind."

"Marriage?" Raleigh caught the sleeve of his shirt and tugged. "You and Liann are getting married?"

A rakish smile curved his mouth. "Yes. What do you think about that?"

"I think it's great." She gave his hand a playful pat. "Am I going to be on the guest list?"

"You bet. You'll be getting your invitation any day now."

"Congratulations." Raleigh sent him a teasing grin. "She's too good for you."

"I know."

"I'm kidding," she said, laughing. "You two were made for each other." Raleigh stood up and tucked her notebook into her purse. "Does Evan know?"

"I told him this morning. When are you two going to tie the knot?"

"What?" Raleigh asked on a note of incredulous laughter. "Me and Evan? Married?" She shook her head. "Now *you're* kidding."

"What's so funny about that?" Cody leaned back in his chair, his eyes dancing. "I think you two were made for each other."

Looking away from him, Raleigh fought the feeling of being cornered. "I'd better get going so that you can get back to work."

"Raleigh, I'm sorry if I stepped out of line again."

"No, don't be silly." She laughed, trying to get out of the situation gracefully.

"It's just that I assumed you two were getting serious."

Raleigh lifted a shoulder in a halfhearted shrug.

"And when two people are serious, they talk about marriage," Cody added.

"That's ridiculous."

"Why?" Cody prodded, his eyes challenging her.

"Because..." She looked around the room as if she'd find an answer there. "Because he's younger than I am." She winced, hearing the stupidity of that statement.

"Oh, well, that makes it out of the question, doesn't it?" Cody chuckled under his breath. "If you don't want to talk about it, I understand."

Raleigh took a deep breath and decided that honesty was the best policy. "I don't want to talk about it."

Cody held up his hand in surrender. "Okay. I won't press it." He stood up and took one of her hands in his. "I'll call you when I hear something."

"Good. See you later." Gently Raleigh pulled her hand from his and left. Outside the large room, she leaned weakly against the wall and breathed a weary sigh, feeling as if she'd just been interrogated by one of Tulsa's finest.

"Raleigh!"

She recognized Evan's voice before she turned her head to the left and saw him. "Hello."

"Hi." He dropped a kiss on her cheek. "I was hoping to run into you before you made your getaway." He paused and his blue eyes narrowed. "Are you okay? You look beat."

"I'm tired." Raleigh pushed herself from the wall. "It's been a long day."

"In other words, you want to go home alone again tonight." Evan leaned a hand on the wall behind her, effectively blocking her path.

"Evan, I'm sorry, but I'm just exhausted." She lifted a hand and let her fingers trail down the front of his chambray shirt. She smiled, remembering how she had decided he didn't dress like a psychologist, and her gaze lowered to view his brush-denim jeans and boots. "How about next weekend?'' she asked, lifting her gaze to his again.

"If that's the best you can do," he said, not bothering to hide his disappointment.

"Mayfest is next weekend." Raleigh's fingers gathered in the material of his shirt. "We can go to the festivities, and then we can go back to your place and you can help me with my résumé."

"Your résumé? That doesn't sound very romantic."

"Oh, but Evan, I could use your help with it." She looked into his eyes and let her lower lip droop in a seductive pout. "Please?"

A wry smile tipped up one corner of his mouth. "Hell, when you put it that way..."

Raleigh laughed and kissed him quickly on the lips.

"I miss you, damn it!" His other hand came up to grasp her shoulder. "Do I have to wait for weekends to see you?"

"Evan, you act as if you haven't seen me in months and it's only been a couple of days." Raleigh lifted her hand and hooked her fingers around his extended arm. "I'm behind on my work. There's...the police beat is hopping these days."

"Okay." He sighed and dropped his head forward in a defeated way that made Raleigh's heart go out to him. "What's Mayfest?"

She lifted her brows in surprise, then laughed. "Oh, that's right. We didn't have Mayfest when you lived here before, did we?" He shook his head and she continued. "It's a celebration of spring. There's arts and crafts and magicians and singers—"

"Where?"

"Downtown along the Main Mall and at the Williams Center." She smiled and leaned closer, lowering her voice to a tempting whisper. "And there are all kinds of food!"

"Sold!" Evan smiled and kissed the tip of her nose. "When should I pick you up?"

"Saturday morning."

"Saturday," he said with a groan as if it were months away. "About nine?"

"Great." Raleigh ducked under his arm. "I'll be looking forward to it."

"Raleigh?"

She turned back to face his worried expression. "Yes?"

"Is everything okay?"

"Sure." She offered a cheery smile.

"I mean, between us."

Feeling herself backing into that corner again, she gave a noncommittal shrug. "Sure. Bye now!" Turning from him, she hurried to the exit.

Outside she chided herself for giving in to the part of her that panicked any time Evan—or anyone, for that matter—pressed her on how deeply she was involved. Why couldn't she listen to the part of her that told her to thank her lucky stars for Evan Younger and give everything she had to the relationship? Why did she have to heed that hesitant side of her?

It would be so lovely to just feel and not think; to go with her emotions and not worry about tomorrow. But Curtis's death had taught her a bitter lesson, she reminded herself sternly. He had been everything to her, and when he'd left her, he had taken so much with him, leaving her to flounder in a world that was suddenly dark and lonely. It was dangerous to give so much to someone else, Raleigh thought as she got into her car and started the engine. It hurt too much and it cost too much, emotionally.

Yet, the conflicting sides of her situation were tearing her apart. She had spent most of her life looking for a man who would love her as much as she loved him, but she was afraid of that kind of relationship now.

"Nothing is forever," she whispered fiercely to herself. But only one part of her believed it.

Chapter Eight

Spring spread a green carpet and raised a canopy of blue across Oklahoma on the second week of May.

The first part of May had brought several consecutive days of rain, which had only now given way to summery temperatures and cloudless skies. Like the unpredictable weather, Raleigh felt carefree after two weeks of nail-biting worries. Walking with Evan along Tulsa's Main Mall, gaily festooned for Mayfest, she tucked her hand in the crook of his arm as her gaze swept a display of original oil paintings.

Evan had been surprised to see the beehive of activity downtown, and Raleigh had explained that only a few years ago Tulsa's downtown area had been anemic. Businesses and the Chamber of Commerce had come to the rescue, however, with the creation of Mayfest. Events of all kinds were scheduled during the celebration to draw citizens to the heart of the city, and the downtown area had been enthusiastically transformed into a "people place." Mayfest had been a success since its inception.

Raleigh looked down the mall to where a banner was spread above a frothing fountain. Youngsters were celebrating the beginning of summer by jumping into the fountain and turning it into a swimming pool. Their parents sat along the edges of the tiered fountain and let their feet dangle in the cool water.

Lifting her gaze, Raleigh stared in awe at the way Tulsa reflected itself in the gleaming skyscrapers. My, my, how we've grown, Raleigh thought with a sense of pride. Catching sight of the Old-English-style letters on the *Times* building, Raleigh frowned slightly. Did Grant have any idea that he was being investigated? she wondered, feeling the burden fall heavily back onto her shoulders.

Waiting for word from Cody on his investigation of Grant Farris was similar to sitting on a stack of dynamite, Raleigh thought. So far she'd managed to avoid Grant at the office, but she knew she couldn't avoid him forever. She wished she could discuss the investigation with Evan, but she'd been sworn to secrecy. She stood back a little as Evan examined a painting done in the art-deco tradition. He'd worn cutoffs today, and his legs were muscled and lightly furred with dark, curling hair. His blue pullover shirt had a red horizontal stripe running from shoulder to shoulder, and it was neatly tucked into the waistband of his cutoffs. Raleigh smiled, feeling good all over. Evan was a miracle tonic, she decided. Time spent with him was trouble free.

She stepped closer, hooking her arms around one of his and resting her chin on his shoulder. He glanced over his shoulder at her and smiled.

"Did you get your invitation to Cody and Liann's wedding?" he asked, returning his attention to the piece of sculpture in his hands.

"Yes."

"Why don't we plan on going to it together?" He turned the clay man in the moon over in his hands so that Raleigh could see its whimsical grin. She laughed in appreciation, and Evan withdrew his wallet from his jeans pocket. "I'll take this."

Raleigh took the funny man in the moon from Evan and smiled at the moon's silly face. "Are you an impulsive buyer?"

"No, I just know what I like." He handed over the money to the artist, then reached for a baseball cap with "Oklahoma—State of the Arts" printed across the bill. He placed it on Raleigh's head. "I'll take that, too. Could you wrap the sculpture and put it in a sack for me?"

"Sure." The young artist took the purchase from Raleigh and wrapped it in a page of the *Times*.

"It's nice to know the newspaper is good for something," Raleigh quipped dryly, drawing a grin from Evan. She fitted the red-and-white cap more securely on her head and looked around at the numerous booths. Artists from around the world had come to Mayfest this year to display their talents. A bluegrass band was playing in Bartlett Square, and a troupe of jugglers and clowns were cavorting along the fountain.

"Are you going to the wedding with me or not?" Evan prodded, taking her hand again.

"Sure." She spotted a fellow reporter and waved to him. "There's Brian," she said for Evan's benefit. "I'm glad I don't have to work weekends anymore."

"So am I. That cap looks cute on you." Evan released her hand and hooked his arm around her neck, pulling her sideways to plant a kiss on her cheek. "You've been preoccupied all week. Is your job getting to you?"

"I've just had a busy week." Raleigh smiled up into his face, wishing she could confide in him. It would be nice to unload all of her worries, but it wouldn't be a smart move. Depending too much on Evan was pure folly, she warned herself. She needed to be stronger and more self-reliant. She needed to shoulder her own problems without help from anyone else. Tilting up her nose, she sniffed the air. "Do you smell those nachos?"

Evan took a sniff and closed his eyes in a moment of ecstasy. "Lead me to that booth and I'll buy us some."

Raleigh zeroed in on the nacho stand. "We can eat them over by the fountain and listen to the bands."

They bought a plate of nachos and a couple of soft drinks and wandered over to the square, finding a seat along the fountain. Sharing the nachos, they listened to the blue grass music and enjoyed the festive atmosphere.

Munching the round chips and melted cheese, Raleigh watched couples stroll arm in arm, realizing that this was the first Mayfest she'd attended as part of a couple. Last year she had envied those twosomes, but this year she was one of them. Loving was more complicated than she had ever imagined, Raleigh thought as she watched a teenage couple neck openly on a bench. The older you became, the more thought you gave to loving and commitments. Circumstances that might have been simple when she was seventeen were now fraught with complications. While she loved the way Evan made her feel, a part of her held back. She couldn't help but remember the loneliness she had experienced when Curtis died.

She'd depended on him, and when he had killed himself, he'd taken a big chunk of her life with him.

Evan examined Raleigh from the corner of his eyes, noting her worried frown. Realizing he was shoving nachos into his mouth as if he were starving, he brushed his hands down his thighs and suppressed the urge to shake Raleigh and demand to know why she was keeping secrets. He loved a mystery as much as the next person, but secrets of the heart shouldn't exist between lovers. Didn't she know that? Didn't she understand that he needed her trust as much as he needed her love? One without the other was worthless; together they were priceless.

She slipped her rainbow-colored suspenders off her shoulders and let them dangle at her hips. Evan smiled, thinking she looked about eighteen today in her faded jeans, white blouse and suspenders. Her hair was gathered by a rainbow-colored ribbon at the nape of her neck, completing the effect.

Raleigh sat up straighter and pointed ahead of her. "Look! They're getting ready for the Mr. Pretty Legs contest!"

The exuberance in her voice interested him more than the activity around a platform a few yards ahead. "What's that?"

She popped the last nacho into her mouth and tossed the paper plate into a trash can. "They pick the prettiest male legs. Last year one of the guys I work with won."

"Can anyone enter?" Evan asked as an idea seized him.

"Anyone who is male." Raleigh brushed crumbs from her jeans and slid off the concrete edge of the fountain. "I've got to watch this."

Evan finished his soft drink, gathered his nerve and decided to give in to his impulse. "I think I'll enter."

"What?" Raleigh turned wide hazel eyes on him. "Are you serious?"

"Deadly." Evan lifted one leg for her inspection. "Don't you think I stand a chance? You've seen the merchandise."

Raleigh stood back, adopting a contemplative pose. "You might have a ghost of a chance."

"Ha!" He tossed his paper cup into the trash can with a flourish. "Step aside, woman."

Raleigh laughed and swept a hand toward the platform. "Good luck."

Evan walked up to a man who seemed to be in charge of the entrants, and Raleigh moved to the front of the crowd of spectators. She ran an eye over the competition lined up on the platform and decided that Evan had more than a ghost of a chance. His closest competition, Raleigh decided, was a muscular blonde who looked as if he spent most of his time in the gym and under a sun lamp. Evan took his place at the end of the line, and Raleigh thought he looked a little nervous. She smiled her encouragement, wishing she had brought along her camera.

"I thought I might find you here," someone said beside her.

Raleigh tore her gaze from Evan and his competition and turned. "Cara!" She hugged her sister. "I'm surprised to see you here."

"I was doing some shopping when I saw the crowd and remembered it was Mayfest, so I decided to check it out." Cara glanced up at the platform and gasped. "Isn't that Evan?"

"Yes." Raleigh laughed at Cara's shocked expression. "What do you think his chances are?"

Cara twisted a strand of hair around her finger absentmindedly as she surveyed the field. "That blond Goliath is the front runner, but Evan is a close second." Cara clamped a hand on Raleigh's shoulder. "Let's sit down and enjoy this."

"Okay." Raleigh sank to the ground and crossed her ankles. She had to tip back her head to watch the competition, but the view was interesting. Most of the contestants went for laughs. Two of them were dressed in drag, their masculine faces smeared with outrageous makeup. Raleigh laughed along with the others, but a feeling of anticipation grew within her. When Goliath was introduced to the crowd as "Sam, the owner of a Tulsa health spa," Raleigh and Cara exchanged a worried look.

"Cheer up," Cara said, placing an arm about Raleigh's shoulders and giving her an affectionate squeeze. "I think Evan is sexier looking."

"You do?" Raleigh asked dubiously as Sam displayed an impressive array of rippling muscles.

"Yes. His personality is more attractive. Sam looks as if he's in love with his mirror image."

"This isn't a personality contest," Raleigh reminded her sister. She scrutinized Sam's muscular legs as he showed them off to the crowd. "I think he's won."

Cara frowned and punched Raleigh in the shoulder. "Have a little faith, Raleigh."

Evan stepped forward, his gaze sweeping the faces before him and lingering for a few moments on Raleigh. An old thrill surfaced within him, reminding him of those evenings when he had lived out a fantasy and danced in a club for women only. He'd realized then that he had a streak of exhibitionism in his character. What would Raleigh think if he let himself go and performed? he wondered, his gaze finding her again. Cara Torrence waved at him, then gave him a thumbs-up sign of encouragement. It was all the extra incentive he needed.

"Last, but not least, we have Evan," the announcer said, touching Evan's shoulder. "He's a psychologist who has recently moved back to Tulsa. Let's see what you've got, Evan."

The announcer stepped back out of the way, and Evan felt a moment of nervous paralysis, but the music from a rock band a few yards away dissolved his momentary shyness. Instinctively, his hips began swaying to the hardrock beat, provoking an immediate reaction from the onlookers. The audience began swaying and clapping in time with the music, and an occasional wolf whistle pierced the air. It brought back memories of hot lights, beseeching hands and uninhibited appreciation. A rakish grin pushed across his lips as he crossed his arms in front of him, grabbed the hem of his pullover and worked the material up his body with slow deliberation.

Checking the expressions before him, he saw that the women had pressed closer to the platform and some of them were reaching out to him. His smile grew as he swept off his shirt and whirled if over his head as he executed a slow, grinding circle. His female admirers begged for more. Evan kept up a grinding rhythm with his hips as he unbuckled his belt.

"Take it off!" Cara shouted.

Raleigh stared at her sister in open-mouthed shock. "Cara! Control yourself!" She looked back at Evan, who was pulling his belt from its loops. "This is indecent exposure!"

"There is absolutely nothing indecent about him," Cara said with a lusty laugh.

Raleigh felt her cheeks flame as she caught Evan's eyes. He unsnapped his jeans and arched an eyebrow as if asking for permission. Raleigh shook her head and clamped a hand over her eyes.

Evan laughed, enjoying Raleigh's show of discomfort. He snapped his jeans again, and when the crowd groaned in disapproval, he hiked up the frayed ends of his cutoffs and exposed his tan lines, then performed a few more seductive gyrations to regain their support. The rock band ended the song and Evan blew a kiss to Raleigh and stepped back into line. Sam looked over and gave him a tight smile.

"Where did he learn to dance like that?" Cara asked as she applauded wildly.

"His master's thesis was on exhibitionism," Raleigh said, feeling a mixture of pride and timidity. She smiled, shaking her head slightly. "What a show-off."

"He's adorable, Raleigh." Cara stood up and helped Raleigh to her feet. "He'll make a wonderful brother-in-law."

Raleigh laughed off the idea, although it jarred her. "You're nuts."

"You love him, don't you?"

Looking away from her sister's keen eyes, Raleigh shrugged. "I don't know exactly what I feel for him. Oh, my gosh!" She lifted a hand to cover her gasp. "He won!"

The onlookers hooted their approval as Evan accepted the winner's spoils—a magnum of champagne and season tickets to the Tulsa Civic Ballet Theatre—and shook the announcer's hand. He lifted the magnum above his head in a salute to the crowd, then singled out Raleigh and winked at her.

"Evan, some of the ladies are asking if you're married," the announcer said, then moved the hand mike toward Evan to catch his answer.

"I'm not married," Evan answered as his gaze locked with Raleigh's again. "But I am spoken for."

Raleigh looked away and felt her skin grow warm. Cara nudged her in the ribs with her elbow, and Raleigh laughed nervously.

"This sounds serious," Cara teased.

"He's just popping off," Raleigh assured her. "It's nothing." She looked back to Evan, who was putting his shirt back on and accepting congratulations from his competitors. "I think he enjoyed that, don't you?"

"What man wouldn't enjoy having women throw themselves at him?" Cara smiled at Evan as he approached them. "Well, if it isn't Gypsy Rose Evan."

"Hi, Cara." Evan kissed Cara's cheek. "It's good to see you again." He tucked the champagne under his arm and looked at Raleigh. "I can't decide which one of you is the prettiest. I guess it's a toss-up."

"Cara's the prettiest," Raleigh said automatically.

"Don't I have her trained well?" Cara asked with a smile, then shook her head and laughed. "I've got to run. I'll see you two later."

"Why don't you have dinner with us?" Raleigh asked, placing a hand on Cara's arm before she could melt into the crowd.

"Thanks, but I've already made other plans."

"Okay." Raleigh's hand dropped back to her side. "See you around." She watched Cara's lithe figure zigzag among the Mayfest crowd until she disappeared from view.

"Is Cara seeing anyone special?" Evan asked, moving closer to Raleigh and lacing the fingers of one hand with hers.

"No. She's very selective and very independent."

"It must run in your family." Evan examined the bottle of champagne and grinned. "Let's go back to my place and open this."

"What about dinner?"

"I'll fix something at home."

Raleigh shook her head. "I've got a better idea. We'll order a pizza—my treat."

Evan pulled her closer and kissed her forehead. "Pizza and champagne?"

"They're as American as Mom and apple pie," Raleigh told him in mock seriousness, then laughed with him.

They had started in the direction of Evan's parked car at the Williams Center when Raleigh spotted Grant. She looked away but knew he had seen her.

"Raleigh!"

She heaved a sigh and turned back to Grant. He gave her a broad smile before shifting his attention to Evan.

"I don't believe we've met," Grant said, extending his hand to Evan. "I'm Grant Farris."

"Evan Younger. It's nice to meet you." Evan pumped Grant's hand once. "You're the editor of the *Times*?"

"That's right." Grant rocked back on his heels and grinned at Raleigh. "Having a good time?"

"Yes. We're just getting ready to leave. We've been here since this morning," Raleigh answered, gritting her teeth when she heard the breathless panic in her voice. Why did she get so worked up around Grant? she wondered. He could be innocent, she told herself. If only Cody would contact her and tell her as much! A mental picture of Grant lifting a revolver and firing two shots formed in her mind, making her shut her eyes for a moment and will away the image.

Grant eyed the magnum of champagne. "What have you got there?"

"I won it," Evan said, hoisting the bottle for Grant to see. "I'm this year's Mr. Pretty Legs."

"No kidding?" Grant chuckled, his brown eyes moving to Raleigh. "I guess you're proud of him."

"I'm busting my buttons." Raleigh laughed, but cut it off when she heard the nervous, high-pitched quality of the sound.

The clock in the square chimed, and Grant looked at it with a slight frown. "Four o'clock? I had no idea it was that late." His fingers wound around a gold chain, and he pulled out his pocket watch and flipped it open. A few cheery notes floated out before he snapped it closed again and pushed it back into his pocket. "Raleigh?" Grant chuckled softly and touched her arm. "Are you okay? You look as if you've just seen a ghost."

"What?" Raleigh shook aside her momentary hysteria and stared blankly at Grant's smiling face. Fear wrapped icy fingers around her heart, and she clutched Evan's hand in a death grip. "It's nothing. I ... I'm just tired. We've got to go." She pulled Evan into a stumbling walk. "See you Monday, Grant."

"Right." Grant lifted a hand in farewell. "Are you sure you're all right?"

"I'm fine," Raleigh said, forcing a smile to her lips. "Goodbye." She turned and pulled Evan with her toward a crowded intersection.

Evan grasped her wrist with his other hand and checked her breakneck speed. "Hey, where's the fire?" he asked with a laugh.

"I'm sorry." She slowed to a stroll. "Grant makes me nervous."

"No kidding? I thought you were going to blow a gasket."

"Was it that obvious?" Raleigh chewed reflectively on her lower lip for a moment. "Do you think he sensed how uneasy I was around him?"

"I don't know how he could have missed it." Evan fished his car keys from his pocket and opened the passenger door for her. "What's the problem? Why does he make you so uptight?"

Raleigh eased herself into the car seat and swung her legs inside. "It's nothing. He just rubs me the wrong way."

Evan closed the car door and went around to his side. When he was settled in the seat, he turned sideways to face her. "It's more than that. If I didn't know better, I'd say that Grant Farris scares you."

"Don't be silly." Raleigh laughed and looked away from Evan's penetrating blue eyes. "He just irritates me. He's such a Don Juan. He treats every woman as if she's a pretty little bauble. I resent that attitude."

"Has he put the make on you? Is that why you're so nervous around him?"

"Yes." She turned her head back to him, seizing the excuse. "That's it. He... he's been flirting with me and I don't know how to handle it."

Evan smiled and smoothed his fingertips down her cheek. "You'll have to learn to handle it. Your chubbette days are over, honey." His lips touched hers lightly. "Grant Farris isn't the only man looking at you with renewed interest. Cody told me the other day that some of the policemen are flirting with you, too."

"He told you that?" she asked, surprised that Cody would talk to Evan about such personal things.

"Yes, and I wouldn't blame you if you were tempted by them."

She smiled, catching the question in his voice. "I'm not tempted. Are you jealous, by any chance?"

"I'm not jealous, just possessive." His mouth nibbled on hers, then grew more aggressive. "I don't want anyone else to have you, Raleigh," he whispered fiercely as his hands moved up her spine.

Raleigh tipped back her head, letting Evan's mouth move down her throat. Her heart beat wildly, making her aware of what an active heart she had. Ever since meeting Evan, her heart had been positively acrobatic—tripping, skipping, fluttering and somersaulting. No wonder it was synonymous with love, she thought distractedly as Evan's hands molded her breasts.

His lips worked their way up her neck, across her cheek and to her waiting mouth. His tongue skimmed across her lips but didn't enter her mouth. Raleigh opened her eyes when his lips lifted from hers and saw that his eyes were alight with mischief.

"What?" she asked, dazed.

"I think we'd better mosey over to my place before this gets out of hand." He set the champagne bottle in her lap and started the car.

Raleigh grinned and let her hand drop to his thigh. "Good idea." Her hand moved upward.

"Raleigh," Evan groaned, "you're going to make me wreck this car if you keep doing that."

Laughing, she removed her hand and enjoyed the pained expression on his face.

"We definitely need to work on your résumé this weekend," he said, glancing at her in time to see her scowl. "I don't see how you can work for Farris and feel the way you do about him."

"He makes my skin crawl." Raleigh crossed her arms as a chill ran up her spine. "Let's not talk about him."

"Are you sure there isn't something else that bothers you about him? I mean, you acted as if he were a convicted murderer or some—"

"Can we *please* change the subject?" she snapped, whipping her face away from him to stare blindly out the car window.

"Okay, okay! I'm sorry."

Raleigh ground her teeth together, fighting off the loathsome fear. Grant couldn't have killed Victoria Rendell and Johnny Stratton, she told herself. He was a strutting peacock, but he wasn't the type of man who could murder people, was he? She closed her eyes as the tension built within her until she thought she might explode. Oh, why didn't Cody call her? He must know something by now!

Chapter Nine

 Will you look over this one more time and make sure I've caught all the mistakes?" Raleigh asked, handing Evan the typewritten pages she'd just finished. She switched off the electric typewriter and grabbed the last slice of pizza. "Could I use your phone while you look those over?"

"Sure." Evan leaned back in the dining-room chair and waved a hand toward the kitchen. "There's a phone in there or you can use the one in the living room."

"Thanks." Raleigh went into the kitchen and stood for a few moments, her hand on the receiver, until she remembered Cody Wakefield's home number. She dialed it and prayed he would be home. Ever since she'd arrived at Evan's house, she'd worried that Grant might suspect why she was on edge around him. It had been apparent to Evan, so Grant must be aware that her attitude toward him had changed. How long was she expected to keep these dark secrets? she wondered angrily as Cody's telephone rang on the other end of the line. Relief flooded through her when he answered on the sixth ring.

"Hello?"

"Cody, it's Raleigh."

"Raleigh, I've been trying to reach you at home."

She clutched the receiver and took a deep breath. "I'm at Evan's. Any news?"

"Nothing you can print yet."

"Great." She frowned and closed her eyes in defeat. "What have you got?"

"All I know right now is that Grant took out a bank loan for half the amount that was paid to Green for his property in Okmulgee."

"That's damaging evidence, isn't it?"

"Yes, but not enough for a conviction. One thing is bothering me about this business."

"Just *one* thing?" Raleigh asked sarcastically, and Cody chuckled sympathetically.

"The deed just has Victoria Rendell's name on it. Why wouldn't Grant put his name on it, too, assuming he is half owner?"

Raleigh turned and leaned back against the wall, her brow furrowed in thought. "Maybe he was worried about conflict of interest."

"How's that?"

"Well, he endorsed pari-mutuel betting in Okmulgee County through the newspaper," Raleigh explained. "Maybe he was afraid someone would see his name on the deed and charge him with conflicting interests. That's a serious charge among media people."

"Oh, I see what you mean." Cody was silent for a few moments. "That makes sense."

"A lot of this is making sense," Raleigh agreed. "I thought it was weird at the time that Grant was so hot to get pari-mutuel betting passed in Okmulgee County when he didn't give a hoot how the other counties voted." She sighed wearily, more convinced than ever before that Grant Farris had murdered Victoria Rendell and Johnny Stratton. "Now all we need is a motive. Why would he kill his partner?"

"That's what I'm working on."

"I saw him at Mayfest today. Cody, this is really getting to me. I can't be around Grant without coming unglued."

"Raleigh, don't tip him off!" Cody's voice was stern.

"Easy for you to say. I have to work around the guy."

"Don't go to work," Cody said matter-of-factly.

"Just like that? I have to pay the rent."

"Call in sick. Do whatever you have to do, but don't make him suspicious. I don't want him covering his tracks or skipping town."

"Okay." Raleigh massaged her neck, feeling as if it were supporting a twenty-pound ball and chain. "Call me if anything else breaks."

"I will."

Raleigh replaced the receiver, then leaned her forehead against the wall while she gathered her self-control. *The next thing that will break will probably be me.* Her mouth twisted into a humorless grin at the thought.

"Raleigh?"

She lifted her head and ran her hands over her face. "Yes?"

"Bring me a beer when you come back in, will you?"

"Okay." She went to the refrigerator and tore one of the cans from its plastic holder as her mind replayed the conversation with Cody. *If Grant had borrowed a lot of* money from the bank, that would account for the rumors that the *Times* was in financial trouble. It certainly proved that Grant Farris was no longer the rich playboy if he had to float a loan to purchase some land. But why would he murder Victoria? Did he simply want to take all the money from the track instead of sharing it? Could he kill someone over simple greed? And why did he shoot Johnny Stratton?

She closed the refrigerator and stared at the cold can in her hands. Maybe he caught Johnny and Victoria in a compromising position and shot them in a jealous rage. She shook her head. No, that didn't wash. What was he doing with a gun when he walked in on them if it wasn't premeditated?

The chill from the can spread over her body, and she shivered as grisly scenes flickered through her mind.

"Raleigh? What are you doing in there?"

"I'm coming." She shook aside the gruesome thoughts and went back into the dining room. Evan tossed the sheets onto the table and grinned.

"I'd hire you in a second. That is one impressive résumé, lady."

Needing a diversion, she hitched up her suspenders and grabbed the sheets. "Do you think so?"

"I sure do." Evan opened the can and drank from it. "Instead of mailing it to Donnelly, why don't I just take it to his office Monday?"

"You wouldn't mind?"

"No. It's on my way to work." He took the papers from her and tapped their edges on the table before fitting them in a black plastic folder. "I'm excited about this, aren't you?"

Raleigh hooked her thumbs in her suspenders and leaned back in the chair. "Yes. The more I think about it, the better it sounds. I hope Donnelly thinks it's a good idea."

"Once he takes a look at this, he will." Evan pushed the folder into the middle of the table. "You're a natural for the job."

"Don't get my hopes up any more than they already are," Raleigh cautioned. "If I don't watch out, I'll be expecting to get the job, and then I won't and I'll be crushed."

Evan propped his feet up on the dining-room table, tipping back his chair at a dangerous angle. "You've got a real hang-up about expecting too much, don't you?"

Pulling her feet up into her chair, Raleigh hugged her knees to her chest and chose her words carefully. "I wouldn't call it a hang-up. I've just learned to be realistic in my expectations." She glanced at him, finding him devilishly attractive when he smiled in that lopsided way. Her fingertips itched to smooth the tumble of dark curls away from his forehead. It would be easy to expect endless love from him, she thought recklessly. As easy as falling into a pot of gold at the end of a rainbow.

"Who made you so wary, Raleigh?" Evan asked in a low, nerve-tingling voice. "Who changed you from a dreamer to a doomsday prophet?"

She rested her cheek on her bent knees and focused her gaze away from those all-too-knowing eyes. "Dreams are for sleeping, not waking."

"Baloney. Dreams keep us moving ahead. They make us achieve what we thought was impossible."

She looked at him. "You believe that?"

"I live by it." His gaze softened perceptibly. "What made you give up on your dreams?"

"I don't know what you're talking about."

"Curtis's death? Is that what made you decide not to expect anything? Did he disappoint you so terribly that you're afraid to put your faith in anyone or anything?"

Raleigh unfolded herself from the chair and escaped into the living room. "Why do we always end up talking about Curtis? He's dead. Let's just leave it at that. I don't like being psychoanalyzed by you."

"If I'm psychoanalyzing you, it's purely personal, not professional," he said, getting up from the chair and following her into the living room.

"I don't like it, personally or professionally." Raleigh sank into one of the chairs and glared at him. "So drop it before we start yelling at each other and I go home alone."

He grinned and sat on the floor beside her chair, hooking one elbow about the arm and letting the beer can dangle from his fingers. "Okay, we'll drop it." He brought the can to his lips and drank deeply. "The past couple of weeks have been tough on me. I was beginning to think you had given me the brush."

Raleigh sighed and pulled the ribbon from her hair. She shook her head in a negative response and felt her hair settle along her shoulders. "I've been busy. I told you that."

"I know what you told me and I know what I felt in my gut." He glanced at her, watching as she tucked the ribbon under her shirt collar and tied it at her throat. He finished the beer and set the can on the end table. "I told myself that you needed a little breathing space."

"I did."

"And that you'd come around and see me again."

"And I did."

He shifted to his knees, his hands clutching the chair arms and making her his prisoner. "And I'm glad you did." He bent his elbows and leaned in to kiss her, his lips warm and reassuring. "I know your work isn't going well. It's got you on edge. Do you want to talk about it?"

Did she want to talk about it? Raleigh bit her tongue to keep from spilling the whole Grant Farris story. The thought of sharing it with Evan and receiving his calm, reasonable advice made her limp with relief, but it was a short-lived euphoria. She couldn't say anything yet. Secrets. Oh, how she hated secrets! Why had she agreed to go off the record? She had known better. It was a journalist's curse. She realized she was shaking her head and that Evan was disappointed at her reaction.

"I don't want to talk about it now," she said, smoothing the lines from his face with her fingers. "I'd rather think about happy things."

"I've got a great idea."

"What's that?" Raleigh placed her hands on his shoulders.

"Why don't you come to Eureka Springs with me next weekend and meet my folks?"

Her fingers bit into his shoulders in a spasmodic reaction. "That sounds serious," she said, and her voice held a quiver of doubt.

"It *is* serious." He sat back on his heels. "I want them to meet you. I've told them all about you and—"

"You've talked to your parents about me?"

"Yes." He tipped his head to one side in a bemused way. "Why should that shock you? Haven't you talked to your parents about me?"

"No." She twisted a pearl ring around her finger, realizing how odd that sounded. She hadn't talked to her parents about him, although she suspected they knew she was seeing someone. She had kept Evan a secret as if she were afraid that once the secret was out, he would disappear. *Secrets.*

"Why haven't you? Are you ashamed of me?"

"No." She shook her head adamantly. "I just . . . You never came up, that's all."

"I think we should let our parents in on this, don't you? We're not playing around anymore. This—we—*are* serious, right?"

She lifted one shoulder in an indifferent shrug. "Sure, I guess so."

"You *guess* so?" He puffed out a sigh of frustration and clutched the chair arms again. "Raleigh, we're not just good friends and we're not just lovers. We mean a lot to each other, and I think it's time we both admit it and let everyone else in on it. You're not still hung up on this age business, are you?"

"No." She lifted her hands in a helpless gesture, feeling insecure and fragmented. "Let's just leave it as it is for now. Why push it?"

Evan bounded to his feet. "Have you heard anything I've said?"

"Yes." Raleigh looked up into his flushed face, realizing with a jolt that he was fuming. "I've been listening."

"You've been *listening*, but you haven't *heard* me," he charged, placing his hands on his hips and glaring at her as if he were a bull and she a red cape. "I've been pouring my heart out to you and what do you have to say about it? Don't push it!"

"What are you so mad about?" Raleigh asked as she scrambled from her chair for equal footing.

He clamped his hands on her shoulders and dug his fingers into her flesh. "I'm mad at you! I'm asking for a commitment from you, Raleigh. I want you to meet my parents. I want to meet your parents. Have you got that?'' He gave her a little shake, making her head rock painfully on her neck.

"Evan," she pleaded, squirming from his hold, "let go. You're hurting me.'' She stepped back from him, unable to face the demand he was making. "I want to meet your parents . . . someday.''

"Next weekend," he ground out between gritted teeth.

"I can't next weekend.''

"Why not?''

"I . . . I just can't.'' She grasped his arms, sensing that he was withdrawing emotionally.

"You mean, you won't.''

"No, that's not what I mean.'' She drew a deep breath and searched frantically for the right words that would appease him for the time being. "Evan, I've got a lot of things on my mind right now. Don't push me into a corner on this.''

"Why don't you share those things with me?'' His hard expression told her that he already knew what her answer would be.

"I can't share them right now.''

"You keep saying 'can't' when you mean 'won't.' ''

"No, I *can't*.'' She shook his arms, desperate for his understanding. "It's stuff that has nothing to do with you. It's . . . it's things about my work that I can't talk about yet.''

"If you were a government spy, I might be able to swallow that.'' His smile was a twist of cynicism. "There's nothing I wouldn't talk to you about, Raleigh. Nothing.'' He jerked his arms from her grasp and turned away from her. "You were the one who was worried about getting involved in a one-sided love affair, but I'm the one who should have been worried about that, it seems."

"No, Evan." She reached out to him, but he moved his arm so that her fingertips only brushed his sleeve. "It's not one-sided."

He looked at her from the corner of his eye. "Then prove it. Go to Eureka Springs with me next weekend."

"Don't do this!" Raleigh held up her hands and pressed them against her throbbing temples as she whirled away from him. "Don't ask me to make a decision about us now. I can't. I've got too much on my mind and I can't think clearly."

"Are you going to Eureka Springs with me, Raleigh?" he asked in a toneless way that made her cringe.

"That sounds like an ultimatum."

"It is."

Raleigh spun to face him and felt her heart crack down the middle when she saw the rigidity in his eyes. She shook her head in a silent plea, but he didn't take back his words.

"I've told you how I feel about you," he said in a voice that was as hard as his eyes. "The ball is in your court now. Either you go to Eureka Springs with me next weekend, or we call it quits."

"Evan, please don't do this."

"What will it be?" he asked unrelentingly.

"Just give me a few more weeks ... a little more time to get my life straightened out and I'll—"

"I've given you enough time," he growled, and his hands clenched into angry fists at his sides. "Are you going to Eureka Springs with me?"

Her heart broke in two. "No, I can't."

A grimace twisted his face before he turned his back on her. "I'll take you home."

"Don't bother." She swallowed a sob and brushed past him. "I'll call a cab."

"Suit yourself."

Evan watched the cab pull away from the curb, and something wicked snapped inside of him. Rage whipped through his body, and with a vicious growl of frustration, he whirled from the window, his arm swinging in an arc that sent the table lamp crashing to the floor and splintering into jagged glass fragments.

Staring at the destruction, Evan blinked stupidly, hardly aware that he had just broken his mother's prized Depression-era glass table lamp. His knees turned to jelly and he sank to the floor, narrowly missing a shard of glass.

"Raleigh...Raleigh..." His voice broke and he cradled his head in his hands, his fingers clutching his hair and pulling until his scalp tingled.

It had been a long time since he'd cried, and it felt so good to release his shattered dreams in a deluge of rasping sobs that burned his throat and cauterized his wounded heart. The last time he had cried was when the woman he'd been living with for eight months had left him for a job in St. Louis. That had been painful, but this was almost more than he could bear. He had waged a valiant campaign for Raleigh's heart, and he'd thought he had won it. He'd been so sure of himself that he'd phoned his parents and told them he was bringing the next member of the Younger family to meet them. What would they say when he showed up empty-handed and broken-hearted?

Better luck next time, son. You'll get over her. You'll forget her. There are other fish in the sea.

A moan tore from his throat as the old clichés roiled up inside him until he thought he would gag.

There would never be another Raleigh, he told himself. He would never love like this again. There were some things that the heart knew with certainty, and this was one. There was no cure for this. Time would not heal the wound completely: a scar would be left, and he would carry it with him to his grave. Just like in those old, mushy novels, Evan thought. When he drew his last breath, her name would whisper across his parched lips.

"Raleigh." He felt an emptiness gape within him at the sound.

If only he could turn back time, he wouldn't have given her that ultimatum. He would have played by the rules and given her more time, but the seeds had been sown and now he must harvest what he had planted. Loneliness. That was his crop. Utter loneliness.

Evan lifted his face from his hands and stared at the shattered lamp. He started picking up the pieces, feeling as if he were placing pieces of his soul into the palm of his hand. He licked the corner of his mouth and tasted his own salty tears. Oh, if she could only see him now, he thought with a twisted smile. On his hands and knees, picking up what was left of his life after she'd ripped through it with all the finesse of an Oklahoma tornado. The trained psychologist—an expert in the mysteries of the human condition—trying to fit the pieces back together and doing a terrible job of it.

"I can't fix it," he mumbled, and threw the fragments of the lamp into the trash can. The sound of them banging against the metal can reverberated inside of him, and he clamped his hands over his ears to keep out the noise.

Scrambling to his feet, he grabbed his jacket from its peg near the door and pushed his arms into it. He shut the door behind him and broke into a jog as he headed down the street toward Webster High School. There was a track there and he was going to run until he got her out of his system or collapsed, whichever came first.

Sinking into the tub of warm water, Raleigh felt the calming effect of the hot milk she'd drunk earlier weave slowly through her taut muscles and troubled thoughts.

Eyes closed, she imagined that she could see her troubles rise from her in the form of ghostly specters, each wearing grins that made her think of Grant Farris.

She shivered and sank lower in the tub until the water lapped at her chin.

Losing Evan had hit her harder than hearing about Curtis killing himself. Did that mean she loved Evan more than she had Curtis? No, she answered herself. There was nothing she could have done to keep Curtis in her life, but she had all but shoved Evan out. That was why she was taking this so hard. She could have prevented this loss.

The significance of the evening crashed down on her, and her hands flew to cover her heart in a protective motion. She gasped, surprised at the pain that shot through her, and then dissolved into hiccuping sobs that seemed to start at her toes and grind their way up her body, leaving her dry-eyed and retching. It was the worst kind of crying: the kind that tore chunks from your soul and ripped through your heart.

She cried for Curtis and the waste he had made of his life. She cried for all the dates she had missed out on during her teenage years when she'd been too heavy to attract a worthy male. And she cried for the man who had offered to make up for those chubbette years.

Why hadn't he given her a few more weeks? Why couldn't she make him understand that she wasn't in the right frame of mind for a proposal?

He'd taken it as a rejection when she had meant it only as a postponement.

"It wasn't my fault," Raleigh whispered, then sputtered when tepid water lapped into her mouth. She sat up a little, feeling lethargic and realizing that the warm milk and hot bath were making her woozy. Afraid that she might fall asleep in the tub and drown, she stood up and dried herself. Her arms felt heavy, and she had to drag her feet across the floor to get to her bedroom.

She sprawled across the bed, unmindful of her nudity as she pulled up the covers and snuggled beneath them. A dull ache settled near her heart, reminding her that her troubles had only temporarily departed and would be back with her in the morning light.

For now, however, the ache had diminished to the point where it was bearable. There would be plenty of time to cry over this mess, she told herself sleepily. Plenty of time to feel sorry for herself . . . to argue that she had been helpless, given the situation . . . that she could still get Evan back if she tried hard enough.

She rolled into a dreamless slumber only to awaken hours later when the sun was just beginning to paint the horizon a rosy hue. She pushed aside the covers and grabbed her new green satin robe from the chair. Belting it at the waist, she went to the window to watch the morning light illuminate the spires of downtown Tulsa.

Dawn brought no hope with it, but it forced her to examine her shortcomings, to see clearly the wasteland that awaited her. Even if she hadn't had the uncertainty of Grant Farris's innocence to wrestle with, she realized, she would still have been reluctant to meet Evan's parents and bring her love for their son out in the open. She was afraid, afraid that once she gave her love its wings, it would fly away and not return.

She recalled a sampler her grandmother had once embroidered, and the words burned in her memory: If you love something, set it free. If it comes back, it is yours. If it does not, it never was.

She hadn't had the courage to test her love for Evan. She had held on to it jealously, and he had ripped it from her selfish grasp.

But that wasn't all, Raleigh admitted. She was afraid to love him because loving him fully meant being completely vulnerable, totally dependent and undeniably captured. She had adored her brother openly, but her love hadn't been enough for Curtis. Would it be enough for Evan?

"I'll never know now," Raleigh told the sun, then looked away when the bright light burned her eyes.

She went back to bed and stayed there until Monday morning, when she got up long enough to eat some toast and drink some coffee. She phoned the newspaper and told the receptionist that she had the flu and wouldn't be in all week. Sheila offered her words of sympathy that twisted Raleigh's heart and made her feel even more miserable.

She hung up the phone and crept back to bed. The blue flu, she thought as she pulled the covers over her head and wondered if she'd ever be able to face a day without Evan. She had a screaming case of the blue flu.

On Wednesday she received a call from Donnelly Wakefield, and it jarred her enough to make her leave the bed and join the living again.

"Am I disturbing you?" Donnelly asked when she answered the telephone, hoping it might be Evan.

"No."

"I called the newspaper and they told me that you were home with the flu."

"Yes, I'm not feeling well." Raleigh pushed her hair from her face and caught a glimpse of herself in the mirror. She looked dreadful, and she glanced away from her reflection, unable to gaze too long at her sunken eyes and pale face.

"I'm sorry to hear that. I wouldn't have disturbed you, but it's kind of important. I've looked over your résumé and—"

"My résumé?" she interrupted, having forgotten all about it. She'd left it at Evan's, hadn't she?

"Yes. Evan Younger brought it by Monday morning."

"He did?" She couldn't believe it. Evan had delivered her résumé after she'd thrown his proposal in his face?

"Yes, and I'm impressed." Donnelly's voice was warm and filled with encouragement. "When you're feeling better, I'd like to see you and iron out the details."

"What details?" Raleigh asked, a few steps behind the conversation.

"I'd like to hire you."

"You're kidding!" She gripped the receiver and felt hope surge through her.

"I don't know why you should be so surprised," Donnelly said with a laugh. "You're qualified for the job and I need a topnotch press agent. You *do* want the job, don't you?"

"Yes!" Raleigh drew a calming breath and forced her tone down to a civilized level. "I want the job very much, Donnelly. You've just... You took me by surprise. I didn't expect to hear from you so soon."

"I can't drag my feet. The campaign is heating up and I need a good speech writer. Do you think you could drop by my office sometime next week? We can discuss salary and your responsibilities then. I guess you'll have to give a two-week notice at the newspaper."

"Yes, I'll handle all of that. It's no problem. Let me call you next week and make an appointment."

"Fine. If I'm not in Tulsa, call my Oklahoma City office and leave a message."

"Okay. Thank you, Donnelly. You don't know how much this means to me."

"It's an even exchange, Raleigh. I'm glad you've decided to join my team. Take care of yourself and I'll talk to you next week."

"Right. Goodbye." Raleigh replaced the receiver, then released a rousing Oklahoma whoop. Her steps were light and springy as she left the bedroom for the kitchen; her appetite had suddenly returned along with her spirits.

I've got the job! she thought in a burst of elation that fizzled with her next thought. She had the job, and she had Evan to thank for it. Sinking into one of the kitchen chairs, she pressed the heels of her hands against her burning eyes as tears squeezed from the corners and rolled down her cheeks.

Chapter Ten

Folding the single sheet of typing paper into thirds, Raleigh felt a stirring of apprehension.

Was she doing the right thing? She slipped her letter of resignation into an envelope addressed to Grant Farris and wondered if she should deliver it personally or mail it. The thought of seeing Grant face-to-face sent her across the living room to a small desk. She took a stamp from one of the drawers and affixed it to the envelope, then brought the letter to her chest in a moment of panic.

Press agent to Donnelly Wakefield. It sounded impressively lofty. Could she handle the responsibilities? If Donnelly didn't win, what then? Where would that leave her? Newspaper jobs were hard to come by in Tulsa. She might have to move to another city for employment, and she loved Tulsa and didn't want to live anywhere else.

She placed the letter on the desk top, refusing to succumb to her doubts. Donnelly would win the governorship, she thought with a spurt of confidence. He was the best man for the job, and the people of Oklahoma would recognize that, especially after they heard the great speeches he would deliver!

Her gaze fell on the desk calendar and she felt a twinge of desperation. It was Friday. She had muddled through six days without Evan. Whatever feeble hopes she had harbored that he would relent and contact her again had withered with each passing day, and Raleigh was beginning to face the prospect of life without the good doctor.

The ringing telephone snapped her from her bleak thoughts, and she dropped into an easy chair as she lifted the receiver.

"Hello?"

"Are you really sick or are you faking it?" Cody asked on the other end of the line.

"I'm faking it, but I've been better. I really haven't felt like working this week. Have you heard from Donnelly?"

"The question is, have *you* heard from Donnelly?"

"Yes!" Raleigh laughed, and Cody joined in. "Thanks for your help, Cody. I just finished typing my letter of resignation."

"Have you seen Grant lately?"

"Not since Mayfest. Have you uncovered anything else?"

"My banking sources told me that Grant is being pressured to pay off the loan. It seems he is temporarily short of funds and can't make his payments. He put the *Times* up for collateral, so I suppose that accounts for the rumors we've heard about the newspaper being financially unstable."

"Boy, am I glad Donnelly hired me." Raleigh closed her eyes in relief, thankful for the Wakefields.

"I've been looking over a financial profile of the *Times*, and it's been steadily losing money for the past few years. I think this racetrack might have been Grant's ticket out of the newspaper business."

"Tulsa isn't big enough for three dailies, and afternoon papers are struggling across the nation. The *Times* won't be the first or the last to sink."

"I'm glad you won't be going down with the ship," Cody said with grave sincerity.

"So am I. Have you got any other news?"

"Just one more item." Cody paused dramatically, and Raleigh prepared herself for the blow. "Mr. Green called me this morning. He remembered what Victoria Rendell called the man she was with."

"He remembered the guy's last name?"

Cody chuckled. "He *thought* Victoria was calling the guy by his last name. She called him Grant."

Raleigh released her breath in a soft hiss. "But that doesn't prove Grant pulled the trigger."

"No, it doesn't, but I'm working on some angles. I should come up with something solid by the end of next week."

"Next week?" Raleigh moaned, wishing this ordeal could be over by tomorrow. "If only I hadn't overheard your conversation with Green, I wouldn't be in this fix."

"It's not that bad, is it?"

"It's worse than bad, Cody." She felt the beginnings of another good cry swell in her chest. "Off the record, do you think Grant is guilty?"

"Off the record, yes."

"But what's his motive?"

"I'm working on a scenario," Cody said, drawing out the words and piquing Raleigh's curiosity.

"Like what? A lover's quarrel?"

"Something like that."

"Do you think it might have been premeditated?"

"I think Grant might have intended to scare Victoria, but things got out of hand. I'm beginning to suspect that Johnny Stratton was just at the wrong place at the wrong time."

"You don't think Howard Rendell had anything to do with this business?"

"No. I never felt that Howard was guilty. He was too obviously suspect. Grant was anxious for Howard to take the fall, wasn't he?"

"Was he ever!" Raleigh rolled her eyes, recalling how livid Grant had been when Rendell had been set free. "You know, I have two weeks' vacation coming to me. I was thinking I might just submit my resignation and take my two weeks' vacation. That way I won't have to see Grant again."

"Do whatever you think is best. I know this has been a strain on you."

"That, my friend, is the understatement of the century."

"Don't tip him off. Be careful, okay?"

"Yes. Keep me posted."

"I will."

Raleigh replaced the receiver with a heavy sigh. The finger of guilt was slowly swinging toward Grant Farris, a man Raleigh had worked for day in and day out. If the guilt landed on her editor, it would shake the weak foundation of the *Times* and the staff would be the innocent casualties. She began forming a scenario of her own that involved Grant and Victoria as ruthless business partners. Enter Johnny Stratton, a good-looking, young golf pro who wins Victoria's favors. Victoria dumps Grant, first as a lover, then as a business partner. Would Grant be angry enough to kill Victoria and her new lover?

Years of covering the police beat had shown Raleigh that passion was the cause of many crimes. Sane, responsible people became crazed and irresponsible when wronged by a loved one. Most of the women in prison had committed crimes in the name of love. The line between love and hate was thin, and many a convicted lawbreaker had crossed that line and lived to pay for it.

It was difficult to imagine Grant Farris killing for love or passion. Greed must have been his motive, Raleigh decided. Money was the only thing Grant had been faithful to in his entire life. He was a lousy publisher because he never gave a fig for responsible communications. He was interested only in the money end of the business. Advertising was his forte, and news ran a distant second.

If Victoria had kicked him out of her bed, Grant would have suffered an injured ego, but he would have survived handsomely. However, if Victoria had kicked him out of a lucrative business deal, Grant would have been out for blood.

Raleigh wrapped her arms around herself, warding off a clammy chill as the scenario gained credibility. He could have done it, Raleigh thought; Grant Farris was capable of murder.

The telephone rang, breaking through the chill silence and the ugly scene in Raleigh's mind. She jerked the receiver from its cradle.

"Hello?" She swallowed the lump of fear in her throat and swept a hand over her eyes to clear them of their inner vision.

"Hi, it's Cara. Are you okay? I called the newspaper and—"

"I've been playing hooky," Raleigh interrupted, wanting to put Cara's mind at ease. "I'm making a career move, but the *Times* doesn't know that yet."

"You're changing jobs?"

"Yes. I've accepted the position as press agent to Donnelly Wakefield."

"Fantastic!" Cara sounded breathless, as if the news had knocked her for a loop. "I didn't even know you were interested in politics."

"I'm not. I'm interested in a better job and in getting Andrew Mathison out of the governor's mansion."

"I'm with you on that score. When do you start work?"

"As soon as I submit my resignation to the paper. I've decided to take my two weeks' vacation and not go back to the *Times*."

"Just like that?"

"I believe in clean breaks." A shaft of pain speared her heart as she remembered another breakup, one that had been messy and devastating. What was Evan doing now? Was he thinking of her? Did he hurt as much as she was hurting?

"Let me be the first to congratulate you."

"What?" Raleigh shook her head in confusion before she returned to her original train of thought. "Oh, right, my job."

"That *is* what we were talking about," Cara reminded her with a little laugh.

"Yes. Thanks. I'm excited about the prospects. I just hope I can handle it."

"You will." Cara was silent for a moment as if gathering her thoughts. "Have you seen Mom and Dad lately?"

"No, not for a couple of weeks. I . . . I've been kind of busy." Guiltily she wondered if Cara had called to lecture her on how to be a better daughter. "Why? Is something wrong?"

"I was over at their place today and they were sort of depressed."

"Why?"

"Tomorrow is Curtis's birthday."

Raleigh's gaze flew to the wall calendar and her eyes widened in shock. "I'd forgotten! The days have just slipped by and—"

"I know. It didn't occur to me until Mom and Dad mentioned it. I guess we've all tried to put it out of our minds and get on with our lives. For heaven's sake, don't feel guilty about it slipping your mind!"

"I'm not," Raleigh lied as guilt rushed through her in a sickening wave. Last year she'd celebrated Curtis's birthday at her parents' home. She and Curtis had gone to see *Lady and the Tramp* that evening and had cried sentimental tears when Lady had shared a romantic spaghetti dinner with Tramp. Curtis had kidded her, telling her that she needed a Tramp in her life, someone a little bit naughty who could make her less a lady and more a woman. An emptiness yawned within her, but she knew she wasn't grieving for Curtis anymore, but for the man who had made her feel like a woman.

"I know what you're thinking," Cara said. "You're thinking about last year when Curtis was with us."

"Yes, I was." Depression edged its way into her. "Weren't you?"

"Yes, but we'll get past tomorrow. Raleigh, why don't you call Mom and Dad and cheer them up?"

"I don't feel very cheery, Cara."

"Fake it."

"Okay. I'll call them."

"Good. I think just hearing from you will make them feel better. Hey, are you okay? You sound so...I don't know...downtrodden."

"How perceptive of you," Raleigh said with a sad little laugh. "I feel like I've been trodden on."

"Are you still seeing Evan?"

"No." She ground her teeth together to keep the tears at bay.

"No?" Cara sounded disappointed. "That's too bad. I like him, and I thought you two made such a cute couple. What happened?"

"It's a long story and I'm not in the mood to rehash it."

"I understand. I'm here when you feel like talking about it."

"Thanks, I'll keep that in mind."

"Well, I've got to go. What time is it?"

Raleigh glanced at her watch. "Six o'clock."

"That late? No wonder I'm starving! I'll talk to you later."

"Okay. Bye." Raleigh depressed the call button, then released it and dialed her parents' number. She had no idea how she was going to cheer them up when she felt as if the world were crumbling around her, but she had to try.

Her mother answered the telephone. "Mom? It's Raleigh."

"Hello, honey. Have you been sick?"

"No, I've just taken a few days off. I'm changing jobs."

"You are?"

"Yes, I'm going to work for Donnelly Wakefield as his press agent."

"Oh, honey, that's wonderful. Hold on and let me tell your father." When her mother spoke again her voice was muffled as if she'd placed her hand over the mouthpiece. "Edgar, Raleigh is going to work in the Donnelly Wakefield campaign.... What? I don't know, I'll ask." Dixie's voice was strong again. "What are you going to do in his campaign?"

"I'll be his press agent and his speech writer."

Dixie related the news to her husband, then returned to the phone. "Your father is so excited. He really likes the Wakefield boys."

Raleigh smiled, thinking that Donnelly and Cody had passed their boy stages years ago. "I like them, too. Mom, I just got off the phone with Cara, and she said you and Dad were sort of depressed. Are you two okay?"

"Of course we are. It's just that ... well, tomorrow is ... would have been Curtis's birthday."

"I know." Raleigh searched for the right words. "We'll get through it together."

"We're going to visit his grave tomorrow. Do you want to come with us?"

Raleigh twirled the telephone cord around her finger, trying to suppress a feeling of dread. Curtis's grave was one place she had avoided. It seemed so cold and impersonal, while her memories of Curtis were warm and vibrant. "I ... I'll meet you there." She closed her eyes, wishing she could get out of this gracefully. "What time?"

"Oh, about noon. If you don't want to, you don't have to."

"No, I'll be there. Are you sure you're okay?"

"We're fine, honey. Really," Dixie replied sincerely. "And we're happy about your new job. I think we're all getting past the tragedy, don't you?"

"Yes." Raleigh shook her head, realizing that she was the only Torrence who hadn't gotten past Curtis's death. It still lingered within her, refusing to let go. It seemed that every time she turned around, she was running into memories of her brother and the happy times she had shared with him.

"We'll see you tomorrow then?"

"Yes, Mom. I'll see you there. Goodbye."

"Bye-bye, honey."

Raleigh smiled wistfully as she hung up the telephone and settled back in the comfortable chair. Dusk stole into the apartment, throwing inky shadows into the room and deepening the darkness within her. The simple need to talk to someone weighed heavily on her mind, making her restless and edgy. She glanced toward the telephone, realizing how ironic her yearning was. She'd been on the telephone most of the afternoon with Cody, Cara and her parents. Why hadn't she talked to them? They would have listened and given her sympathetic advice.

It was strange how a person's life was divided into neat compartments. She could talk to Cody about Grant Farris, but she wouldn't have felt comfortable talking to him about her personal life. She could talk to Cara about Curtis, but she had excused herself from talking to her sister about Evan. She could talk to her parents about her new job, but she couldn't talk to them about the passion she'd felt for Evan Younger and the loneliness she knew now.

There had been one person in her life whom she could really talk to about everything, and that person had been Curtis. She'd bent his ear about everything from her career goals to fantasies of being swept off her feet by a man who made Prince Charming look like a wimp. Curtis had always been there for her, lighting her way when it was dark, encouraging her when she doubted herself and making her laugh when she'd wanted to cry. She had shared so much with him, but he had shared so little with her. That knowledge made her realize how one-sided their relationship had been. She had entrusted Curtis with her deepest, darkest secrets, but he'd never trusted her with his. She had been his fair-weather friend, but he had avoided her when his skies were cloudy and he needed a friend. He had turned to alcohol, instead of her.

One-sided relationships. Were they to be her curse? No one had ever offered to commit themselves totally to—

Raleigh brought herself up short, realizing the lie she was forming in her mind. Someone *had* offered to share himself, his dreams, his goals, his ambitions with her, and she had rejected his offer.

Tears filled her eyes and overflowed onto her cheeks as self-pity consumed her.

"Oh, Evan, what have I done?" she asked the empty room.

She curled into a little ball and burrowed into herself, trying to escape the loss of her best friend.

Raleigh awoke with a jerk and struggled through a few moments of disorientation before her eyes grew accustomed to the darkness. She realized she was sitting in her living room.

Switching on the table lamp at her elbow, she narrowed her eyes against the light and stared at her watch. It was after midnight. It was Curtis's birthday, but there would be no celebration.

When she unkinked her legs, her muscles were tight with fatigue. A mantle of depression slipped over her like a thick rain cloud, and that desperate yearning to lean on someone overwhelmed her. It was a weakness, but one that persisted, and Raleigh knew she didn't have enough strength to fight it off. She'd been wrong to give in to her irrational fears when Evan had offered his love to her in exchange for her trust.

If only Curtis were here! She could talk about this, get it out in the open, examine it and be done with it! Bottling it up inside was dangerous. Curtis had put a cap on his problems, and they had blown him apart. Raleigh could feel the pressure building up inside of her, and it frightened her.

Before she knew what she was doing, her fingers had curled around the telephone receiver. She stared at her hand, realizing that she was about to dial Evan's number, and she released the telephone and balled her hands into her lap. She couldn't call him! What would she say?

Her gaze was drawn magnetically to the telephone again, and her heart urged her to make the call while her mind told her she was crazy for even contemplating such a foolish notion. The battle raged within her until she wanted to scream. Suddenly the conflict ended and she grabbed the receiver and dialed Evan's home. She held her breath as the telephone rang and rang. He wasn't home! Was he with someone else? Had he found another lover so soon?

"Yes? Hello?"

She released her breath, and her heart tripped over itself at the sound of Evan's sleep-dazed voice.

"Hello? Is someone there?" he demanded grumpily.

"Evan, it's me." She waited, listening to his breathing at the other end. Didn't he recognize her voice? "It's Raleigh. Raleigh Torrence."

"I know."

The icy, unrelenting tone of his voice brought tears to her eyes. Loneliness walked into the room and sat beside her with eerie familiarity, and Raleigh wondered if it would be her constant companion from now on. She turned her back on it and clutched the telephone that had suddenly become her lifeline.

"Did I wake you?"

"It's after midnight, what do you think?"

"I'm sorry." She bit her bottom lip to keep from sobbing into the phone. "I wanted to talk to you."

"It's a little late for that."

"Is someone there with you?" She closed her eyes as despair engulfed her.

"What do you want, Raleigh? If you called to check up on my sex life, then I'm hanging up right now—"

"No!" She gripped the telephone so hard her nails bit into the palm of her hand. "Don't hang up!" She listened, but couldn't hear anything. "Are you still there?"

"Yes."

Tears rolled down her cheeks, and she swallowed the lump of emotion in her throat; when she spoke, her voice was husky and broken. "I know you don't want to hear from me, Evan, but I had to call you. I . . ." She swallowed again and groped for the words that would keep him on the line. It was so hard to talk to him, so hard to make him understand. "Can you hold on just a minute?"

No answer.

"Evan?"

"Yes. I'll hold."

She drew a deep breath, all too aware of how important the next bit of conversation would be. Grabbing a tissue from the box on the table beside her, she dabbed at her eyes and nose before pressing the receiver to her ear again.

"I'm back. Thanks for holding."

"What's on your mind?"

"I wanted to thank you for . . . for taking my résumé over to Donnelly's office. He hired me."

"I'm glad, but why did you wait until after midnight to call me and thank me?"

"I . . . I don't know." She pressed the tissue to her trembling lips.

"Well, I've got to get some sleep because I'm getting up early tomorrow . . . this morning."

"It's Saturday."

"I know. I'm driving to Eureka Springs to see my parents."

"Oh." She closed her eyes and felt hot tears tickle her cheeks. Eureka Springs. That's what had gotten her into this mess.

"So, if that's it—"

"No!" She straightened up and wiped away the new flood of tears. "There's something else."

"I'm listening."

"Well, I have a problem, and I thought you could help me with it." She waited, but he didn't say anything. "You see . . . I mean . . . well, it's Curtis's birthday and I need to talk to someone. I used to talk to him, but I can't do that anymore. He was my best friend, but he's gone, and I need to talk to someone about my problems." She drew a deep breath, wishing Evan would say something. "I'm under a lot of stress right now, and I'm about ready to crack. Everything is all black and ugly. I promised Cody I wouldn't tell anyone about Grant, but it's driving me crazy, and I lost my best friend and my lover this week, and I need to talk to somebody about it. Evan, I need to talk to my best friend, but you're my best friend, and you don't want to see me again, do you?" With a sob, she broke off her disjointed explanation, wondering if any of it made sense to the man on the other end of the line. "Evan? Evan!"

His sigh whispered across the line. "I'll be right there."

The receiver dropped from her limp fingers, and she fell back in the chair as a sunny shaft of hope lit her soul and loneliness took its leave.

Chapter Eleven

Evan picked dead leaves off Raleigh's philodendron plant while she poured hot herbal tea into thick mugs. The clock on the mantel chimed, announcing that it was two o'clock in the morning.

"It seems we've played this scene before," Evan said, tossing the dried leaves into the ashtray as he turned to face her. "Are we going to hurt or heal each other this time?"

She glanced up at him from her seat on the couch, then added a spoonful of honey to her tea. "I'm for healing. I don't think I could hurt any worse than I do right now."

The lamplight spilled over her face, highlighting her wan coloring and the dark circles beneath her eyes. Her hair, usually shiny and fluffy, was tangled and hung limply against her pale cheeks. When she glanced up again, Evan saw how puffy and bloodshot her eyes were.

"I have to admit that you look like hell." He smiled, trying to soften his honesty.

"You should," she accused him, smiling in return. "How dare you show up here looking as if you hadn't a care in the world! You should at least look as if you've been suffering."

"I have been." He took one of the mugs and sat beside her. "I thought I'd run into you at work, but I was told that you've been sick."

"Heartsick." Her lips twitched into an uneasy smile. "And I didn't want to see Grant."

"Why? Did he do something to you?" His heart stammered to a halt, then slammed against his ribs when an evil thought sliced through him. "Raleigh, he didn't force himself on you or anything?"

"No." She shook her head and giggled. "I wish it were that simple. I could have handled that."

He relaxed, chiding himself for jumping to silly conclusions. "So what is it?"

Her hazel eyes met his shyly. "It's so sweet of you to come over her at this time of night. I feel better already."

He took a sip of the mint-flavored tea. "You sounded as if you were at the end of your rope when you called."

"I was, I think." She shook her head again. "I am." Pulling her legs up on the couch, she shifted sideways and visibly relaxed. "I promised Cody I wouldn't talk to anyone about Grant, but if I can't trust you, who can I trust?"

"What does Cody have to do with Grant?" Evan asked, bringing the rim of the mug to his lips again.

"He thinks that Grant might have murdered Victoria Rendell and Johnny Stratton."

The tea went down the wrong way and Evan coughed, his eyes watering. Concerned, Raleigh slapped him several times on the back with the flat of her hand. Evan held up a hand to ward off another blow.

"I'm okay," he croaked. "Stop hitting me."

She giggled and placed a hand over her mouth. "I'm sorry. I didn't mean to hurt you."

"It's okay." He swallowed the burning sensation in his throat and gasped for breath. "Why would Grant Farris kill Victoria Rendell and Johnny Stratton?"

"Jealousy, greed, passion." Raleigh shrugged helplessly. "I don't understand the motive, but the evidence is pointing in his direction. Cody is keeping a lid on it until he can get something more concrete. At Mayfest you said that Grant would have to be blind not to notice how strange I acted around him." Her hazel eyes seemed even larger behind the lenses of her glasses. "Do you think I've tipped him off?"

"No. Why would he think you'd know anything about it?" He gave her a reassuring smile. "I wouldn't worry about that. Do you think he did it?"

"Yes, I'm beginning to think it's possible. I'm sure that he and Victoria had a thing going."

"You mean they were having an affair?"

"Yes, and it went sour. They were in business together—they bought some land to build a racetrack on—and I think she might have tried to cut him out of the deal."

"Did you know all of this the other night when you were at my place?"

"Yes." She removed her glasses and rubbed her eyes with her thumb and forefinger. "It's been eating at me. It's spooky to think that I might be working for a man who committed a double murder and then tried to get another man convicted for it.''

''I'm sorry I pushed you.'' He set his mug on the table and bowed his head, feeling like an ogre for making demands on her when she'd been so distraught.

''I needed a push, so don't be sorry.'' She adjusted the knot at the waist of her robe and frowned thoughtfully. ''Ever since I met you it's been hard for me to believe this is happening.''

''What is happening?''

She ran her hands up and down her arms and smiled. ''I have black-and-blue marks from pinching myself. I just couldn't believe that you wanted me and that you might even love me.''

He was silent, content to study her face. She looked all of sixteen with her hair tumbling to her shoulders and her eyes bright as if she had a fever. She pulled the lapels of her robe together at her throat and looked away from him.

''You were right about me not expecting much from people. I learned not to. When I was younger I expected fairy tales to come true. I lived for the day when Prince Charming would ride into my life, kiss me and I'd wake up and realize that all that had gone on before had been a bad dream. I'd be beautiful and slim and live happily ever after.'' Her eyes were brimming with tears when she looked at him. ''Isn't that silly?''

''No. Everyone dreams.''

''Well, I stopped dreaming. I got tired of waiting and being disappointed. I threw myself into real things like my job and my family. I started depending on Curtis. I thought that together, we could be strong for each other and get past the rainy days.''

"But that didn't work out," Evan said, finishing the thought for her.

"No, it didn't." She ran a hand across her eyes in an impatient gesture. "My love wasn't enough for him. He...I guess he couldn't talk to me the way I could talk to him."

"Raleigh..."

"I know. I understand that he couldn't tell me things. I was his little sister and he didn't want to appear small in my eyes. I understand that now."

"I'm glad." He pulled a handkerchief from his back pocket and handed it to her. "If I were you, I'd believe in dreams. Yours have come true. You're slim and beautiful, and even though I'm not a real prince, I'm a prince of a guy." He grinned when she giggled and gave her a comforting hug. "I like to hear you laugh."

"Thanks." She blew into his handkerchief and balled it up in her hands. "I want to explain why I didn't trust my feelings for you or yours for me."

"Okay. I'd like to know."

"I was afraid that we wouldn't work out and you'd leave and I'd be back where I started before I met you." Her eyes were bright and pleading. "When Curtis died he took everything beautiful with him. It felt as if he'd torn a big chunk out of me. You stepped in and made me happy again, and I just couldn't take the chance.... I was afraid...."

"I understand." He pulled her into his arms and let her cry softly against his shoulder. It felt wonderful to hold her again, and he relished the feel of her frail shoulders and narrow back. Her hair was downy soft against his cheek, and he turned his lips into it. "I was a little frightened myself."

"What were you afraid of?"

"Of losing you."

"I'll go to Eureka Springs with you." She lifted her head to look at him, and desperation edged into her voice. "I'll go anywhere with you. I just want to keep you in my life. I don't want to let you go. I was so lonely without you. I didn't want to depend on you, but I already do and I—"

"Shhh." He touched her lips with his to silence her and held her head between his hands. "I understand. I think you should get some sleep and we'll talk more later."

She stared at him, her eyes wide with disbelief. "You're not leaving me alone? Stay here with me tonight, Evan."

The temptation was strong, but his resolve was stronger. He shook his head and spoke before she could. "Listen, Raleigh. You've been through a lot and so have I. Let's get some rest and piece this back together when we're stronger and can think more clearly. We're both too shaky now to accomplish much." He chuckled and rolled his eyes heavenward. "I don't know about you, but I'm exhausted!"

Her lower lip trembled and her eyes brimmed with tears. "You don't want me anymore."

"That's not what I'm saying." He gripped her shoulders and made her look at him. "I *do* want you. I just think it would be better if I went home now to give us both a little time to think things through." He placed a tender kiss on her trembling lips. "I'll be back in a few hours."

"What about Eureka Springs?"

"I'll call my folks and tell them I'll be there next weekend. Now promise me that you'll get some sleep. I'll be back before you know it with doughnuts and coffee."

He could tell that she didn't like the idea, but she nodded anyway. She'd turned his world topsy-turvy and he needed a few hours to adjust to what she'd told him. Grant Farris a murderer? He shook his head as he stood up and started for the door. He turned and smiled at her worried expression.

"Raleigh, you're dead on your feet," he admonished as he pointed toward the bedroom. "Get in there and sleep!"

"Promise you'll be back?"

"I promise."

"I'll set my alarm for eight o'clock."

"I'll be here by eight-thirty."

"I told my family I'd meet them at Curtis's grave tomorrow at noon to pay my respects, but I don't know if I'll be up to it."

"I'll go with you."

"You will?" Her eyes shimmered with hope.

"Sure. It will be good for you. You should make peace with him, Raleigh. He didn't kill himself to hurt you. Forgive him, and let go of it."

"I guess you're right. His death was such a waste." She sighed and looked around the room in a distracted way that made his heart constrict painfully. She looked so lost and confused.

"Maybe not. The police officers seem united and supportive of each other, and I think Curtis's death had something to do with that. It shook them up and made them think." He saw the weariness in her eyes and knew that she was more exhausted than she realized. "Go to bed—now!"

She sighed and nodded. "Okay. Thanks for coming over."

"Thanks for calling me." He winked and closed the door.

The room grew colder with his leaving, and Raleigh pulled the robe tightly around her. She stumbled into the bedroom and fell across the bed. Evan was right, she thought as she closed her eyes. She was dead on her feet. She thought briefly of setting the alarm clock, but sleep washed over her before she could transform the thought into action.

Raleigh awoke with a start, sensing that a sound had awakened her. She held her breath and listened, then glanced at the clock to find that it was a little after eight. She sat up in bed and tried to gather her senses just as someone pounded on the front door.

Evan! She jumped from the bed and tied the sash of her robe as she raced to answer the door.

"You came back, thank heavens!" She threw open the door and gasped when she found herself staring at Grant Farris. "Grant, what are you doing here at this time of the morning?"

"Did I wake you?" He frowned and shook his head. "I'm sorry. I'm an early riser and..." His voice trailed off and he looked over her head pointedly. "Can I come in? I just wanted to check on you. Sheila said you have a nasty flu bug."

"That's right, and I'm contagious, so—"

"I won't stay but a minute."

She gave a little nod and stepped back to let him enter the apartment. The urge to refuse him entry was great, but she told herself to get it over with. She couldn't tip him off now. It was important to keep his suspicions at bay. Grant glanced around him as he adjusted the fit of his gray suit jacket.

"I didn't know you made sick calls on your employees, Grant." Raleigh gave him a quick, unamused smile as she sank into one of the matching armchairs.

"I usually don't, but I realized I was near your place and I decided to stop by and see how you're feeling."

"I'm better."

When she offered nothing more on the subject, Grant adjusted his striped tie nervously and laughed. "I put David McCormick on your beat, but he ran into some problems."

"Oh? What kind of problems?"

"He said that Cody Wakefield wouldn't even talk about the Rendell case. What's going on? Why is Cody so touchy?" He unbuttoned his jacket and swept it back, planting his fist at his waist in a dapper pose.

Raleigh shrugged off the questions. "I'm resigning from the newspaper, Grant. I've already mailed my letter of resignation."

He seemed genuinely shocked; his dark eyes widened, then narrowed swiftly. "What brought this on? I thought you enjoyed your work."

"I need a change. I'm bored with the job. I've accepted the position of press agent for Donnelly Wakefield."

"Wakefield again. You're really thick with them, aren't you?" One corner of his mouth lifted in a sneer.

"Not really. Cody was a good friend of my brother's, but I don't know Donnelly that well. Do you have something against the Wakefields?"

"No," he said quickly, then chuckled. "No, of course I don't. I just hate to lose you to Wakefield, that's all. You're a good reporter."

"Thanks." She laced her fingers and felt her nerves stretch and quiver. What was she supposed to say now? Why didn't he just leave?

"Have you talked with Cody lately?"

"I've been ill, Grant," she reminded him, evading his question.

"Do you think he's investigating anything new on the Rendell case?"

"When he has something, he'll contact McCormick. He's always been good about working with the press."

"Who do you think killed Vicki and Johnny Stratton?" he asked in a quiet, chilling tone.

Raleigh kept her head bowed, her gaze locked on her hands. His familiar use of the woman's first name registered in her mind before she answered, "I haven't thought about it that much. Do you have a suspect?" She glanced up to see that he was leaning forward a little in an intense scrutiny of her, but he straightened quickly when she caught his eye.

"I've always thought that Howard Rendell looked as guilty as sin."

Unable to stand another moment of his plodding interrogation, Raleigh stood up and went to the door. "It was nice of you to drop by, Grant. I'm feeling better, as you can see." She opened the door and looked over her shoulder at him.

"Why is it that I keep getting the feeling that you're not telling me something?" Grant asked slyly. "You didn't use to be so jumpy around me. Has someone been carrying stories behind my back?"

The fine hairs on the back of her neck stood straight up as apprehension stirred within her. She tried to laugh, but it was a nervous, flighty sound. "I think you're paranoid, Grant. What would I be keeping from you?"

"What, indeed?" he asked, moving close to her. "Did you know Victoria Rendell?"

"No." Raleigh swallowed and tasted copper. "Did you?"

"You know that I did and you made sure Cody knew it, too, didn't you?"

"Grant, I—"

"Hi there!"

Raleigh faced the open door and felt relief wash over her at the sight of Evan. He held up a sack from a doughnut store and shook his finger at her.

"Have you been waiting for me after you promised you'd get some sl—" He bit off the last of the sentence when he saw Grant. "Grant, what are you doing here?"

Raleigh sent a grateful smile to Evan. "Good morning, Evan. I'm so glad to see you."

"Good morning." Evan's eyes were icy blue as they shifted to Grant. "Is something wrong?"

"No. Grant stopped by to check on me." Raleigh shrugged in a bewildered way as Evan entered the apartment and stood at her side.

Grant frowned and flicked his jacket open and closed in an impatient gesture before he buttoned it. Raleigh tensed as she realized what her eyes had caught a glimpse of when Grant had adjusted his jacket. In the inner pocket was a long folder with a Trans Global insignia on it. Airline tickets.

She lifted her gaze to his and saw that he knew she had seen too much. Raleigh took a step back from him, and that coppery taste coated her mouth.

"Goodbye, Grant." Her voice was weak and breathless.

Grant looked at Evan again, then turned back to Raleigh with a scowl on his face. "Goodbye, Raleigh, and be careful." His dark eyes bored into hers. "Be very careful."

Raleigh closed the door behind him and bolted it. She leaned her forehead against the door until her heart slowed to a normal pace.

"Are you okay?" Evan asked, gingerly touching her shoulder.

"Yes." She straightened and went to the telephone. "I've got to call Cody," she said, already dialing the number, grateful when he answered on the first ring. "Cody, it's Raleigh."

"Good morning. I was just—"

"I think I tipped Grant off just now."

"What?" His voice sharpened, cutting across the line.

"He was here at my place asking a lot of stupid questions and I got nervous. Cody, he has Trans Global airline tickets in his pocket. I think he's flying the coop." She glanced at Evan and saw his brows lift at the news.

"I hear you. Thanks."

Raleigh blinked when the line was abruptly severed. "He hung up on me. Just like that!" She slowly replaced the receiver. Was Cody dashing to the airport to arrest Grant? At the thought, her eyes flew to Evan.

"What?" he asked, setting the sack on the coffee table.

"Let's go to the airport." She started for the bedroom to get dressed.

"Now?" Evan asked, following her. "Don't you think you should let the police handle this?"

"Yes, but I want to be there if this goes down." She grabbed a pair of jeans and a shirt from the closet. "We'll take your car."

"Do you think Cody will arrest Grant?"

"We'll never know if you keep asking questions and stalling." Raleigh pulled on her jeans and stuck her arms into her shirt.

"Okay," Evan said with a sigh. "I'll start the car so we can make a quick getaway. Meet you outside."

"I'll drive. We'll need to put the pedal to the metal."

"Not in my car," Evan called back to her. "And *I'll* drive. I'd like to get there in one piece."

There were several police cars at the airport's main entrance when Raleigh and Evan arrived. Evan let Raleigh out, then went to park the car. Rain fell from the sky in a heavy sheet, and she hurried into the terminal and made her way to the Trans Global ticket counter. A number of flights were posted, and Raleigh decided to head for the gates and look for Cody or Grant. Trans Global gates were on the lower level, Raleigh was told by the woman at the ticket counter.

"Just follow the blue lines," she added, pointing to the floor. "They'll lead you to the Trans Global gates."

"Thanks." Raleigh took the escalator to the lower level. Following the blue lines on the floor, she ran along the corridor and felt like Dorothy looking for the Land of Oz. Just follow the blue lines, she chanted to herself, stopping when the lines stopped. She looked up to find herself at the Trans Global gates.

"Now what?" she whispered, gazing down the long corridor and seeing only strangers. She started walking slowly, her gaze darting left and right in search of something or someone familiar. Had she been wrong? Maybe those hadn't been airline tickets in Grant's pocket. Maybe he'd purchased tickets for someone else or for later in the week.

There was activity at two of the departure gates. She approached the first and looked over the boarding area where people waited for their flight. A Trans Global plane taxied outside the plate-glass window, and most of the people were watching it. A baby wailed mournfully, and its mother spoke soothingly. The crying scraped across Raleigh's nerves, making her even more tense. Giving the area one more sweeping examination, she moved to the next crowded gate several yards farther on. There she approached a cluster of people who were in line to have their boarding passes checked. The flight at the first gate, she knew, had been destined for St. Louis and New York. Looking past the boarding attendant to the flight announcement, she noted that this fight was headed for Nassau. The Bahamas, she thought with a sudden smile. This had to be it. Grant had to be here.

Edging around the people, she looked into the boarding area and was disappointed when Grant was not among those who waited for the plane. And where was Cody? She started feeling foolish, thinking now that Cody had probably checked the airlines by telephone and discovered that Grant Farris wasn't a scheduled passenger. Cody wasn't here. Grant wasn't here. There wasn't going to be a big showdown.

Raleigh started back toward the escalator, intent on finding Evan and going home. She lifted a hand to her forehead, realizing that she had a headache from too little sleep and too much excitement. She suddenly felt bone weary.

Spotting a sign for rest rooms ahead, Raleigh headed for the ladies' lounge. A splash of cold water on her face would revive her enough until she could get home and fall into bed, she thought. She stopped just short of the rest-room doors to remove her glasses and tuck them into her purse. One of the earpieces clung to the outside of her purse and Raleigh struggled with it a few moments before the glasses finally slipped inside. Swinging the strap over her shoulder again, she looked up and froze.

Notes chimed faintly but loudly enough for her to hear them clearly, and a chill ran up her spine. Raleigh felt a momentary faintness before she shook her head to clear it and shifted her eyes sideways in the direction of the chiming tune.

He was no more than a foot away from her, smiling as he closed the watch and slipped it back into his vest pocket.

"Grant." She was surprised she could get his name past the paralyzing fear in her throat.

He took two steps to stand right in front of her. His smile mocked her, telling her that she was all alone and he knew that she had double-crossed him. *If he could kill once, he can kill again,* the voice in her head whispered, and Raleigh felt her heart pound in her chest. She looked into Grant's eyes, realizing that she didn't know him very well at all. She'd never seen his eyes darken to such a pitchy shade before, and she'd never before noticed the vein in his temple that throbbed with his pulse.

Raleigh swallowed hard and glanced toward the escalators. Where was Evan? Would he show up in time...in time for what? To save her?

"What are you doing here?" Grant asked, reaching out and seizing her wrist as if sensing she was about to make a mad dash for the escalator.

"I...I'm picking up a relative." Raleigh glanced toward the escalator. No Evan. Act normal, she told herself. She might be able to fool Grant. "What are you doing here?"

"I think you know."

Raleigh shook her head. She wasn't fooling him: she was the fool. Why had she come here? Why wasn't she at home with Evan . . . safe and sound? "No, I don't. Are you meeting someone?"

"You told Cody I was having an affair with Victoria, didn't you?"

"I don't know what you're talking about." Frantically she jerked her arm, trying to escape from Grant's strong fingers. "Let go of me!"

He gave her arm a savage jerk, making her stumble and fall against him. His face was close to hers and his eyes seemed to glow with a dark secret. *Secrets.* Raleigh shut her eyes for a moment and watched her life flash before them. Grant shook her and Raleigh opened her eyes to witness his madness again.

"She laughed at me. So did he. I was just going to scare her and make her see that she couldn't push me around, but she laughed at me!" His lips drew back from his teeth. "It was all his fault. If he hadn't told her that she could pull off the deal without me, everything would have been fine. Just fine."

"Grant, you're hurting me." Raleigh pulled back, desperate now to get away from him. "Let go!" She looked around, but panic blinded her. All she could see was the danger in Grant's dark eyes. Did he have a gun or a knife? Could she get away from him before he could reach his weapon if he had one? Couldn't the people passing by see the fear on her face?

His eyes took on a distant gleam and his expression hardened to hatred. "Women are all alike. You're all double-crossers. You're no different. I didn't want to hurt her and I don't want to hurt you, but you leave me no choice. I'll have to shut you up." His fingers bit into her wrist, closing like a vise on the fragile bones.

"Let go!" Raleigh cried out, certain that the bones in her wrist would be crushed.

"There he is!"

"Police! Freeze!"

Raleigh's head whipped around at the shouts, and relief poured through her when she saw Cody and two other plainclothes officers. Three uniformed officers stood behind them.

"Let go of her, Grant," a calmer voice beside her insisted.

A whimper of relief escaped her when she saw Evan standing next to her. He looked blessedly calm and in control as he pried Grant's fingers from Raleigh's wrist with persistent patience, then draped his arm protectively over her shoulders. "That's it, Grant. You've hurt enough people."

Grant shook his head as if to clear it. A dazed expression flickered across his face as Cody came up behind him and snapped handcuffs on his wrists. Then he seemed to grasp the situation, and he smiled sadly at Raleigh.

"Don't make me sound too crazy in the story you write for the *Times*."

Raleigh wrapped her arms around Evan's waist, needing his security. "I don't work for the *Times* anymore. I won't be writing that story."

"Oh, yes. That's right." A policeman clamped a hand on his shoulder and Grant glared at him, then looked at Cody. "What made you suspect me?"

"The land you bought with Victoria," Cody answered.

"She backed out on our deal. Stratton told her that she didn't need me. She could build the track and take all the money."

"So you killed her," Cody said disdainfully.

"I didn't mean to." Grant's face twisted pitifully. "She laughed at me and I..." He paused, gathering in a shaky breath. "She pulled a gun out of the dresser drawer and threatened me with it. I tried to get the gun from her and it went off."

"What about Stratton? Was that accidental, too?"

"No." Hatred lined his face. "I didn't even know he was there until he came running in after hearing the shot. He started screaming at me and I had to shut him up."

"So you killed him." Cody shook his head in bewilderment. "Grant Farris, I'm arresting you on suspicion of murder. You have the right to remain silent...."

Raleigh closed her eyes, letting Evan guide her away from the others. Cody's voice grew distant, but she could still see the mad glint in Grant's eyes when he'd threatened her. The newspapers would have a heyday with this, she thought, and she was glad she wouldn't have to take part in it. This was one story she didn't want to write.

She was barely aware of the drive back to her apartment and was stunned to learn that it was only nine-thirty. Evan made coffee and heated the doughnuts, then made her sit down on the sofa and relax.

"He's nuts," Raleigh said, taking a cup of coffee from Evan. "I saw the madness in his eyes."

"Crimes of passion." Evan sipped his own coffee and sat beside her. "Grant's not the first or last person to cross the line between love and hate."

Raleigh set the cup on the table and rested her cheek on Evan's shoulder. "I love you so much."

The simple, honest way she said it made it all the more special to him. Evan tipped back his head, feeling his heart swell with love. He set his cup beside hers and tightened his arms around her, reveling in the splendor of being loved by Raleigh Torrence. He felt her gaze on him and it snapped him from his silent celebration.

"Is something wrong?" she asked, worry marring her lovely face.

"No, something's right." He pulled her up to receive his kiss. "I love you, Raleigh. I love you." It was good to hear the words, but it was better to feel them in her kiss and touch. "We're going to be okay now."

"I'm sorry I put you through so much misery. I was so afraid you wouldn't come back to me this morning."

"I told you I would. I drove around for a while and thought about everything that's happened. I'm amazed that *you* didn't go crazy, what with knowing about Grant and having to keep it to yourself."

"It wasn't easy, especially when it came down to losing you."

"You never really lost me." He smiled and kissed the tip of her nose. "I'm sorry I was so hard on you. Forgive me?"

She began unbuttoning his shirt, pausing to press her lips against the patches of skin she exposed. "There's nothing to forgive. I'm surprised you kept seeing me."

"It was out of my hands. I fell in love with you and there was no turning back."

"Did you call your parents?"

"Yes. I told them you weren't feeling well."

"That's true." She spread her hands across his chest and rained kisses there. "But after a few hours in bed with my doctor, I'll be a new woman."

He laughed, then sucked in his breath as Raleigh angled her body upward until her mouth covered his. His openmouthed kisses made Raleigh remember the first time she'd experienced his raw passion. She had known even then that this man was special and unforgettable.

"Oh, Evan, make love to me again." She stood up and held out her hands.

"You don't have to ask twice," he said with a rakish smile as he took her hands and stood up. "Who's your best friend?"

"You are," she answered, smiling up into his face as he bent her arms behind her, arching her body into his.

"Who's your pal?"

"You are."

"Who loves you?"

"You do."

He grinned and backed with her the entire distance to the bedroom, never once taking his eyes from her face. When his legs bumped against the bed he fell backward, taking Raleigh with him. Laughing, she settled on top of him and smoothed the curling hair on his chest with her fingertips.

"My life has completely turned around since I met you," she said, musing aloud. "When we met I was still in shock over Curtis's suicide, I didn't have enough confidence in myself to look for other employment even though I was miserable at the newspaper, and I had decided that what I needed was an older man who would treat me more like a daughter than a wife." She kissed his mouth, then sprinkled kisses across his collarbone. "Look at me now. I've got a new job, self-confidence, a new lover and a whole new outlook on life. You're good for me, but am I good for you?"

He framed her face in his hands and laughed, a bewildered expression covering his face. "I'm not the type of man who enjoys being alone. I knew at a young age that I couldn't be happy until I found a lasting love. I see forever in your eyes, Raleigh. Even when you acted as if our first night together was as casual as a handshake, I knew better.''

"That was stupid of me," she said, frowning. "I just didn't know how to act the next day. I didn't want to be all serious and mushy and scare you off."

"No more games." His eyes embraced her. "From this moment on let's be honest with each other. Let's trust each other."

"It's a deal, doctor."

She rolled off him and let him undress her. He exposed her creamy breasts and moved his hands over them, his fingers gently kneading the firm, ripe flesh. He took one rosy crest in his mouth and scraped his tongue across the sensitive center. Raleigh reacted instinctively by parting her thighs so that his hips could settle comfortably between them.

Desire licked through her as her fingertips explored the angles of his face and found the dimples that grooved his lean cheeks. Closing her eyes, she saw him with her fingers: the arch of his brows, the straight bridge of his nose, the soft brush of his lashes and the curve of his upper lip. He smiled against her fingers, and she opened her eyes to be caught momentarily in those clear blue pools.

"You're beautiful," he whispered against her fingers.

"And you're overdressed," she reminded him gently as she moved her hands down his body to the waistband of his jeans.

He left the bed long enough to remove his clothes, then came back to her. Lying on his side, he kissed the slope of her stomach and the sensitive skin of her inner thighs. Evan's need for her was overwhelming and uncontrollable as he grasped her waist and joined his body with hers. Her lips clung to his and her tongue was bold, darting into his mouth and undulating against his. Her legs slipped around him, binding him tightly to her, and her fingers dug into his upper arms.

Evan moved within her, content to study the rapture on her face. Her hair fanned out in a golden halo around her head, her lashes were crescents against her cheeks, her skin gleamed with a sheen of perspiration and her lips were wet and rosy from his kisses. He bent forward at the waist for another taste of her sweet mouth, and she trembled and quaked against him. His lips moved tenderly upon hers as her breathing grew shallow. His own desire soared, and his pulse quickened, pounding a primitive beat in his inner ear.

Raleigh clutched his elbows as Evan pulled her up his body until her hips rested on his thighs. She leaned forward until she could wrap her arms about his neck and stare deeply into his eyes, eyes that were glazed with passion. His hands spanned her waist and guided her into a slow, grinding movement that sent spirals of pleasure through her and reminded her of his winning performance during the Mr. Pretty Legs contest.

She'd thought she had nothing left, no remaining source of energy, but he tapped a hidden supply and Raleigh began climbing toward the summit again, this time with Evan.

His lips moved against her throat, then slid to the pulse beneath her ear. Raleigh tipped back her head, her arms tight around his neck, her eyes closing as ecstasy consumed her. His hips drove up against hers, and with each plunge Raleigh felt her love for him spill over.

Their feelings were fragile and wondrous, and they looked deeply into each other's eyes, eloquent in their silent adoration. Evan grew still, then filled her with a molten fire that made her cry out his name and pull his face to her breasts in a moment of frenzy. When she was limp, he eased her backward to the bed again. His hands caressed her and his lips traveled from eyelid to eyelid.

"Wonderful . . . wonderful." Evan ran the tip of his tongue across her full lips and smiled when she opened her eyes. "I love the way you love me."

She slipped her fingers through his hair, her gaze following their progress. "I never thought I'd ever be this happy." She kissed his mouth, then slipped her arms under his as he snuggled against her, his head pillowed on her breasts.

"What time is it?"

"Why?" he asked, ready to fall asleep and dream of her.

"I've got to meet my folks, remember?"

"Oh, right." He raised his arm and peered at his watch. "We've got time to snuggle for a while."

"Are you sure?" She started to look at his watch, but he removed it from her view by wrapping his arm around her waist.

"I'm sure. Trust me."

Raleigh smiled and snuggled closer to him. "I do. You know I do."

Raleigh placed the yellow mums near the headstone and stood back, her gaze moving over the simple inscription: Curtis Torrence, Beloved Son and Brother.

"Your parents just drove up, honey," Evan said, curving his hand at the back of her neck.

"Okay." Raleigh stepped forward, feeling drawn by an invisible bond, an intangible need. She touched the cold marble and smiled. Curtis seemed very close to her, and she no longer felt angry or guilty. The gaping tear in her soul seemed to have closed magically. "I forgive you, Curtis," she whispered as a tear spilled from the corner of her eye and trickled down her cheek. "I'm still mad at you for leaving without saying goodbye and for lying to me, but I forgive you." A weight lifted from her heart, and she breathed in deeply. The air smelled clean and zesty coming right behind the rain.

"Raleigh?" Cara placed a hand on her arm. "Are you okay?"

Raleigh smiled and nodded. "I'm fine. I was just squaring something with Curtis." She looked over her shoulder and waved to her parents as they approached the grave. "Mom, Dad, I want you to meet someone." She linked her arm in Evan's and looked at him with open admiration. "I want you to meet the man I love."

Chapter Twelve

Don't they make a lovely couple?" Raleigh nodded toward Cody and Liann, who were cutting the first slice of their five-tiered wedding cake. Poor Cody was having trouble with his bulky cast, making the guests laugh when he almost toppled over a bottle of champagne with his awkward arm.

"Yes." Cara gave the couple a cursory glance. "So why didn't Grant put his name on the land deed?"

Raleigh enjoyed the sight of Cody and Liann a few moments more before she turned her attention to Cara's persistent questioning. Liann McDowell Wakefield was a gorgeous bride. Her chestnut hair and dark eyes contrasted nicely with her groom's blond hair and blue eyes. Cody was dressed in a white suit, and his groomsmen were in gray. Liann's wedding party wore long dresses of violet edged in old ivory lace. Liann's wedding dress was of antique lace, and Raleigh had heard someone say it had been Liann's grandmother's wedding gown. It looked fragile and elegant.

Cody didn't attempt to disguise his rapt devotion to his bride. He kissed her mouth tenderly before offering her a bite of cake. Raleigh felt sentimental tears sting her eyes as she witnessed the scene of devotion. It reminded Raleigh of how, when Cody and Liann had recited their vows, Evan had held Raleigh close and kissed her tear-stained cheek; his expression had reflected the heart-swelling devotion a groom feels for his bride.

"Raleigh!"

"Okay!" Raleigh puffed out a sigh. "This is a wedding, Cara, or hadn't you noticed?"

"The wedding is over. This is the reception. Now tell me about Grant. Why didn't he put his name on the land deed?" she repeated.

"Because it would have been a conflict of interest. He endorsed betting in Okmulgee County through the *Times* and it was a clear case of using the newspaper's influence to fill his own pockets."

"Oh." Cara watched Cody and Liann share a wedding toast, then applauded politely when the toast had been honored. "Then why did he kill Victoria? That knocked him out of the deal because her daughter inherited the land."

"Grant wasn't thinking clearly, Cara." Raleigh glanced around her, searching for Evan, who had left a few minutes ago to get them glasses of punch. "He didn't go to Victoria's house that day to kill her. He just wanted to threaten her because he knew she was getting ready to give him the bum's rush. Victoria pulled the gun on him, and one thing led to another. Johnny Stratton was outside in the hot tub when he heard the shot and ran upstairs.'' Raleigh caught sight of Evan and waved. "He surprised Grant, and Grant shot him.''

"Good grief, what a mess!" Cara moaned, then smiled brightly when she saw Evan. "Refreshments, at last!"

Evan handed them each a cup of punch. "Sorry I took so long.''

"I was filling Cara in on all the gory details concerning Grant Farris," Raleigh said. "I talked with Mike Allison yesterday and he said the *Times* is for sale."

"Surprise! Surprise!" Cara said dryly. She turned her head and gazed out the floor-to-ceiling windows that took up one wall of the Arrowhead Country Club's reception room. Watching her, Raleigh thought her sister looked stunning in a mint-green dress of filmy chiffon. "Oh, my gosh! Look!" Cara pointed out the window. "There's Howard Rendell!"

"Where?" Evan asked, pressing closer to gaze out the window at the stretch of golf green.

"Down there. That man in the red-and-white-checked pants.''

"Yes, I see him," Raleigh said. "I bet he's glad Grant Farris is behind bars.''

"That poor guy.'' Evan straightened, shaking his head from side to side. "Can you imagine the misery he's gone through over this murder case? I imagine that there were times when he was sure he was going to prison for something he didn't do.''

"I hope he can get his life back together," Raleigh said, feeling sorry for the man.

"I'm going to get a piece of that cake," Cara said. "Do you want me to get a slice for you while I'm at it?"

"No, thanks," Raleigh said, and Evan shook his head.

"Okay." Cara left them, moving with the liquid grace of a panther.

"Hello, Raleigh."

Raleigh turned toward the voice and smiled when she saw Donnelly Wakefield.

"Hello, Donnelly. You know Evan, don't you?"

"Of course. Good to see you again, Evan." Donnelly shook Evan's hand and offered a friendly smile. "I wanted to officially welcome you aboard the Wakefield political train, Raleigh."

"Thank you. I'll be ready to start work June first as promised."

"That's just a little over a week away," Donnelly noted. "Time sure is flying." He grimaced. "I'm already getting nervous about this."

"You're Oklahoma's next governor," Evan said with a broad grin. "You have a right to be nervous."

Donnelly laughed and his blue-green eyes sparkled, drawing Raleigh's attention to the fact that he was a handsome man.

"I need people like you on my side," Donnelly told Evan. "Confidence is a necessary quality in this business." He glanced in the direction of his brother and new sister-in-law. "Looks like they're getting ready to take off on their honeymoon." Donnelly smoothed his hands down the front of his gray suit, then looked back to Raleigh. "It's good to see you again, Raleigh. I hope I won't be too difficult to work for."

"After Grant Farris?" Raleigh gave a short laugh. "You'll be a cream puff."

Donnelly grinned and gave a jaunty salute before making his way across the room to his brother.

"Do you think he's handsome?"

Evan's casual question brought Raleigh's gaze to him, and she smiled. "Are you jealous?"

"No, but do you think he's handsome?"

"I wouldn't know." She stood up on tiptoe and kissed him. "I only have eyes for you."

"You're a wise woman, Raleigh Torrence." He glanced toward the bride and groom. "Go catch the bouquet."

"I'll give it my best shot."

"You'd better catch it if you know what's good for you." He took her by the shoulders and gave her a little push in the right direction.

Raleigh went to the circle of women who stood a few feet from Liann Wakefield. Liann turned her back on them, counted to three, then let the bouquet arc into the air over her shoulder. The ribboned flowers fell neatly into Raleigh's hands, almost as if by magic. Raleigh laughed, feeling a little shocked at having seized the flowers so easily. Liann caught her eye and waved.

"You always were a good catcher," Cara said beside her. "I'm leaving now. Tell Evan goodbye for me."

"Okay. I'll talk to you later this week." Raleigh hugged Cara. "It was a lovely wedding, wasn't it?"

"They always are," Cara said over her shoulder as she made her way to the exit.

Raleigh shook her head, wondering if Cara would ever find a man who could stay on equal footing with her. She hoped so, but it would have to be a special man to make Cara's heart flutter.

"Let's go over to the club and have a drink," Evan said, slipping an arm about Raleigh's waist. "You know what it means when you catch the bouquet, don't you?"

"Free flowers?"

He gave her a fake smile. "Cute. No, it means that—"

"I'll be the next bride," Raleigh finished for him. "I've heard the old saying, doctor."

He guided her toward a table for two near the front of the club and helped her into her chair.

"Order me a Scotch and soda, okay?"

"Where are you going?" Raleigh asked.

"I've got to make a telephone call." He kissed her cheek. "I'll be right back."

"Okay."

Raleigh ordered the drinks, and as she waited for Evan to return, her thoughts circled back to the wedding. Cody had arrested Grant less than a week ago, and he'd told Raleigh that he was glad to close the case before his wedding. Raleigh smiled to herself, remembering how lovely Liann had looked during the ceremony. She bore some resemblance to her late father, Captain Roger McDowell, Raleigh thought. Liann had had quite a year. Raleigh gave a little laugh. We've *all* had quite a year!

But the year hadn't all been bad, she reminded herself. She had Evan. She smiled and sniffed the bouquet before laying it on the table. Though the courtship had been rocky, she had learned that her love for Evan and his for her was tenacious and binding. They had gone through a lot of stress together, had weathered some thunderous misunderstandings and had found roses among the thorns. Raleigh caressed the violets in Liann's bouquet and wondered if she would be carrying a wedding bouquet some day soon....

"I'm back." Evan sat in the chair across from her and took a sip of his Scotch and soda. "You're going to start working for Donnelly June first, right?"

"Right." Raleigh reached across the table for his hand. "I'm so excited! Thanks for helping me get the job."

"I didn't help you get the job," Evan said, squeezing her hand. "You got the job all by yourself because you're a qualified, talented writer. Donnelly Wakefield is lucky to get you, and so am I."

Raleigh's heart swelled with love, and she pursed her lips and blew Evan a kiss across the table. "I love you."

"And I love you."

Minutes passed as they held hands and looked deeply into each other's eyes. The world slipped away and time slowed to a seductive pace. Evan was the first to break the spell. He released one of Raleigh's hands to finish his drink, and his action bespoke a man who was suddenly in a hurry.

"We're going to have to get a move on if we're going to make that flight."

Raleigh blinked, releasing her thoughts of love and trying to make sense of Evan's announcement. "What flight?"

"The flight to Las Vegas this evening. Are you ready?"

"Wait a minute!" She laughed and grabbed his hand. "Why are we flying to Las Vegas tonight?"

"To be married, of course."

"Evan!" Her lips curved into a happy smile, and she felt her eyes fill with tears.

"Don't cry," Evan pleaded. "You're not losing a lover, you're gaining a husband."

Raleigh half rose from her chair and leaned over the table to kiss him. "I can't believe I'm actually going to get married! It's weird!"

"What's so weird about it?"

"I was just thinking that it might not be in the cards for me."

"Well, that's how much you know." He stood up and pulled her to her feet. "I'm a liberal feminist, so you can keep your maiden name, if you want."

She considered it for a few moments, then shook her head. "No way!"

"Why not?"

"I'm not going through the rest of my life being introduced as 'Here's Miss Torrence, and the man with her is Younger.'"

He laughed and hugged her closer. "Don't worry, kid. Besides, who will care one way or the other when I'm seventy and you're seventy-four?"

"Who cares now? In fact, I think if you'd been born a day earlier, you'd be too old for me." Raleigh pressed her hands at the back of his head and brushed her lips against his. "Where are you taking me for our honeymoon?"

"Where would you like to go?" His lips moved against hers as he spoke, sending sparks of passion showering through her.

"Eureka Springs."

He leaned his forehead against hers and frowned. "You're kidding."

"No, I'm not."

Evan laughed and, unmindful of the other customers and employees in the club, he swept her up into his arms and started for the exit. A waitress stopped him.

"Your check, sir," she said, holding the slip of paper toward him.

"Oh!" He set Raleigh on her feet and pulled his wallet from the inside pocket of his jacket. "I'm sorry. I had other things on my mind." His lips twitched with humor as he handed a bill to the waitress. "Keep the change."

"Thanks." The waitress glanced at Raleigh, her curious gaze sweeping over Raleigh's pale pink dress and the bouquet she held in one hand. "Did you two just get married?"

Raleigh's surprised gaze flew to Evan's, and they both laughed in delight.

"No, we're on our way to get married," Evan explained as he swept Raleigh back into his arms with a gallant flourish. "So please excuse us."

He carried her outside, where the sun poured over them in a shower of warmth. Evan placed a tender, clinging kiss to her lips as he let her slip slowly from his arms.

"What a beautiful day," Raleigh said, bringing the bouquet to her nose and breathing in the sweet perfume. Feeling Evan's intense gaze, she looked at him and smiled.

"We're going to have a wonderful life together, Raleigh," he promised solemnly.

Touched by his vow, she nestled in his embrace. "I know we are, Evan. We just can't miss."

COMING NEXT MONTH

CHEROKEE FIRE—Gena Dalton
It was Sabrina Dante's silver spoon that Cherokee cowboy Jarod Redfeather couldn't trust. The two lovers came from opposite worlds, but the Indian heritage taught them to overcome their differences.

A FEW SHINING HOURS—Jeanne Stephens
Fifteen years ago, Quinn left for Vietnam, not knowing about the daughter he had given Kathleen. Now he was back, hoping that love could make time stand still.

PREVIEW OF PARADISE—Tracy Sinclair
Travis couldn't resist rescuing Bettina from being sold at an auction by nomad chieftains. But a valuable amulet had been stolen, and his damsel in distress was the number one suspect!

A PASSIONATE ILLUSION—Tory Cates
Tempers flared when Matthew accused Lissa of not being able to act. He wanted her to bring illusion alive with passion—passion as real as the hunger he could no longer deny...

ALL MY LOVE, FOREVER—Pamela Wallace
They were adults now—not lovestruck teenagers. But even after the hurt of raising their child alone, Carolyn still loved Rafe. She only knew she wanted him...more than ever before.

FORWARD PASS—Brooke Hastings
Federal drug agent Liz Reynolds never intended to win a trip to Hawaii with star quarterback Zack Delaney. But now Zack was in for the most challenging game of his career.

AVAILABLE THIS MONTH:

RIGHT BEHIND THE RAIN
Elaine Camp

SPECIAL DELIVERY
Monica Barrie

PRISONER OF LOVE
Maranda Catlin

GEORGIA NIGHTS
Kathleen Eagle

FOCUS ON LOVE
Maggi Charles

ONE SUMMER
Nora Roberts

AMERICAN TRIBUTE

Where a man's dreams count for more than his parentage...

Look for these upcoming titles under the Special Edition American Tribute banner.

CHEROKEE FIRE
Gena Dalton #307—May 1986
It was Sabrina Dante's silver spoon that Cherokee cowboy Jarod Redfeather couldn't trust. The two lovers came from opposite worlds, but Jarod's Indian heritage taught them to overcome their differences.

NOBODY'S FOOL
Renee Roszel #313—June 1986
Everyone bet that Martin Dante and Cara Torrence would get together. But Martin wasn't putting any money down, and Cara was out to prove that she was nobody's fool.

MISTY MORNINGS, MAGIC NIGHTS
Ada Steward #319—July 1986
The last thing Carole Stockton wanted was to fall in love with another politician, especially Donnelly Wakefield. But under a blanket of secrecy, far from the campaign spotlights, their love became a powerful force.

American Tribute titles now available:

RIGHT BEHIND THE RAIN
Elaine Camp #301–April 1986
The difficulty of coping with her brother's
death brought reporter Raleigh Torrence
to the office of Evan Younger, a police
psychologist. He helped her to deal with
her feelings and emotions, including love.

THIS LONG WINTER PAST
Jeanne Stephens #295–March 1986
Detective Cody Wakefield checked out
Assistant District Attorney Liann McDowell,
but only in his leisure time. For it was the
danger of Cody's job that caused Liann to
shy away.

LOVE'S HAUNTING REFRAIN
Ada Steward #289–February 1986
For thirty years a deep dark secret kept them
apart—King Stockton made his millions while
his wife, Amelia, held everything together.
Now could they tell their secret, could they
admit their love?

The Silhouette Cameo Tote Bag Now available for just $6.99

Handsomely designed in blue and bright pink, its stylish good looks make the Cameo Tote Bag an attractive accessory. The Cameo Tote Bag is big and roomy (13" square), with reinforced handles and a snap-shut top. You can buy the Cameo Tote Bag for $6.99, plus $1.50 for postage and handling.

Send your name and address with check or money order for $6.99 (plus $1.50 postage and handling), a total of $8.49 to:

Silhouette Books
120 Brighton Road
P.O. Box 5084
Clifton, NJ 07015-5084
ATTN: Tote Bag

SIL-T-1

The Silhouette Cameo Tote Bag can be purchased pre-paid only. No charges will be accepted. Please allow 4 to 6 weeks for delivery.

Arizona and N.Y. State Residents Please Add Sales Tax

Offer not available in Canada.